A COWBOY TO CALL HER OWN

CARI LYNN WEBB

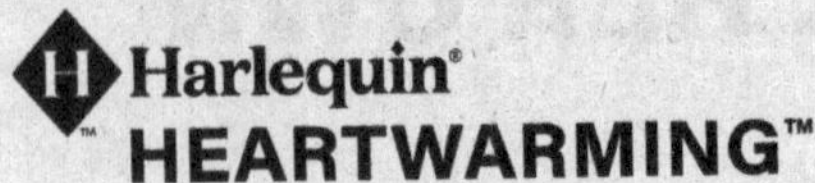

Recycling programs for this product may not exist in your area

ISBN-13: 978-1-335-60513-9

A Cowboy to Call Her Own

For questions and comments about the quality of this book, please contact us at CustomerService@Harlequin.com.

Harlequin Enterprises ULC
22 Adelaide St. West, 41st Floor
Toronto, Ontario M5H 4E3, Canada
www.Harlequin.com

HarperCollins Publishers
Macken House, 39/40 Mayor Street Uppe
Dublin 1, D01 C9W8, Ireland
www.HarperCollins.com

Printed in U.S.A.

1 2 3 4 5 6 7 8 9 10 HDC 28 27 26 25

“It’s not exactly easy, cooking in this place,” Asher said.

But Kelley felt at ease with him. The more time she spent with her cowboy, the longer she wanted to stay and share secrets. “Once I figured out the quirks around here, there was nothing to it.”

Asher eyed her like he didn’t believe her. “You aren’t like most people I know.”

You aren’t like I expected either. And she was not certain if she was happy about that. “Is it good or bad that I’m not like most people?”

“It was a compliment.” Asher finished his drink and added, “I imagine most chefs would have walked in here and then walked out. Probably even most home cooks.”

“I like a challenge,” Kelley said.

“That’s not it.” Asher shook his head. “You see the best in things, not the worst.”

“Not always,” Kelley confessed. “Especially not after my divorce.”

“What changed?” he asked.

I met a cowboy.

Dear Reader,

If ever there was a character that holds a piece of my heart, it is Elias, *aka* Big E Blackwell. So, it is a thrill to be sure that I get to kick off another Blackwell series featuring the clever and sometimes meddlesome cowboy. I'm even more excited to be writing with my very close friends again.

Now it is time to join Big E in Gold Finch, Kentucky, where Big E steps in to oversee his dead cousin's horse racing ranch. Only, Big E finds himself facing old rivalries and new scandals, and quickly realizes he needs to bring his cousin's estranged sons back home. Good thing Big E is somewhat skilled in mending the broken branches on the Blackwell family tree. Now if Big E can show these Blackwell brothers that family is worth fighting for, then they just might discover that the greatest victory isn't winning the race, but rather finding lasting love.

Big E has the RV tuned up and his sights set on Kentucky. So, step inside and buckle up. After all, matters of the heart are never a smooth ride.

Happy reading!

Cari Lynn

Cari Lynn Webb lives in Florida with her husband. She's been blessed to see the power of true love in her grandparents' seventy-year marriage and her parents' marriage of over sixty years. She knows love isn't always sweet and perfect. It can be challenging, complicated and risky. But she believes happily-ever-afters are worth fighting for. She loves to connect with readers.

Books by Cari Lynn Webb

Harlequin Heartwarming

A Three Springs, Texas Romance

A Proposal for Her Cowboy
The Rancher's Secret Crush
Falling for the Cowboy Doc
Her Cowboy Wedding Date
Trusting the Rancher with Christmas
The Texas SEAL's Surprise
His Christmas Cowgirl
Falling for the Rodeo Cowgirl

The Blackwells of Eagle Springs

Her Favorite Wyoming Sheriff

The Blackwell Belles

A Cowgirl's Christmas Reunion

Visit the Author Profile page at Harlequin.com for more titles.

For the readers who have embraced Big E
and the Blackwell family. I am so very grateful.

Special thanks to my editor, Kathryn Lye, for wanting
more Blackwell books. To Amy, Anna, Carol and
Melinda—you make my world better. To my family—
there aren't enough words to tell you how much
I appreciate your support and encouragement.
Love to you all.

PROLOGUE

It was a good day for a race.

Elias Blackwell stood on the flower-bedecked terrace of the Champions Club on the third floor of the grandstands at Rosehaven Downs in Gold Finch, Kentucky. His gaze followed the curves of the wide, mile-long track that glinted like a copper ribbon in the afternoon sun.

Inside the exclusive wood-paneled lounge behind him, generations of horsemen and -women in their pressed finery and spotless felt cowboy hats sipped bourbon and laughed easy. While below, a mix of tourists, locals and avid bettors clutched programs and filled the grandstands.

Movement from across the terrace caught Big E's attention. A pair of the equestrian world's elite with horse roots as deep as the Blackwell family appeared in the open French doors. Sullivan Connelly and Patsy Richmond owned and operated stables of the same caliber as Big E's dead cousin, Walter Blackwell.

They all had stories of success, knew the value of digging in, and always raced to win. Their children had grown up right alongside Walter's six sons. Their paths crossed on racetracks across the Bluegrass countryside and everywhere in between. However, Sully and Patsy were not Walter's friends. They were respected rivals. And it did well now that Big E recognized the difference.

Sully strolled over, his exotic leather cowboy boots hitting hollow on the hardwood floor. His smile fell far short of reaching his eyes. "Good luck out there today."

"Same to you both," Big E replied then tipped his cowboy hat up to better catch their gazes. "Although Walter once told me that it isn't luck that takes a horse past the wire. It's heart."

And before Walter's unexpected death one month ago, Big E's cousin had sworn his colt had the heart to outrun all of them. Today was the third and last race in the Triple Laurel Legacy Circuit. And Walter's horse, Sovereign's Pride, would find his name and Blackwell's in the storied history books if the colt won. There had not been a triple crown winner in the Triple Laurel Legacy Circuit in over forty years. Not even that had discouraged Walter or shaken his belief. Big E was there now to honor his cousin's memory and ensure Walter's legacy stood the test of time.

"Well, even if Sovereign's Pride loses today, no one can take away his first two wins." Patsy brushed her hand over her sapphire-blue pantsuit, the tailoring as sharp as the glint in her green eyes. "There's consolation in that, I suppose."

And Big E sensed there would be something more like satisfaction from this pair if Pride came up short. "If he wins today, I imagine the good folks of Gold Finch will have quite the celebration."

"Plenty of worthy horses have stumbled here at the Rosehaven," Patsy said, a hint of a smile on her face. "It's more diamonds in the rough for the Dust and Diamonds Derby. I've lost count of the horses with so much hidden promise who failed to shine on this track when it mattered most."

"The young ones tend to burn too hot, too fast. On account of getting pushed too hard, too soon." Sully swirled the large ice cube in his bourbon glass and added, "They get here for the Diamond Derby only to fade out by the first turn."

"Some fires settle deeper and when it's time, they blaze," Big E countered and hoped today was that day for Walter's prized horse.

"It's been my experience that history does not like to be beaten," Patsy said, her words smooth and polished like the silver streaked through her hair.

"Or it could be that history has been waitin' on the right horse," Big E said casually then touched the brim of his hat and walked away. He spotted Edie Kincaid, one of Walter's longtime exercise jockeys and the friendliest face in the bunch, near the French doors.

"I can bet you none of the hats in here have seen a day of honest work," Edie said, her voice pitched low with disapproval.

"Every cowboy has got a hat reserved for big occasions." Big E chuckled and added, "The kind that tells everyone this day matters."

"I'm wearing mine now." Edie pointed a lean finger at her black cowboy hat then frowned and said, "But these around here are worn for show like shiny ornaments, not for life."

There was certainly prestige and spectacle mixed in with the tradition at Rosehaven Downs. And Big E supposed that was all part of the show and the draw.

"Well, if silk ties and polished shoes are your preference, you're welcome to stick around here," Edie said.

"What's your preference?" Big E asked the straight-talking cowgirl.

"I'm more suited for dirt and saddle leather." Edie's grin gleamed in her gaze.

Big E smiled wide. "Where are we going next?"

"To the only place that mattered to Walter." Edie handed Big E a paddock pass and told him to clip it on his shirt.

Then she led him through the club past the oil paintings of former champions and down the stairs. The air was different at the ground level.

Scented with leather and fresh-cut grass and anticipation. The energy was restless and unmistakable.

"The stretch looks longer from down here," Big E mused.

"Funny thing is most people look at a racetrack and only see a circle," Edie said beside him. "But for folks like Walter and me, it is the whole of our lives. Where we start and finish."

Big E supposed the race ended sooner than Walter ever expected, unfortunately. Big E said, "But it's the stretch between the poles that counts the most. That's what makes life worth all the dust."

Yet, when Big E considered Walter and his estranged sons, well, there was more than dust-covered distance there. But today was not about fixing a fractured Blackwell family branch. It was about racing.

Big E stepped to the paddock rail and watched a familiar chestnut colt circle. Sovereign's Pride danced a little, neck arched, ears pinned, hooves striking sure. There was fire in Walter's favorite horse, no doubt. His cousin's colt was proud, confident and ready to blaze.

Then Big E saw the trio of officials heading straight their way. Two stewards in sanctioned dark uniform jackets and a third that Big E suspected was a state veterinarian trailing behind. The stewards' boots cut a sure path across the grounds. Their faces were set. Their gazes were trained on Sovereign's Pride.

Tension suddenly thickened the air. Even the crowd in the grandstands seemed to have gone completely quiet as if they held a collective breath. Big E gripped the rail.

Joe Allcott, Walter's best friend and stable operation manager, lifted his head at the officials' arrival. His expression fell flat. Words were exchanged, low and intense.

Then Joe met Big E's stare, his voice tight as if his jaw was locked. "They're scratching Pride." A pause or a grind of Joe's teeth, then the head trainer added, "They claim a drug test came back dirty."

Dirty. Big E straightened. His grip on the rail tensed.

Edie shook her head. The cowgirl's words came slow and hard. "Walter would never run a dirty horse. Never."

Big E agreed. Blackwells did not cheat to get ahead. It was not their way.

"I know it," Joe said and jerked his chin toward the officials. "But they get the final say."

Suddenly, there were papers to sign. Words like *steward's scratch* and *fines* and *sanctions* bantered about. Pride pawed the ground and tossed his head as if he knew what was being stolen from him.

The crowd craned for news; the hushed murmurs leveled up.

A hand suddenly landed on Big E's shoulder. Big E shifted to find himself face-to-face with

Patrick Connelly, Sullivan's oldest son and current stable operation manager.

"Shame about Pride. Walter always seemed more careful with his horses. Funny how things change when a man's gone, huh?" Patrick leaned in as if to offer support and said, "Don't let it weigh you down. At least Walter wasn't here to see it."

But the colt had been pulled in plain sight of owners, trainers, fans, bettors and announcers. All eyes were on the Blackwells now and for a different sort of newsworthy story. Big E held his peace and gave Patrick the smallest nod of dismissal.

A woman came into view, her stature petite and her auburn hair coiled in a braid on top of her head. She shook her head sadly. "Bad business, that. Walter was the heart of the stables. Without him, who can you trust?"

With those cryptic words, the woman walked away. She joined Patsy and Sullivan near the stairs leading up to the grandstand where the duo watched over the proceedings. Big E met Sully's gaze. Sullivan's mouth curved slightly, not quite a grin and not quite *not*.

Tipping his hat lower, Big E shifted his attention toward the groom leading Pride back to the barn. Joe and his team followed close by. There was a definite shadow over his cousin's reputation and legacy now. And unfortunately, the woman was not wrong. Big E was not certain who he could trust.

But he knew two things for sure.

The colt was innocent.

And an attack on one Blackwell was an attack on the whole family.

Nothing for it now. It was time to bring Walter's sons home. After all, it was about more than Walter's legacy. The Blackwell family name was at stake, too.

CHAPTER ONE

"KELLEY, STOP WHAT you are doing."

Not again. Kelley Munroe winced and watched her older sister barrel through the front doors of the Galloping Fork Diner well ahead of the sunrise and the diner's early-bird regulars.

"Now. I need you." Laura-Beth flipped the open sign to Closed, relocked the doors that Kelley had only just opened moments ago and rushed on, "I need Frannie, too." LB hollered for their younger sister to get a move on and join them.

Frannie pushed through the swinging door from the diner kitchen, clutching an apron and frowning. "LB, you don't work here. You can't order me around. Only Kelley can."

Laura-Beth made a *pfft* sound that carried across the entire seating area. "We are t-minus ten days until my walk down the aisle. My fiancé's business trip got extended this morning for several more days. Wes is currently en route from San Francisco to Los Angeles." She tossed her arms over her head, escalating her newfound flair for the dramatic and added rather empathetically,

"And there are decisions to be made. Today. Right now, in fact."

Kelley nodded, although Laura-Beth was once again in motion and busily rearranging the furniture in the main dining area.

"You need to make her leave," Frannie grumbled beside Kelley. "All her bridal fuss and wedding frenzy will ruin the breakfast service for the customers."

Their big sister had been *wound up* since her surprise engagement to local boy and successful tech entrepreneur Wes Taggart last month. Yet, it was the couple's subsequent decision to fast-track their nuptials that set the usually even-keeled middle school English teacher off in something of a bridal whirlwind. Kelley mumbled, "She will just come back. We have to deal with her now."

Frannie wrapped the straps of her apron around her waist and tied them tightly. "She's getting worse."

Kelley didn't disagree. Laura-Beth's wedding ambushes were becoming daily occurrences, especially with Wes's recent back-to-back business trips. As Wes was, in his own words, *clearing the decks* to spend the entire month of July after their wedding with his new bride and no work distractions, Kelley cut him some slack.

Still, Kelley checked the time on the wall clock behind the counter and said loud enough for Laura-Beth to hear, "We've got a few minutes to spare for our sister who needs us."

Frannie looked less than convinced.

Kelley squeezed Frannie's shoulder. "I know what I'm doing, *little fig*." Frannie's childhood nickname earned Kelley a glower from her younger sister.

"You've been saying that since you gave up your New York restaurant, signed your divorce papers and moved home to work here at the diner," Frannie groused, giving her usual morning grump free rein.

Kelley hadn't given up. Quite the opposite. She had fought for her marriage and their restaurant. The same could not be said about her ex-husband. But that so-called chapter of life was finished, and it wasn't worth rereading now. Besides, the bride-to-be was the focus, not Kelley, thankfully.

"We can discuss Kelley's situation and her next move later," Laura-Beth said offhandedly, then motioned to them. Her engagement ring sparkled under the fluorescent lights. "Come over here and help me move this last table. It's the heaviest."

Frannie stayed rooted to her spot near the cash register.

Kelley helped Laura-Beth scoot the largest table to the side then asked, "LB, what are we doing anyway?"

"Isn't it obvious?" Laura-Beth paced a small circle around Kelley and added, "We've got a wedding party dance to choreograph." At Kelley's arched eyebrow, her sister said, "If it helps, think of it more like a dry run-through."

Kelley took in the open space Laura-Beth created in the dining area and said slowly, "You want to dance here."

"What did you think she was wanting?" Frannie asked, feigned disinterest in her tone.

"I thought we were going to sit down, have coffee and talk through the final wedding details." At which point Laura-Beth would return to her calm and collected persona who exuded confidence rather than panic and pandemonium. The daily urgent phone calls and around-the-clock texts would cease. And Kelley could go back to running the diner's breakfast service as usual.

"Well, we can sip and chat later. Right now, we need to practice our multitasking skills." Laura-Beth grabbed Frannie's arm, tugged her away from the counter and over to Kelley then ordered, "There's no reason we can't decide my other wedding things while you two dance."

Her big sister was petite, her heart-shaped face delicate and pretty. Only now there was a decided determination in the set of Laura-Beth's pointed chin and a stubborn glint in her pale green eyes. It would be easier to convince a goat to stop climbing than to change Laura-Beth's mind. Kelley sighed and extended her arm toward her little sister. Smiling, she asked, "Can I have this dance, Ms. Francine Marie?"

Frannie blew a raspberry at Kelley and said, "I knew I should've hit snooze on my alarm this morning and driven myself to work."

"But then you would have missed all this." Kelley bowed low to her grumbly little sister and asked again, "Now, may I please have this dance?"

Frannie's eyebrows pulled together and lowered. But the spark in her vibrant green eyes was more than evident. Frannie mused, "Actually, if this morning is about deciding things, we've got Fourth of July decisions to make. Like are we participating or not."

Kelley should have seen this coming. Being a part of the town's Fourth of July celebration was something of a family tradition. Kelley liked watching the parade and fireworks show well enough. It was the participation part that gave her pause. That conversation definitely required more caffeine and preferably something extra sweet.

"It's the first time we are all together for the Fourth in what seems like forever," Laura-Beth stated. "So, of course we are taking part like we always did as kids."

That earned Laura-Beth a satisfied smile from their youngest sister. Frannie eyed Kelley. "How about it, Kiki? Are you floating with us or not?"

Kelley never liked saying no to her sisters and disappointing them. Still, she said, "I think we should keep this morning about wedding things."

"But LB already declared it a day for decisions," Frannie challenged.

"Fine," Kelley sighed. "We can discuss the parade."

Frannie considered her and pressed, "Then you're doing it, right?"

"I'm agreeing to discuss it." That was all Kelley allowed. At her sister's frown, Kelley whispered quickly, "If we dance now, LB will leave us alone the rest of the day and just perhaps all the remaining days until the wedding."

"That would be a very good thing," Frannie muttered.

"Dance with me, *Little Fig*." Kelley grinned and added, "Let me sweep you off your boots."

Finally, Frannie's smile broke through her morning grump. Her little sister curtsied all grace and elegance despite her worn cowboy boots, rumpled shirt, black pants and heather-green waist apron. Frannie set her hand in Kelley's and said, "Why, my darling *Kiki*, I'd be delighted."

"Can you two stop with the theatrics and get dancing, please? We don't have all day." Laura-Beth pressed a button on her phone, and a slow country ballad filled the diner.

"Right. Some of us have jobs we should be doing now," Frannie shot back.

Kelley seized her little sister's hand and started into a country waltz before her two sisters could start in bickering.

Only two songs later, Laura-Beth called a halt and said, "The pair of you are a hot mess. You've rammed into no less than four tables and toppled three chairs."

"It's Kelley's fault." Frannie frowned and crossed her arms over her chest. "She doesn't know what *swept off your boots* even means."

Kelley could not recall ever being swept off her feet in boots or otherwise. It was a silly turn of phrase in her opinion. After all, if she got swept off her feet, she would literally fall down. Nothing fun about that. Kelley shot back, "Well, I lost count how many times you stepped on my toes, which are throbbing now, by the way."

"That's because you don't know how to lead correctly," Frannie challenged.

"Fine." Kelley bowed to her sister. "You lead this time."

"Gladly," Frannie said.

"Let's try a different dance this time," Laura-Beth said. "Like a simple two-step. You can't possibly get that wrong."

One verse later, they bumped into another chair. Frannie yelped. And Kelley tried not to rub her sore toes.

Laura-Beth slapped her hand on her forehead and groaned. "You're ruining the wedding party dance."

"Maybe we don't need it," Frannie offered.

"You can't be serious." Laura-Beth set her hands on her hips and confronted Frannie. "I won't have my entire reception ruined because you can't follow a simple two-step."

"This is not my fault," Frannie retorted. "Don't you dare blame me."

"I didn't crush Kelley's toes," Laura-Beth charged.

Frannie fumed, "No one can be expected to think straight let alone dance at such a ridiculous hour, LB."

A pair of headlights flashed across the front windows. That had to be Lenny Culver. The older cowboy was always the first of the early-bird regulars to arrive. Len preferred his first cup of coffee extra hot, straight and sipped in silence. It was well into his second cup of coffee when Len would claim he was finally fit for company and then he'd step up his conversational game with the other regulars.

But Kelley was not interested in the retiree's conversational skills right now. Len told Kelley more than one story about how he used to wear his boots out on the dance floor in his younger days. Still, Kelley was going to owe the good-natured widower free breakfast for the inconvenience.

Kelley beelined toward the entrance and called over her shoulder, "Frannie, you get up even earlier for your horse."

"My mare requires affection and care at this time of the day," Frannie shot back. "Not conversation or coordination."

"So wake up, little sister," LB snapped. "My wedding day is on the line here."

"Hold up, you two," Kelley cut in before her

sister could ramp up their bickering. "I've got a solution."

Laura-Beth closed her mouth and arched an eyebrow at Kelley.

Frannie spun around and watched her.

Kelley opened the front door and caught sight of a cowboy turning away as if to head back to the parking lot. *Not so fast*. Kelley called out a hasty good morning, latched on to his arm and tugged him quickly inside. The cowboy behind her, she faced her sisters and announced, "To be clear, I have a cowboy solution."

Surprise flashed across Frannie's face. Then her smile turned mischievous.

Laura-Beth gaped and swiftly recovered.

Confused, Kelley twisted around to greet Lenny Culver. Only her gaze didn't connect with Len's kind brown eyes like it should. After all, Kelley and Len literally saw eye to eye seeing as they both topped the height chart at five feet eight and a half inches. Len celebrated the half inch. Kelley, not so much. It only made her stand out that much more next to her two petite sisters.

But this was not one of her early-bird regulars. Her pulse kick-started.

The top of Kelley's head barely reached this cowboy's rather sturdy, all-too-fit-looking shoulder. Kelley lifted her gaze slowly past a chin and cheeks covered in a neat and close-trimmed beard and up to a familiar pair of bold blue eyes. *Oh my.*

Before Kelley could backpedal and talk her way out of her cowboy mix-up, Laura-Beth exclaimed, "Asher Blackwell, you're certainly a sight for sore eyes."

Asher Blackwell was certainly a sight. His sun-streaked blond hair and vivid gaze contrasted against a chocolate-brown suede jacket over a fitted black T-shirt tucked into a pair of charcoal-colored jeans. Asher Blackwell was handsome in that effortless, not a care in-the world sort of way. The sort of way that made any cowgirl take notice.

As for Kelley, she could not look away.

"Now you have a proper dance partner, big sis." Frannie gave Kelley a close-lipped grin as she sashayed past Kelley and gave Asher a quick welcome-home hug. Then Frannie said, "What an excellent morning this is turning out to be."

Not so excellent was Kelley noticing the hint of reserve beneath Asher's polished style. As if the former carefree cowboy now came with a silent warning that he had secrets and no intention of sharing.

Don't worry, cowboy, I'm not asking.

These days Kelley was all about keeping things to herself, too. Especially those things that could get broken like her dreams and her heart. And when it came to Asher Blackwell, he was always something of a wildcard, and her first marriage taught Kelley the folly of rolling the dice. As for her old crush on Asher, well, that was nothing more than a blip in the memory books. Kelley swallowed, but her throat was suddenly too dry.

"What are we doing exactly?" Asher asked, his words casual and light, as if he always found himself partnering a cowgirl for a sunrise two-step in a small-town diner.

Kelley was trying to remind herself that reconnecting with a handsome cowboy was not on her priority list. A relationship wasn't even on her nice-to-have or some-other-time list. Besides, there were more than enough hopeless romantics around Kelley to pick up her relationship slack.

"You two are going to dance together," Laura-Beth instructed, using her firmest, no-nonsense middle school teacher voice.

Asher's eyebrows twitched.

Kelley held her breath, waiting for his hasty apology and even quicker exit. Who could blame him? Kelley was tempted to hightail it out of there herself.

Instead, Asher's all-too-direct gaze settled on Kelley and stuck.

Something flashed in his blue eyes. Interest, perhaps? Only if Kelley was one of those overly optimistic, quick-to-fall hopeless romantic types with a well-established crush on a cowboy. She was definitely not that. She was levelheaded and sensible and no longer allowed her emotions to lead. Still, now seemed like an appropriate time to excuse herself and get back to her job of managing the morning shift at the diner. Kelley opened her mouth.

Laura-Beth eased right in and said smoothly, "Asher, please tell me you haven't been in New York so long you forgot how to do a simple country swing dance."

"I think I can manage." Asher chuckled and had Kelley's hand in his before she could retreat to the kitchen. A small tug and he guided her straight into his arms as if she was exactly why he had come home.

Kelley sidestepped that foolish thought. Then Asher's other hand settled on her lower back, gentle yet steady. The warmth of his touch was unmistakable. Awareness jolted inside her, tempting her to update the status of her crush to current and active.

One verse later and no bruised toes, Asher drew Kelley even closer and said quietly, "It's finally coming back to me now."

Things were coming back to Kelley, too. Things like how long it had been since she danced. Or even wanted to. And just how much she enjoyed dancing, especially with a capable partner. "I'm sorry about this, but welcome home."

"Not exactly how I pictured my first morning in town," Asher mused, his expression slightly bewildered. "Not that I'm complaining."

Neither was she. He turned them several times quickly, swirling her perilously close to breathless. *Breathless in a cowboy's arms*. How long had it been? And why was it *so* compelling with Asher? Wanting to regain her footing and avoid any unintentional missteps of the heart kind, Kelley blurted, "I'm sorry about Walter."

Asher's gaze dimmed instantly at the mention of his dead father. It was almost as if he'd become suddenly guarded. No more devil-may-care attitude. His steps slowed. That earlier reserve dropped firmly back into place.

Kelley winced.

"No. No. No." Laura-Beth appeared beside them and shook her head. Her words were hasty and earnest. "This is a wedding dance. You can console each other later. Hug it out and all that afterward."

"Did you lose someone, too?" Concern crossed Asher's face. Then he pulled Kelley back into his arms as if to comfort her and asked, "Are you okay?"

Very okay. But she was in the arms of Asher Blackwell—the charismatic cowboy turned New York businessman. And that should not be okay. Asher was everything her ex-husband was: career driven, ambitious and focused. Yet, with Asher focused completely on her, Kelley struggled to find his flaws. Finally, Kelley nodded.

"It's the opposite, actually," Frannie chimed in from behind the counter where she refilled sugar shakers for the tables. "Kelley's ex-husband lost the best cowgirl he will ever find when he walked out on my sister."

"Kelley is way too good for him anyway," Laura-Beth added.

And that was why Kelley came home. Her family had her back. No matter what. Kelley knew who she could count on. Always. Still, she held Asher's gaze.

Asher considered her.

"Trust us. Kelley is way better off without him," Laura-Beth continued, certainty in her words.

There was a time Kelley had not been quite so certain. But that was in the months following her separation from her husband and the fallout of owning a restaurant together. Back when she had lost both her professional and personal futures in one fell swoop. Her words were soft yet resolute. "I'm fine." *And you should know, I'm even better on my own, cowboy.*

Asher nodded, yet concern lingered in his gaze.

Nice that, but entirely unnecessary. Kelley squeezed Asher's fingers and said, "Really. I'm good. The divorce was finalized earlier this year and that is all officially behind me as they say."

Asher searched her face for another beat then said, "I'm sorry you had to go through all that."

It was not the sincerity in his words that got to Kelley. But rather the almost imperceptible change in his hold around her waist. It was suddenly somehow tender yet protective as if he held something precious. She wanted to sigh all the way down to her sore toes. Or she would have if she wanted to feel special to a cowboy. But after her split from her husband, she decided romance was a luxury she could no longer afford.

"Asher, you should take Kelley to dinner," Frannie called out. "Then maybe you can find out if my big sis is as good a catch as we claim."

Kelley shook her head.

"But don't take her to dinner here at the diner," Laura-Beth added. "It's too hard to keep her focused on you when she is here."

Funny. Kelley was having no problems focusing on Asher. "Don't pay my sisters any mind."

One corner of his mouth lifted.

And all Kelley suddenly wanted was his full smile. Aimed at her. Talk about a misstep.

"Pay me every mind." Laura-Beth stomped her boot. "This is a wedding party celebration, not a condolence gathering. We are supposed to be blissful and excited and so very delighted."

"Cheerful and oh so very hopeful," Frannie chimed in.

"Absolutely. That, too." Laura-Beth motioned toward Kelley, and Asher then ordered, "Now, get happy."

"Yes, ma'am." Asher twirled Kelley away then spun her back into his embrace, turned them in a tight circle and twirled her out again. That move he repeated flawlessly until Kelley's laughter floated around the dining area like so much homespun sugar.

"Yes. Exactly like that. Now, take it from the

beginning." Laura-Beth started the song again, turned up the volume and called out, "Frannie, make a note. We need to add that spinning move to the dance."

Three more twirls and Kelley released her hold on Asher then lifted her hands to call a stop to catch her breath.

"No. You have to see it through to the end." Her sister was suddenly beside them. Laura-Beth continued, "There are no breaks in wedding bliss."

Kelley inhaled and stepped back into Asher's arms.

"From the top," Laura-Beth announced and restarted the music.

The dance came to a close with no interruptions and Asher completed it with a perfectly executed dip. Kelley couldn't remember ever being a part of a movie-style ending. *Be still my heart.* Her eyes locked on Asher's and that awareness fired all over again.

There was a high-pitched happy whistle from the direction of the kitchen. Hayes Stroud, the diner's longtime cook, had clearly arrived. Outside, applause and cheers filled the parking lot. Asher shifted and drew Kelley slowly back up to standing. His gaze never left hers.

"That was perfect." Satisfaction streamed across Laura-Beth's face then she added, "I've got a final dress fitting to get to and a meeting with the wedding coordinator. But first, coffee and a blackberry pastry." With that, Laura-Beth breezed through the swinging doors into the kitchen.

Kelley ran her palm over Asher's chest as if searching to see if his heart was beating as rapidly as her own. *How about an encore, cowboy?* Kelley snatched her arm away and blurted, "Grab a seat. Breakfast and coffee are on me for all your assistance this morning."

Kelley didn't stick around to hear Asher's reply. Instead, she boot-scooted to the diner entrance and finally greeted her early-bird regulars clamoring to get inside. The sign flipped back to Open, Kelley turned around only to pull back to avoid bumping into Lynette Arber.

The older widow fluffed her silver bangs and said, "Breakfast and a show should be the way we start every morning here."

Beatrice, Lynette's sister and a widow, too, beelined for her stool at the counter and called out, "I'll take my usual, Kelley, and a turn on the dance floor with your cowboy."

"He's not mine," Kelley said quickly and watched Asher slip through the swinging doors into the kitchen.

"He oughtta be." Lynette waggled her eyebrows at Kelley. "You two got what they called chemistry back in my day. It's not only good for the dance floor, either."

Chemistry wasn't sustainable for more than a night out on the town or perhaps through the honeymoon phase. Kelley learned that much with her ex-husband, and they had shared a lot more than chemistry. Kelley held on to her grin and greeted Lenny Culver with a quick apology for the delayed opening.

"As long as the coffee is piping hot, there is nothing to apologize for." Chuckling, Len headed for his usual seat at the end of the counter and asked, "Are you going to tell us who your cowboy suitor is, Kelley? Or are you going to make us guess?"

"Don't tell us," Lynette said and plopped onto the stool between Len and her sister. Her gaze gleamed. "We could use a good mystery to spice things up around here."

That earned a hum of agreement from both Beatrice and Len.

Kelley kept silent. The mystery wouldn't last much past their first cups of coffee. Someone was bound to recognize Asher Blackwell when he walked outside to his car. The cowboy was hard to miss and even harder to mistake. Asher might have been out of sight for the past eight years but he was far from out of mind for the locals. It seemed everyone had a take on what drove Asher out of town for good all those years ago. Those stories had picked up steam again after the death of Walter Blackwell when none of the Blackwell sons returned.

But now Asher Blackwell was home. And the town was sure to be abuzz all over again.

Coffee and tea mugs filled and the dining area put back to rights, Kelley stepped through the swinging doors and stopped short of stepping back into her cowboy's arms. Whether to warn him or protect him, she wasn't quite sure. She swallowed and said, "There's room at the counter for you."

"My uncle is expecting me for breakfast at the house. Frannie got me the caffeine boost I stopped in for." Asher lifted a to-go cup toward her and added, "But I appreciate the coffee and dance."

"Anytime." She was surprised to realize she meant it.

Asher arched an eyebrow.

She lifted one shoulder and worked to keep her expression and words casual. "What can I say? It was not the worst way to start my morning." There was only one way it could have been better. A good-morning kiss with a cowboy. *Her cowboy.*

"Until next time, then," he said, his grin one-sided. At the exit, he glanced back at her and added, "Save a space on your dance card for me, Ms. Kelley Munroe."

There would have been a time she would have saved her entire dance card for a cowboy like him.

Except Asher Blackwell was a city cowboy now.

And Kelley left those behind when she signed her divorce papers, headed back home and hung up her heart for good.

CHAPTER TWO

INSIDE HIS RENTAL SUV, Asher took a sip of his coffee and sighed. Proper temperature, full-bodied yet balanced, not too bitter or too sweet. It was official. The Galloping Fork Diner still served the best cup of coffee from here to the east coast. It was good to know some things had not changed in Gold Finch after all.

As for things that were better than Asher remembered, well, the sunshine in a certain cowgirl's laugh was a rather refreshing surprise. Not that Asher could linger, even if he wanted to. He wasn't home to make new memories, especially not with the former wallflower turned colorfully carefree chef, Kelley Munroe. Besides, no amount of sunshine could possibly blaze through his dark cloud of cynicism.

A few miles outside downtown, Asher drove by a set of ornate glossy steel gates with a striking polished steel sign overhead that read Blackwell Stables. Towering wide, square twin stone columns added to the grandeur of the stable's main entrance along with the sturdy triple post fence bordering the property that at last count totaled more than two thousand acres. Top-of-the-line stables, state-of-the-art indoor and outdoor practice tracks and well-tended pastures were not only the core of the impressive horse farm. They were also the first things visitors saw when they arrived.

You get one first impression, boys. Make a statement and no one will doubt you ever.

Ironic that Asher always wondered what exactly he could have done differently at his own birth. He was the second-born twin, and his birth order had seemed to make the wrong sort of statement with his father. When it came to his dad, one thing was clear to Asher. Walter Blackwell always doubted Asher. *Mark my words, son. You are nothing without the Blackwell name. You'll realize that soon enough.*

Asher stepped on the gas and avoided that potential pothole. For the past eight years, Asher and his dad shared nothing more than silence. He had no intention of arguing with his father's ghost now. Instead, he opened the call log on his phone and pressed the first name on the list.

His boss answered before the second ring and as was Pierce Rylan's way, Pierce skipped straight to the point and said, "If you're calling because you are locked out of the company network, I already know. I told the IT Department to do it."

"You can't do that." Asher frowned at the cell

phone. "I've got clients and deals in the pipeline. You can't just cut me out completely."

"It's not permanent so don't be getting any ideas in your head," his boss replied then added softly, "This is for your own good."

Asher doubted that very much. Work was what Asher did best. Where he felt his best. "How long are you blocking me?"

"Seven days," Pierce said, his words curt. "Business days."

That was the rest of the week and all of the following one, too. Asher flexed his fingers around the steering wheel and turned onto a private road a few miles past the stable's main gates. He drove through the nondescript wrought iron gates and followed the curvy one-lane road.

"Now go vacation like my wife tells me to do." Amusement smoothed the edge from Pierce's words. "Reconnect with nature or some such thing. You'll be better for it."

Asher rolled his eyes even though he was alone. The only person who worked more than him was his boss. He asked, "Would you give me access to my work email if I told you I was home? Back in Gold Finch, Kentucky."

"No," Pierce replied flatly and without hesitation. "I would tell you to find your cowboy boots and get on with vacationing."

That was the problem. Asher was not sure how

to *get on* in Gold Finch. He was much better at *getting gone*. He sighed, loudly and irritably.

"You'll thank me for this." Pierce chuckled and added, "No more work texts, either. Send me a photo of you on a horse if you feel the need to text me." With that last order, his boss ended the call.

Asher parked in the horseshoe-shaped driveway and reached for his cell phone. Only there were no unanswered work emails to distract him. He snatched the coffee cup from the console and finished the last of it in one swallow. He should have lingered at the diner. Accepted Kelley's breakfast offer. But he was not home to reconnect, especially not with an intriguing cowgirl chef.

Silence crowded around him. His thoughts tumbled. And suddenly, the already compact rental car became all that much smaller. Asher got out. Only now he was in a face-off with the sprawling single-story ranch house where he'd grown up.

The family rambler needed a fresh coat of paint. The garden beds a good weeding. He'd bet the last brick on the second step of the front porch was still loose. Same as it had been since his twin knocked it loose trying a new trick on his skateboard when they were kids. Their father had assumed Asher was the careless one and the brothers hadn't bothered to correct him. Asher blocked the memory before it could trip into another and then another. He was not there to revisit his childhood, either.

Asher eyed the front entrance. On the other side

of the ornate wood double doors was a decades-long collection of family photographs decorating every available space on the foyer walls and extending into the hallway. Short of closing his eyes, there would be no way to escape walking through snapshots of favorite family moments on his route to the kitchen.

An ache built inside his chest. Making him realize he wasn't quite as numb as he pretended to be.

Asher veered toward the stone path that led to the detached garages and back door for quick access to the mudroom and far fewer painful flashbacks. Besides, it wasn't like Walter was there to stop him. That ache expanded.

One rap of his knuckles on the glass pane in the back door, Asher stepped inside and was officially home. He braced his legs wide and waited for that sadness to engulf him. It saturated the very air the last time Asher was there for his twin's funeral eight years ago. Back then he had struggled to draw a decent breath around the tightness in his chest. Now the air was tinged with a distinct bitterness.

Asher inhaled. Not bitter but rather burnt. He sniffed again. Definitely a burning smell.

Hurrying into the kitchen, Asher found his father's cousin, Elias Blackwell, and his father's best friend, Joe Allcott, eyeing a smoking toaster on the kitchen island. Asher asked, "Everyone okay in here?"

"We're fine, but I can't say the same for the toast." Big E frowned and used a pair of tongs to fish out a blackened piece of bread. Shaking his head, Big E chuckled. "I believe this toaster is more vintage than me."

Joe coughed and waved his arm, dispersing the smoky air wafting from the toaster. "Walter was never much for unnecessary upgrades, especially if they didn't benefit the stables."

The horses always came before everyone and everything in Walter Blackwell's heart and mind. There simply was very little space left for anything else. Especially a son who refused to bend to his father's wishes. *You're a Blackwell, Asher. It's time to see if you can prove you know what that means.* Asher knocked the past aside and moved farther into the kitchen.

Joe made his way around the island, shook Asher's hand then added, "Looks like you made it without any issues."

The only issue was Asher suddenly second-guessing his decision to come home. What help could he possibly offer? And judging from Joe's cool reception, his father's best friend and the stable's longtime manager was thinking along the same lines. Asher cleared his throat and said, "It's good to see you, Uncle Joe."

Joe only gave a small chin dip in acknowledgment of the Blackwell boys' endearing name for him.

Now Asher knew where he stood. That was to

be expected. Joe always sided with his father for as long as Asher could remember.

Big E tossed the toast into the sink and wiped his palms on a towel. Then he shook Asher's hand and drew him in for a quick, albeit hearty welcome-home embrace. Big E grinned and said, "You're taller than I remember, son."

"My mom called me a late bloomer," Asher replied.

Freshman year of college Asher finally grew tall enough to look his twin in the eyes, and suddenly it became even more challenging to tell the identical twins apart. Of course, Dylan and Asher used that to their advantage and enjoyed more than one laugh when they had confused friends and family over the years. What he wouldn't give for a twin swap right about now. That ache built again.

Asher flattened his palm on the butcherblock countertop decades past its prime and anchored himself in the present. So much time to heal and yet Asher still missed his twin on the daily. He asked, "Did we miss the staff breakfast already?"

"This is breakfast." Joe frowned and added, "Vicky was poached by Sully over at Connelly Stables. She gave her notice last night. The crew is eating donuts this morning."

But Vicky was a staple around the ranch and known for her extensive culinary creativity with a Crock-Pot. There was not a meal Asher could recall that hadn't been served in a Crock-Pot of some sort whenever Vicky was on duty. And Asher was always elected the taste tester by his brothers. He scratched his cheek. "What now?"

"Can you cook, son?" Big E asked, hope in his steely gaze.

"Not well enough to feed an entire stable of employees." His lack of skill aside, the more pressing problem was the collection of outdated appliances and whether any even worked properly. Given the state of the toaster, Asher was betting no.

Joe crunched on the last of his toast and added, "Unfortunately, we've lost more employees than Vicky to our rivals recently."

No surprise there. Cheating allegations tended to spook both the clients and the staff. He looked from Joe to Big E and asked, "How bad is it?"

Big E lifted his chin and held Asher's stare. "Folks will calm down now that one of Walter's own is home."

Except Asher was not one of Walter's. That much Asher's father had made perfectly clear when Asher refused to step into his dead twin's place, take over the stables and pretend it was all business as usual.

You might have the Blackwell name but that hardly means I have to call you my son anymore.

Those were the last words spoken between Asher and his dad. Silent, Asher had walked out of the house for good. The memory left a sour taste that lingered even now. Asher rubbed his throat and said, "I wouldn't be too certain about that."

"Well, you answered my call and chose to come home." Big E smiled at Asher, acceptance in his gaze. "That counts for something to the folks still here."

Asher nodded even though this was mandatory time off after Asher made two uncharacteristic mistakes at work. Big E's phone call had given Asher a landing pad other than white sandy beaches where Asher feared his workaholic self would have been more likely to stir up a sandstorm than build a sandcastle.

"There isn't enough butter to fix this bread and there's more than enough work needing to get done." Joe tossed the last of the toast into the sink and returned the butter container to the refrigerator.

"Come on, we'll show you what we're dealing with." Big E waggled his eyebrows. "And if we're lucky there might even be a donut or two left for the taking."

Asher followed Joe and Big E out to the UTV parked behind the garages and climbed into the back passenger seat. Joe took the trail through the forested area, kept the pace of the conversation slow and filled Asher in on which local stables hired Blackwell employees, and which stables took in Blackwell clients. Big E hadn't exaggerated when he had phoned Asher. The vultures were circling.

Minutes later, Joe stopped beside the main stables and glanced back at Asher then asked, "When were you last in the saddle?"

Longer than he cared to admit. Asher held Joe's steady stare and said, "I haven't forgotten how to ride if that's what you're getting at."

"That's good." Joe cut the engine. There was a challenge in his words. "Now it is time to prove you haven't forgotten what I taught you about proper conditioning all those years ago."

"You want me to exercise horses?" Asher climbed out of the UTV. They should have called Nathan for help, not him. Asher's youngest brother was a horse breeder of all things. Asher excelled in the art of corporate negotiations and being the first in his company to recognize lucrative investment opportunities. Not exactly a necessary skill set around the stables. And yet, he was the only brother there.

"We've got a training schedule to keep and minimal staff to keep it," Big E explained. "Joe and I agree we must keep things as normal and routine as possible. It's good for the well-being of the horses and the employees."

Joe adjusted the cowboy hat on his head and remained silent.

While Asher questioned how much Joe really agreed. He said casually, "Business as usual, then."

Joe nodded, resolve in his gaze and stance.

Except there was nothing typical about Asher working in the stables. And they both knew it. Dylan should be there. His twin would have been able to calm the staff and their fears in minutes. His brother always had a knack for finding the right words in any situation. Asher often skipped the pleasantries, cut to the chase and viewed just about everything as a potential business transaction. That meant constantly gauging the return on investment and always keeping his emotions in check.

Big E stepped into Asher's view and said simply, "Son, we need you."

There were those words again. The same ones Big E used when he phoned Asher not three days ago at his office in New York. The same ones Asher couldn't seem to ignore. Big E eyed Asher as if he already knew Asher would not deny him now, either. Asher sighed. "Where do you want me?"

"The practice track." Joe's smile widened yet lacked any warmth as if he was not overly keen on accepting Asher's help. Joe added, "Don't worry. It's slow miles today. Let me know if it's too much. We'll manage either way."

The words *without you* left unsaid. Right. Asher understood Joe's reluctance yet bristled all the same.

"You'll settle right in after the first walk." Big

E lifted his eyebrows and grinned. “By the time you pick up to a trot, it’ll be like you never stopped riding.”

Joe’s indifference faltered. He reached up and squeezed Asher’s shoulder. Affection flashed in his gaze. “It’s nothing you haven’t done before on these same tracks.”

But that was a lifetime ago. When Asher completed his stable chores simply to get to his adventures faster. The ones that included racing on horseback across open pastures and daring his twin to jump his horse over anything they could find out on the land. These days, the adrenaline rushes came from investment risks paying off better than expected and handshakes that closed seven-figure deals. It was custom business suits and leather chairs in boardrooms and a world away from Gold Finch, Kentucky.

Asher scrubbed a hand over his jaw, unable to shake the feeling that they’d definitely called on the wrong brother. Too late now. It was time to get to work. Besides, he was there, after all, and he suddenly wanted that to mean something.

THE LUNCH RUSH was gone and her morning dance with a cowboy more like a distant yet pleasant memory when Kelley hit Submit on the inventory reorder for the upcoming weekend. Closing the laptop, she caught sight of her sister rushing into the prep kitchen. Kelley pushed out of the creaky office chair she was lounging in, moved into the doorway of the storage area that doubled as the back office then called out, “Frannie, please don’t tell me you got the orders wrong at your last table.”

“Okay.” Frannie snapped her mouth closed and set the plate she was holding on the order counter ever so gingerly.

Kelley tried to keep the frustration from her words and feared she failed. “You did, didn’t you?”

“Does it help if I told you I didn’t get the entire table wrong?” Frannie countered, her hands clasped behind her back. “Just this double-decker club that should be on white not wheat.”

Hayes Stroud returned from his break and cast a look of sympathy toward Frannie. Then the retiree turned full-time cook tossed his support behind Frannie and said, “Everyone should really include more wheat in their diet. It’s good for the digestion.”

Frannie grinned and piled on. “Whole grains are recommended by nutritionists for a well-rounded, heart healthy diet.”

Kelley ground her teeth together. The benefits of whole wheat aside, this error made thirteen tables with incorrect orders in one shift. Her little sister had collected a baker’s dozen of mistakes, which was two more than yesterday’s shift. Kelley washed her hands in the sink and dried them. “But wheat bread is not what the customer wanted.”

Frannie lifted her chin and argued, “Well, big

sister, if you would just make your blackberry bacon grilled cheese, everyone would want that and not the same old, boring double-decker club."

Hayes murmured something that sounded like agreement.

"It's not my menu." Kelley made her way to the food line and set about making the correct double-decker club sandwich. A minute later, Kelley held the plate toward her little sister, who waited at the service counter.

Frannie never reached for the plate and asked tentatively, "Can you deliver it, please?"

Kelley glanced through the pass-through window into the dining area and frowned at the two familiar twenty-something cowboys seated at a window booth. Luke Connelly was the nephew of Sullivan Connelly of Connelly Thoroughbred. Luke always made sure to let anyone within hearing distance know he'd recently been promoted to assistant manager, right under Sully's son, Patrick. Kelley glanced at her sister and asked, "What happened?"

Frannie's chin jutted out. Irritation made her words all the more brisk. "Nothing happened. And do you know why?" Frannie leaned forward. Her gaze narrowed. Her arm cut through the air. "Because Luke laughed at me when I asked if he would talk to his family about me possibly apprenticing there."

Her sister's bottom lip trembled. Kelley stiffened.

"Luke told me that I'm not good enough," Frannie added, a quiver in her chin. "And that I'm not cut out to be a jockey." That miffed tone in her words gained momentum. "*And* that I will have more success waitressing."

There were suddenly things Kelley wanted to tell Luke on behalf of her very talented, athletic little sister, who was more than capable of being a very good jockey. "What did you say to him?"

Frannie's gaze sparked. "I told Luke that girls can be jockeys, too."

Hayes added, "That, they sure can."

Kelley appreciated her little sister's mettle and said dryly, "I'm sure Luke had a response for that, too."

"He told me that being a girl has nothing to do with it." Frannie's bottom lip quivered again. She brushed the end of her ponytail back off her shoulder and avoided looking at Kelley. "He claims I'll never be as good as a real jockey because if it was in my blood, I wouldn't need to ask a favor from him. I'd already be *in*."

Kelley sighed. How many times had her ex-husband gently reminded Kelley that her cooking roots came from a diner, not an upscale urban restaurant? Culinary school aside, Kelley's pedigree was forever lacking in her ex-husband's eyes, too. *Watch out. I promise I will be more than a footnote in the culinary scene.* Her ex-husband had given her a half smile and a bland, *I hope so* before handing her divorce papers.

Frannie sniffed and blinked away her tears. Kelley was quite skilled at that, too. Kelley set the plate back on the counter, wrapped her arms around her sister and said, "What does Luke know anyway?"

It was true the Munroe family did not have an established equestrian racing lineage. Horseracing was definitely not in their bloodline like some of the families in town. The Munroe family provided support services to those racing families throughout the generations. Their family tree was full of firefighters, deputies, schoolteachers and even a mayor. But that did not make Frannie less-than. Kelley would argue Frannie had more passion than most of the locals with racing in their DNA.

Kelley added, "I can't even remember the last big race any of the Connelly racehorses took first place in."

"You wouldn't know." Frannie rested her head against Kelley's shoulder and sniffed. "You haven't been to the racetrack since you've been home, and you never followed it in New York."

"Well, I will definitely follow it when you are in the starting gates." Kelley pulled away and looked her sister in the eyes. "And I do know this. It is still light out. If you leave now, you can get a ride in before dinner."

Frannie sniffed again and said, "Seriously?"

"Yeah. Go on." Kelley released her sister, motioned toward the cookline then said, "Hayes and me have got this."

"Thanks." Frannie hugged Kelley, took off her apron and paused long enough to accept the triple chip cookie Hayes snuck her from the secret staff stash. At the back entrance, she called out, "Kelley, text me when you are finished here and I'll come back to pick you up. But not before six. I want to squeeze in a gym workout after my ride."

The door clicked shut before Kelley could tell Frannie not to worry about it. She would catch a ride home with Hayes.

"You can't keep cutting that girl loose," Hayes said, a slight scold in his words. Yet, there was kindness in his gaze. "She's never going to learn how it works around here that way."

"And you can't keep sneaking her cookies whenever she's upset," Kelley said then added, "Besides, we need to face the facts. My little sister has got a head for horses, not food service."

"Truer words," Hayes muttered and handed Kelley a triple chip cookie.

Kelley broke the cookie in two and gave half to Hayes then she shrugged. "It's fine Frannie left early. We're already well past the lunch rush anyway."

Hayes frowned around a bite of cookie and said, "I would call it more of a trickle than a rush."

Truer words. Kelley polished off her cookie half

and rewashed her hands. Then she delivered the double-decker sandwich to Luke in a to-go bag and said pleasantly, "You'll need to leave now. This section is closed."

Luke tipped his chin toward the stools at the counter and said, "We can eat over there, then."

Kelley held on to her smile and said, "That's closed, too."

Luke eyed her. "You're telling me the entire dining room is closed."

Closed to cowboys who made her little sister cry. Most definitely. Kelley kept her words upbeat. "You can give any complaints to the shift manager." She never blinked and added, "Oh wait. That's me." She set the check on the table and smiled all the way back to the small office. Only she lost her moment of good humor after she pulled out the adding machine and began totaling the cost of her sister's mistakes for the day.

"You do realize that every time you pay to cover one of your sister's meal mix-ups, you're really only lightening up your own bank account, right?" Hayes watched her from the doorway.

"Frannie would barely have any money if I deducted each incorrect meal from her paycheck. And she needs the money for her horse. The boarding and the care aren't cheap," Kelley argued, hit the total button and tore off the thin printed tally sheet. "Besides, I'm her big sister. I'm supposed to look out for her."

"Not at your own expense and this is getting costly," Hayes countered and reached over to answer the retro yellow push button telephone attached to the wall outside the dry storage area.

Kelley glanced at the printed total and cringed. It wasn't quite as dire as Hayes implied. Still, Frannie was clearly trending in the wrong direction with more mistakes each shift, not fewer. Kelley needed to correct that sooner rather than later.

After all, Kelley was rebuilding her own bank account. The longer that took, the longer she would be living at home and nowhere closer to getting on with her life. Not that she knew her next step exactly. She knew only that it would be big. If only to prove she was every bit as talented as her ex-husband and finally make her mark on her own terms.

Hayes hung up the phone and said, "Boss wants you to meet her at Lucky Lane in an hour."

"Why didn't Pauline call me?" Kelley frowned, stashed the calculator back in the side drawer of the metal work desk and checked her cell phone. No missed calls.

"Pauline misplaced her cell phone," Hayes explained.

"Again?" That seemed to be a common occurrence for the diner owner. And it explained why Pauline had not replied to Kelley's texts about approving invoices for payment and signing off on purchase orders for the weekend supply delivery.

"That must be the fifth time this week she lost her phone and it's only Wednesday."

"Pauline has been booked up going on all sorts of dates," Hayes explained. "It seems she recently put herself back in the marriage mart."

"What does that have to do with her lost cell phone?" Kelley snapped her fingers and grinned. "I got it. Pauline left it when she was sneaking out on an awkward blind date. If she went back to get her phone, she would have been stuck on her date."

"Pauline has better manners than that," Hayes countered.

"When was the last time you were on a blind date?" Kelley tapped her chin and considered Hayes. He was a father of two and claimed to be friends with his exes. Kelley added, "Or any sort of date for that matter."

"I've been on my fair share of dates. Now, never mind all that." Hayes braced his hands on his hips and eyed Kelley. "You need to focus. This is your chance."

"My chance for what?" Kelley asked slowly. Because she was not joining Pauline back on the marriage mart. Been there. Divorced that.

"This is your chance to pitch your ideas to Pauline and fix this place." Hayes pulled a small worn notebook from the wide pocket in his apron and handed it to her.

"What is this?" Kelley asked.

"I wrote down your recipes," Hayes said unapologetically. "Although I guessed at some of the ingredients. Not that it matters. These are your creations, so you know full well what goes in them."

Kelley flipped through the lined pages and scanned several recipes. "But this was all in fun." A few weeks ago, at Pauline's request, Kelley and Hayes spent an entire weekend deep cleaning the walk-in refrigerator and freezer and then inventorying the entire restaurant from top to bottom. Hayes challenged Kelley to create her own diner menu while they were reorganizing the walk-in refrigerator. Kelley explained, "I wasn't serious."

"Well, it is serious now," Hayes replied, his words firm. "We need more customers around here. We gotta give the locals a reason to come back for more than just your Wednesday mystery bakes." Hayes pointed at the notebook and said, "There are more than a dozen reasons right inside there."

Kelley hedged, "But don't forget Pauline wasn't all that interested in my ideas for rearranging the cookline to improve the service flow."

"That was bad timing," Hayes mused.

"Pauline accused me of wanting to change everything and erase her mom's very essence from the entire place," Kelley said dryly.

That would have been near to impossible. Trudy Riggins had always been the heart of the Galloping Fork Diner. It was Trudy who had hired and trained Kelley back when Kelley was a freshman in high school. Trudy had been demanding of her employees and particular about every detail of her diner. However, she'd recognized Kelley's passion for cooking and never stopped nurturing it.

"You'd been working here less than a week." Hayes brushed his hand through the air and continued, "Pauline was still in the worst of her grief from her mom's death and couldn't see nothing else. It's been six months."

"And time heals," Kelley said mildly. At least it was supposed to.

"That and it's time to show Pauline what you can really do," Hayes said. "This place needs a refresh, and you need to be back in the kitchen doing more than rolling out dough for a limited pastry run once a week."

It had been over a year since her divorce and since the last time Kelley ran a full dinner service. She'd come home and taken a much-needed step back. It was for the best while she and Pauline found their new normal; at least she hoped it was. Otherwise, she might be concerned she was going backward in life. Kelley smiled at the older cook. "I appreciate the vote of confidence. Now, let me finish up some paperwork so I can meet our boss on time."

"Trudy would tell you that if you see an opening, take it and make your pitch." Hayes turned and walked out, adding, "Swing for the stars. And you will go places you never imagined."

That was just it. Kelley had swung for the stars and the moon. And believed she had it all, too. A dream job working beside the man she loved. It was everything her heart ever wanted.

Yet love, she knew now, had an expiration date. After all, she had ended up back where she never imagined she would be. Home in Gold Finch.

So when she swung again, she would use her head and not follow her heart. Surely then she would get everything she needed.

CHAPTER THREE

BACK IN THE SADDLE. For most of the day. One more thing Asher had not anticipated for his first day home in years. And he could not say he minded all that much. Now, a last dance with a certain cowgirl to close out his day, well, he would not mind that, either. Shaking his head, Asher blamed the heat and his lack of a cowboy hat and proper sun protection for scrambling his thoughts.

He dismounted from Derby Dreamer and complimented the two-year-old thoroughbred on a solid workout then handed the reins to Owen, the stable's hotwalker. Owen was less than shouting distance away when Derby Dreamer reared, broke loose from Owen's hold and sprinted out of the pasture. Fortunately, the spirited colt darted in Asher's direction, and he had the racehorse under control fairly quickly.

Owen jogged over, his cheeks the same flame-colored red as his hair. He exhaled hard, his words coming out in a puff. "I'm sorry. I don't know what happened."

This was the third time that afternoon Owen

had told Asher the very same thing. And the third horse who spooked with the twenty-some-year-old groom.

Owen added, “I can take him now.”

“It’s all right.” Asher ran his palm over the colt’s sleek gray neck and shook his head. “Me and Derby Dreamer seem to have bonded. I’ll cool him down and take him to his stall.”

Owen chewed on his bottom lip and eyed Asher. “Are you firing me, then, for too many mistakes?”

“Not today,” Asher said.

Owen’s shoulders lowered. “What should I do?”

Asher checked the walking ring, noted the horses already there cooling down and said, “Come with me. We can hand-walk Derby Dreamer together.” Asher turned the colt toward a path that circled the perimeter of the property and asked, “How long have you been here, Owen?”

By the time Asher led Derby Dreamer into his stall, he knew Owen’s entire history. The kid was working to pay for his classes at the local college. He wanted to be a veterinarian but needed large animal experience on his application. He’d been working at the Blackwell Stables for two weeks, was bright and eager to try. Asher walked Owen through a proper rubdown, left the kid with Derby Dreamer and went to find Joe to figure out how to get Owen the proper training he needed.

He found Joe in the tack room, inspecting a broken bridle. “I know Owen is new around here, but the colts I worked with today seemed more than a little high-spirited."

"They are," Joe acknowledged. "They are all on the younger side of two."

Asher frowned. "But those workouts today are meant for a more mature two." One that was able to focus and compete.

"We've accelerated our training program slightly," Joe admitted. "The twos have not been sanctioned. We need to get them racing sooner rather than later."

But Asher's father was meticulous about every stage of his training program. He had personally curated and designed the program over years of breeding and racing to produce elite racehorses capable of winning. There was no skipping or rushing through any phase. Ever. Asher said, "Dad would not like this."

"Your father was focused entirely on Sovereign's Pride. And that is why the twos are behind in their training." Joe shook his head and continued, "Now we need revenue, and the juvenile races are our chance until the sanctions are lifted on the threes."

If the sanctions weren't lifted, the juvenile races were their only chance not just for revenue, but to prove the Blackwell Stables still produced quality racehorses.

A trainer shouted for Joe. He grabbed a different bridle from the wall, then eyed Asher. "Don't forget to stretch yourself. You need to be back in the saddle first thing tomorrow morning."

Asher rolled his shoulders against the stiffness already tightening across his lower back from the hours spent riding and said, "Then I proved myself."

Joe nodded and stepped around Asher then glanced back. "You look like you might have even enjoyed yourself, too."

"I did have fun," Asher admitted.

"You don't have to look so surprised." Joe chuckled and shook his head. "It's allowed around here, even for a serious-minded business guy like you."

Asher had fun twice in one day. First, dancing with Kelley at the diner and then riding. That had to be some sort of record. He took it for what it was—a moment to clear his head. After all, he'd long since outgrown making a habit out of fun.

Besides, he was serious now about preserving his twin's legacy, and chasing fun would not lead to reliable revenue streams or the reputational damage control they needed to survive the doping allegations. Of that much Asher was sure.

Asher walked down the stalls until he found the one marked Sovereign's Pride. The colt was sleek and muscular, standing at 16.2 hands. His coat was a deep golden brown. His mane and tail black. His blaze pure white. At first glance, the colt was perfect. A racehorse in its prime, ready to work. Asher could envision Pride rounding the bend toward the finish line and crossing first for an impressive and indisputable win. There was something regal about the horse, as if he knew he was meant to be the best.

Yet, on second glance, there was something fragile about the horse. Asher extended his arm over the stall door, palm open and fingers extended in the same way Joe had taught him when he was four and his father decided it was high time the twins learned how to ride. Pride watched him with caution and flattened his ears, alerting Asher that all was not well with the champion.

Big E joined Asher at the colt's stall.

"Pride is too agitated and very unsettled." And that bothered Asher a lot.

"Hasn't been the same since we came back from the Dust and Diamonds Derby. We've tried everything we know," Big E mused. "Dr. Eisler checked him. Got Doc Julia's treatment plan right there." Big E tipped his head toward the clipboard hanging on the outside of the stall then he added, "Doc says the drugs need time to work out of his system."

"How long does that take?" Asher asked.

"Each horse is different." Big E shrugged. "Could be days or weeks."

Asher watched Pride and held the horse's gaze as if the colt was going to let him in on his secrets. *I know a little bit about how you feel.* And like the racehorse, Asher was not certain quite how to cut through his own discontent. He supposed they were both waiting for the feeling to pass. Asher only hoped it wouldn't be much longer for both of them.

"Maybe you've got an idea," Big E suggested.

"I'm the wrong brother." Asher took a step back. "You want Nathan or Caleb. They've always had a sense for horses and their needs." Nathan bred horses and Caleb was something of a horse whisperer; at least that was what the family always called him.

"But you've got the sense for numbers." Big E tapped his temple. "From what I've heard and learned about you and your job in the city."

Asher lifted one shoulder. "I've managed well enough."

"More than well," Big E stated. "You've got an MBA with a concentration in finance from a renowned university. You're a director at your firm and you closed more deals than any of your peers by almost double last year. If I'm not mistaken, you're on pace to do the same this year."

He was. Until Asher got a call about his father's sudden death. Asher had been standing in front of the floor-to-ceiling windows in his corner office in a downtown high-rise, working late as usual. He had listened to the voice mail from Joe twice. The first time buckled his knees. The replay found him dropping onto the leather couch as if he didn't know how to stand on his own anymore. Asher had sat on that couch until the sun came up, certain the start of a new day would see him back to rights. And yet, like Pride, Asher had been out of step ever since.

Asher scratched his chin and said, "You've done your homework on me."

"You're family." Big E chuckled. "I like to celebrate my family's successes. Also, I find it helpful to know who I can count on and for what."

Asher shifted and studied the older cowboy. "Why do I get the feeling you called me here for more than exercising and conditioning the horses?"

"Because I did," Big E said, his voice low. He glanced around the stables, nodded at a pair of stable hands and Joe, then he added, "Let's take a stroll. With this many ears in the building, there's sure to be some listening in going on."

Asher walked beside Big E until they reached the pasture the farthest away from the practice tracks and stables. A trio of horses grazed in the far corner, their tails swishing and their ears flickering.

Big E hitched his boot on the bottom fence post and considered Asher. His words were frank and matter-of-fact. "I need you to do an in-depth review of the stable financials."

Now, that was cutting to the chase. Asher liked Big E all the more. He asked, "Is there a problem?"

"That's what I want you to find out," Big E said and tipped his hat back. "Given you didn't flinch at my request, I'll keep it plain and direct. We need to figure out if Walter was desperate enough to dope his own horse to win the Triple Laurel Legacy Circuit."

There was no way to misunderstand that directive. Asher exhaled, low and hard. "Do you believe Walter cheated?" Asher's father was many things. Set in his ways. Stubborn. Gruff. But dishonest in business was not one of them, was it?

"I've seen good cowboys so desperate they've done far worse," Big E mused. "If a cowboy has got nothing to lose then it seems anything is possible."

"Joe mentioned that Walter was focused solely on Pride," Asher said. "But he never put one horse above the program before." Walter always preached about building a sustainable program with quality horses as its foundation. He asked, "Why now?"

"Your dad told me that he finally had a rare colt who could cement his place in the racing history books and guarantee his legacy for generations to come," Big E said.

"So, Walter drugs Pride to ensure his horse wins the Triple Laurel Legacy Circuit," Asher said, testing out the theory. "All to make history."

"Don't forget. Winning all three races in the Triple Laurel would have been the first for any horse in Gold Finch," Big E explained. "The town, and more specifically Blackwell Stables, would have been put on the map and no doubt gained national recognition."

"And gained more influential clients," Asher

mused. And those types of clients translated to higher training and boarding fees and more income for the stables. That brought them right back around to the financials. Asher added, "If my father needed money for the business, winning the Triple Laurel would have ensured it."

Big E frowned and nodded. "This is where you find out if the business was in some sort of financial crisis that only Walter knew about."

Asher winced, unsure if he wanted to believe his father would intentionally dope his own horse rather than ask one of his sons for help. Asher had the financial means, yet would he have even taken his dad's phone call?

He pushed away from the fence post and that answer then rounded on Big E and asked, "Why me? I'm a Blackwell in name only according to Walter."

"According to your father's legal documents, you're a stakeholder and a shareholder with a board seat in Blackwell Stables, Inc," Big E explained further. "You and your brothers own equal shares."

But his father disowned him all those years ago. Asher had not misunderstood those harsh words. Asher gaped at the older cowboy. "That's not possible."

"I've got all the legal paperwork at the house," Big E said. "You can read it over yourself."

Asher widened his stance and steadied himself.

"You should know it's already been fully vetted by Walter's attorney," Big E continued. "It is legal, binding and correct."

Asher was stunned. "Do my brothers know?"

"I don't know what Walter told them about his will or the business ownership." Big E hooked his thumbs in the pockets of his jeans and considered Asher. "You were the first of Walter's sons I contacted."

Asher nodded.

Big E pushed away from the fence and said, "Now might be time to reach out to your brothers yourself and start those sorts of conversations."

Asher agreed yet said, "I'm going to hold off until we know more."

"Even if Walter is guilty, there is still a legacy to save here," Big E stated. "One that goes beyond just your dad."

Saving a legacy was one thing. It was ensuring the legacy continued—the looking after the legacy day in and day out—that worried Asher. "We get the stable's reputation back and then what happens? My life is in New York. Yours is in Montana. Not to mention my brothers all have lives—good, successful ones outside of Gold Finch, too."

"There's no sense getting ahead of ourselves." Big E adjusted his cowboy hat on his head and continued, "Like you said, we need more information before we can decide on a proper direction."

"Sounds like I need to get to work on those financials as soon as possible."

"You let me know how I can help."

"A take-out menu or two would do." Asher grinned and added, "The staff will need dinner soon." Because no matter what, the racehorses were the very core of the Blackwell legacy in Kentucky. The stables needed to stay up and running and that required a happy staff.

Big E chuckled. "I think I'll head back and hunt down those menus."

"I'll see you later at the house," Asher said and hopped over the fence into the pasture. "I'm going to introduce myself to this trio that's been watching us very closely."

And he was going to take a moment to clear his head. *Again.*

He was a shareholder. Not disowned as he long believed. A surprise to be sure yet not the biggest one.

He had a true place at Blackwell Stables all this time. No reason to keep standing on his own.

And there it was. The biggest surprise yet. He wasn't certain if he was more happy or mad about that.

Because despite it all, he made his own way. Cut his own path. And cowboys like him didn't shift easy—not for new boots. Not for anyone.

OUTSIDE THE GALLOPING FORK, Kelley checked for traffic as if she were back in New York, then crossed the empty street at a pace more consistent with the townsfolks' preference to leave the racing around for the horses. She walked the one block to the corner of Hitch Post Avenue and Derby Hollow Road where the Lucky Lane Tavern had sat for almost a century.

Kelley stepped inside, waved to the hostess and scanned the bar area. She spotted Pauline Riggins propped on a bar stool right smack in the middle of the long, wide old-fashioned bar. Pauline was a former professional dancer on Broadway and now managed several dance studios closer to Louisville. She was a self-proclaimed designer cowgirl with the fashion sense to back up her claims and always seemed the most comfortable when she was center stage. At just shy of her fiftieth birthday, Pauline was age defying with an air of mystery about her.

Pauline caught sight of Kelley and waved her over, then patted the empty bar stool beside her. "I've got your seat saved."

Kelley slid onto the stool and twisted to face her enigmatic boss.

"I was in the mood for light and fruity." Pauline lifted a tropical cocktail and grinned. "If only we were meeting at the beach instead. What can I get you?"

"I'm good. Thanks," Kelley replied. "I need to get back to the diner."

"Well, if you change your mind, my tab is open," Pauline offered then checked her rose gold-colored watch and mused, “If I’m not mistaken, your shift is over.”

That it was. Kelley said, “I told Hayes I would be back.”

“You’re a good one, Kelley Munroe,” Pauline said and sighed, then lifted her cocktail in a toast. “Mama T knew it and so do I.”

Was this that opening Hayes challenged Kelley to look for? Kelley was not sure this was the swing she even wanted to take. The melancholy in Pauline’s usually vibrant brown eyes caught her notice. Kelley left her purse and the notebook inside untouched then asked, “Are you okay, Pauline?”

“I’m fine.” Pauline gave a quick shimmy on the stool as if shaking off her mood, then focused on Kelley again. “We should probably get straight to the reason I asked you to meet me.”

Kelley searched Pauline’s face, yet her pretty features gave nothing away.

“Mama T raised me to stretch my wings beyond Gold Finch. She’d tell me: *You go on and soar, Pauline. Don’t ever come down unless you want to.*” Pauline stretched her arms out to either side and pulsed them in a rather elegant slow wave as if she was the fairy queen in the ballet. “Mama did the same with you, too. You were always more like a granddaughter to her.”

Kelley smiled. She attended culinary school thanks to the encouragement from Pauline’s mom, Trudy, and Kelley’s grandpa. Kelley would always be grateful Trudy took a chance on her when she was just a shy, quiet teenager whose imagination soared in the pages of books and in the kitchen.

"You know what I've realized recently?" Pauline lowered her arms then plucked the maraschino cherry off the paper umbrella in her drink. Her gaze sparkled once again. "I've realized that mamas are always right."

In Kelley's case, it was Grandpa who was always right. Kelley's mom always wanted Kelley to follow in her librarian footsteps. It was years in the making, however, Kelley finally won her mom over with her literary-themed desserts she provided for her mother's weekly book club meetings.

"I've realized something else, too." Pauline leaned forward, clasped Kelley's arm then said, "We don't belong here."

Not Kelley. She intended to move on. But Pauline… Kelley asked, "What about the diner?"

"Oh, I'm selling it." Pauline plopped the cherry into her mouth and smiled as if she hadn't just tossed a conversational jaw-dropper between them.

"What about preserving everything your mother built here?" Kelley asked around the sudden buzz in her head.

"I'm what my mother built." Pauline pressed her palm over her heart and tipped her chin toward Kelley. "I don't need the diner to know where I came from and where I belong."

Okay. But sell the diner? Kelley curved her fingers around the glass apothecary jar, shook the snack mix inside onto her palm and worked to collect her reeling thoughts. Finally, she asked, "Do you have a buyer in mind?" *Not me, of course. Or maybe me. No. Never mind.* Would that be a step forward or not?

Purchasing the diner made Kelley's temporary move home more permanent. Definitely not what she wanted, right? Surprised. That was all Kelley was. And she knew all too well the folly of impulse responses when in a startled state.

Marry me, Kelley, and our dreams will have to come true. If only Kelley hadn't gotten swept up in that moment. If only she had pressed Pause and gotten her head and her heart aligned.

The diner was being sold. An end of an era for certain. But change wasn't always welcome or easy, and most of the time it didn't ask for an opinion or feedback. Kelley tossed the snack mix into her mouth and crunched down on a spiced nut.

"There is no buyer as of yet, but I'm sure my Realtor will find someone meant to thrive in a quaint small-town diner." Pauline's gaze fixed on Kelley, her mouth twisted to the side. "That's not you, by the way, if that is what you're thinking."

Kelley coughed and pushed the apothecary jar away.

Pauline patted Kelley's knee and said, "Darling, you need to get to baking your return into your ex's heart and then you can get your beautiful life in New York back. Everyone knows that's where you belong anyway." Confidence was there in Pauline's tone and expression. "It's time for you and me to stop hiding out here."

Talk about stuff to unpack. Where to begin? Kelley decided to start with the most obvious misconception. She cleared her throat and said mildly, "You know I'm a trained chef. I graduated from culinary school."

"Of course I know that." Pauline wiggled her ring-bedecked fingers between them. "But culinary school is behind you and if I've learned anything since Mama T's death, it's that we must keep looking forward, not backward."

Kelley nodded slightly, locked her grin in place and her focus on her boss then asked casually, "What's ahead for you then after the diner sells?"

Pauline's gaze flickered toward the end of the bar and narrowed. "I'm going to find myself a cowboy who knows how to treat a cowgirl right."

Eric Grahame, the bartender and tavern owner, stepped closer to them and drawled, "Spoiling a cowgirl with things like fancy dinners and flashy sportscars that have no meaning is not treating her right."

Pauline sniffed and swiveled her stool until her back faced the bar.

Eric chuckled then set a glass of white wine in front of Kelley and said, "This one is on the house. Don't get too carried away by this cowgirl. She's always been full of whimsy and unpredictability."

Pauline muttered, "It is better than being full of passivity and regret."

Eric laughed and said, "Hmm… Now, that depends on your point of view."

Kelley thanked Eric and took in the stiff set of Pauline's shoulders. Too bad she could not recall if there was history between the handsome fifty-something bartender and her boss. There was certainly something between them right now.

Eric moved on to greet new customers and Pauline exhaled slowly. Finally, she looked at Kelley, her bright smile once again on display. "I think that's enough about me. Let's discuss you."

"I think I'm good," Kelley hedged.

"That's up for debate," Pauline insisted and held up one finger. "I approve of your sunrise dance with a cowboy at the Galloping Fork to make your ex jealous. However, it would work exponentially better if you were dancing in New York, not Gold Finch."

Funny how the locals moved at meandering speed and yet gossip traveled lightning quick around town. Kelley opened her mouth to correct her boss again.

"Although I must tell you that I am rather pleased to see you are making an effort. It's important to keep looking forward," Pauline said again. "When do you plan to head to New York to make a case to get your ex back?"

"I'm not. I don't…" Kelley paused. Her gaze skipped around the bar as if she had suddenly lost track of her direction and no longer knew which way was up.

The front doors opened, and an all-too-familiar cowboy walked inside. His gaze locked on hers and his private smile came easy and slow as if it was all for Kelley. Now, that was some whimsy and foolish thinking. Still, Kelley held Asher Blackwell's stare as if he was her anchor and her new direction. She held her breath as she watched him head straight for her.

Asher approached, touched the brim of his hat and said, "Evening, ladies."

"If it isn't Asher Blackwell. You're certainly one cowboy I would not have predicted seeing here." Pauline plumped her teased hair and said, "Welcome home."

"Thanks." Asher gave his name to the teenager manning the to-go station then leaned against the bar top and said, "I hope I'm not interrupting."

He was not an interruption Kelley minded. Not even a little.

Pauline swiveled around on her stool to face Asher fully. "Kelley and I were just discussing her plans for her big return to New York City."

Asher glanced at Kelley. "That sounds like you intend to make a splash."

She didn't even plan to dip her toe back in New York waters. But if Asher was there waiting for her. She might be tempted. *No.* Not tempted. Not even interested. But her pulse picked up. Same as it had that morning when she'd been in his arms dancing around the diner.

Her hopeless romantic stepped out of hiding and pointed out the dance floor not more than a grapevine and sashay behind them. *Ready for take two, cowboy?*

Kelley muted her hopeless inner romantic. Yet, she was flustered and fidgety on the bar stool. And convinced her eagle-eyed boss would notice. Suddenly, she blurted, "I was just about to tell Pauline that I can't go back to New York anytime soon because I'm catering for Blackwell Stables."

Kelley snapped her mouth shut. That was exactly what rattled and impulsive got her. *Lies. Lies. Lies.*

Asher arched an eyebrow at Kelley but remained silent. His expression was mildly curious.

Pauline tapped a nail against her mouth. "I heard a rumor about your cook, Vicky Sumner, swapping kitchens and heading over to Connelly's place."

Kelley had heard the same story from her regulars during the breakfast service. Between guessing wrong about who Kelley's mystery dance partner was, her favorite trio of retirees had filled Kelley in on the latest buzz zooming along the grapevine. The Blackwell cook jumping ship to one of Blackwell's biggest rivals after decades at the Blackwell stable was a highlight.

"Not a rumor." Asher leaned in closer as if he intended to keep the conversation going.

"Bad business, that," Pauline murmured.

"It's certainly been a day of surprises," Asher admitted good-naturedly as if aware the entire bar was trying to listen in on their exchange.

"Other than your unexpected cook setback, I hope the others were good." Pauline lifted her glass in a toast.

Asher held Kelley's gaze. A corner of his mouth tipped into his close-cropped beard. "As it happens, I prefer some more than others."

Kelley never much liked surprises. But Asher Blackwell, she…

"Now, tell me about this catering business going on between you two," Pauline insisted, her gaze shifting from Asher to Kelley. Speculation flashed in her brown eyes.

Pauline made *business* sound like something more personal than professional. Kelley's palms suddenly felt damp. And she was definitely warmer than usual. No turning back now. Besides, catering gave her extra money for her next career move. Kelley plunged ahead, "Pauline, I promise this won't interfere with my shifts at the diner. You can still count on me."

"I intend to," Pauline said, a hint of a warning in her words.

Kelley shifted and regarded Asher. "Are you still available this evening so that we can go over the menus?" She was pleased her voice sounded even, not pitchy. Fibbing always seemed to tangle up her vocal cords. It was the worst sort of tell.

"Come up to the ranch house whenever you are finished here." Asher gathered his to-go bags from Justin at the take-out counter then added, "We can talk more then."

Kelley held on to her smile and watched Asher leave.

Pauline picked up her cocktail and chortled. "Well, once again this would all be a much more effective 'win back your ex' strategy if you were in New York and your ex could see you spending time with a fine-looking cowboy. But I suppose needs must."

Kelly picked up her wine and took a deep sip rather than try to convince Pauline there was absolutely no "win back her ex-husband" scheme.

Pauline clinked her glass against Kelley's and smiled wide. "Here's to more surprises. May they all be as easy on the eyes as Asher Blackwell."

He was a fine-looking city cowboy indeed. *City* being the key. He was a not-here-for-long cowboy to be sure. And that suited Kelley to a T.

Kelley finally relaxed. After all, Kelley doubted Asher Blackwell would stick around long enough for his boots to leave a footprint. The last thing she needed to worry about was her heart getting lassoed.

CHAPTER FOUR

TO STARTING AND ENDING the day with his unexpected dance partner. That idea wholeheartedly appealed to Asher. After all, when he left the diner that morning, he was already intrigued by Kelley Munroe. And now he was all too curious about the cowgirl chef who had plans to return to New York City. *His city.*

And *returning* meant Kelley had been there. Asher had questions, and if he had to use a fabricated catering meeting to learn more about Kelley, he had no qualms about that. Although, hiring Kelley to cover the meals for the stables was on his mind, too.

He polished off the cheeseburger from Lucky Lane Tavern and tossed the wrapper into the trash can in the quiet ranch house kitchen. The rest of the large to-go order he had dropped off at the employee break room in the filly barn down at the stables where Big E and Joe were also currently eating.

Asher hadn't stuck around. Without knowing the state of the stable's financials, he hadn't wanted to make promises to the employees that he could not fund. And if his father was guilty, that was a stain he didn't want to spread to the remaining staff who were proving their loyalty now. He realized that included Kelley, too. How could he hire Kelley if he could not pay her?

Did you do it, Dad?

The burger sat heavy in his stomach, making Asher wish he had opted for a side salad instead. If his father had gotten himself into some sort of financial crisis that made him desperate enough to dope his own horse, well, they would have more headaches than sanctions from the National Racing Compliance Agency to contend with.

Asher left the sweet potato French fries untouched in the to-go container on the kitchen island and headed for his father's office. It was time to get to work on finding out those answers, even if a part of him did not really want to know.

Inside his father's office, he flipped the light switch on the wall and immediately closed his eyes. But that only seemed to set his memories on hyper-focus. The last time he saw his father was in this office. Father and son had squared off against each other with only the cherrywood desk as a buffer between them.

His father had expected Asher to step right into his dead twin's role as heir apparent. Asher had refused and told his dad that Dylan could never be replaced. And then Walter lobbed his first jab. *On that, we agree. Your brother always knew what mattered most and never let me down.*

Asher hadn't flinched. But his father was not finished. *All I need you to do is get in line and do exactly what I tell you. That's how these stables will endure with a Blackwell at the helm.*

Asher hadn't been able to simply get in line and silently follow in his father's bootsteps. Honestly, he hadn't been able to see past his grief that afternoon and it seemed to be trailing him ever since.

Asher snapped his eyes open and scanned the room for something to hold on to. He grabbed the scuffed baseball from the nearest shelf with photographs of his brothers from their school days all dressed in their baseball uniforms. Each one was smiling wider than the next. His gaze skipped to another shelf with a picture of his mother in front of the Christmas tree, laughing as a squirming golden Labrador retriever licked her cheek. The puppy had been the boys' gift to their mom and it was a toss-up who was more excited that day—the brothers, their mom or the puppy. Happy times—they were in there, too.

Asher exhaled, collected his emotions and pushed the past into the to-be-dealt-with-at-a-later-date column. Then he made his way over to the desk and dropped into the worn leather chair to find those answers. Only an hour later, Asher realized he was more confused than ever. He stacked his hands behind his head, leaned back in the chair and stared at another empty document folder on the computer screen.

He heard the front door open and close softly. Heard the footsteps on the wood floors. Then glanced toward the archway, expecting to see Big E. Only it was Kelley. She had changed from her diner uniform into denim shorts with a muted plaid button-down shirt over a soft purple tank top and cowboy boots. She looked comfortable and relaxed. And suddenly, Asher knew what a *breath of fresh air* truly meant.

"Bad time?" she asked then shifted the box she carried to one hand and motioned toward the foyer with her other. "Big E was on the front porch having a rather lively video chat with his great-grandkids. After he introduced me to them, he told me to go on in."

"Sorry." Asher washed his hands over his face to stop staring at Kelley. She was enchanting for sure, but that was no reason for him to act like a tongue-tied teen with his first crush. He cleared his throat and stuck to the business side of things. "I'm just stumped. This computer has not been touched since Dylan bought it a decade ago." That only happened because Asher told his brother what model to get that would handle the business books and accounting software. He added, "It seems my brother was the last person to log in."

Kelley tipped her head and considered him.

"Don't mind me. You aren't here to listen to

all this. You wanted to know if it's a bad time." He stood and moved around the desk then leaned against the front edge. "No. It is not a bad time. I could use a break."

"I brought after-dinner sweet treats as an apology for earlier at Lucky Lane." She moved toward him. "I should not have put you on the spot like that."

He never moved to accept her offering and said instead, "Look, Kelley, about that. I don't want to be the one keeping you from whatever is waiting for you in New York."

"That's just a misunderstanding between Pauline and me." She shook her head. "There's nothing for me in New York anymore."

Loaded statement there. And there once was something in New York for her—he could see that much in her guarded gaze. He nodded and asked, "How long have you been home?"

"Since Christmas." She adjusted her hold on the treat box and fluttered her fingers as if brushing away a gnat and continued, "It's not a very interesting story."

Now, that, he doubted. He found her very interesting. Yet, he could tell from the subtle jut of her chin and pushback of her shoulders as if bracing herself against the memory, that whatever happened in the city was not pleasant. *You can keep your secrets, cowgirl. And I'll keep mine. We can call it even.*

"Tonight is supposed to be about the food." She flipped open the top on the box and said quickly, "Please don't say no to the catering until you've tried my food."

"I'm thinking it might be possible I already have," he said quietly. "Back in New York."

"If you ever ate at Verona Heights in SOHO, then you've tasted my food before." She lowered the lid on the box and said, "I was the Chef de Cuisine there."

He had, in fact, eaten there. On more than one occasion. It was a favorite lunch spot for his firm's legal team. He scratched his chin. "I don't recall seeing you there."

Her smile was small and brief. "I preferred to stay in the back of the house. My ex-husband worked the front of house."

That explained why Asher hadn't recognized her name on the menu. And he assumed her ex-husband was part of that not-so-interesting story she didn't want to share. He wasn't asking, either. Getting to know her would tip this evening into something it was not meant to be. He preferred to keep the personal out of his business. And this was about business. It always was. He said, "It seems I have already tasted your food. There's no doubt I will like whatever you cook. That's not the issue."

"You need a cook and I'm offering to cater for you." Her eyebrows pulled together. Confusion shifted across her face. "I'm not seeing the issue."

"It's simple." And yet, so very complicated now that he realized for the first time in a long while he was reconsidering his moratorium on dating. Of course, that implied he was going to ask her on a date and that she would even accept. *I don't recommend it, cowgirl.* He braced his arms on the desk behind him and said, "To be completely transparent, I don't know if the stable can afford you."

Her mouth formed an O shape.

He tipped his head toward the old but never used desktop computer and focused on the real problem at hand. After all, his success depended on knowing his strengths and his weaknesses. And relationships had never been part of his skill set. "The financials, it seems, are not where I expected them to be."

"Maybe Walter used an online app for his banking and accounting records," Kelley suggested.

Asher shook his head then picked up an old-school flip-style cell phone that he'd discovered in the desk drawer earlier. "The last text Walter sent was more than a year ago. He never much cared for tech things."

"What about Joe?" Kelley asked.

"Joe only deals with the horses and the employees. Walter handled all the money, including the accounts receivables and payables as well as the payroll. They both called it a beautiful partnership." Asher stood, opened the accordion-style closet doors and revealed a four-drawer metal filing cabinet. Cardboard filing boxes were stacked on both sides of the cabinet like crooked bookends. “It seems Walter might have had something of a manual process.”

Kelley set the dessert box on a round table between the two tall-backed chairs near the wall. If she noticed his suitcase stashed there, too, she didn’t give anything away or press him. As if she understood it was one of his not-so-interesting stories about how he was avoiding the bedroom wing. Most specifically the room he used to share with his twin. No matter really. He was there for a week. There was little sense in making himself at home.

Kelley joined Asher at the closet and stood close enough that he caught the scent of vanilla and spice. Fitting for his chef, he supposed. Asher tugged on the piece of paper sticking out from the top drawer of the filing cabinet and grimaced. “I don’t think I’ve ever seen a paper bank statement.”

“Never,” Kelley said, disbelief tingeing her words.

“My entire life is digital.” Asher tossed the paper statement onto the pile of paperwork strewn on the top of the stack. Frowning, he said, “Everything I need is either in an app or in the cloud. I don’t do paper.”

“Seriously. No paper.” Kelly chuckled and asked, “What if you’re at work and you need to take a note? Surely, you've got a notepad or sticky note pad on your desk?"

Asher saw the spark in her hazel eyes but refused to be drawn in. He pulled out his phone and flashed it at her. "I have digital notes. There is literally an app for just about everything these days."

"Then this must be difficult for you." She smoothed out her expression, yet her grin slipped out, granting him a glimpse of her matching dimples.

She had no idea. "This is horrifying," Asher said. "I don't even know where to begin."

All he knew was that he seriously needed to stop noticing every little thing about her. It would do no good later when he was back in the city and trying to forget her.

"There's only one thing to do," Kelley said, her tone matter-of-fact. "You're going to have to organize everything first."

"I was afraid you were going to say that." Asher frowned then brightened. "Please tell me there is an app for that. There has to be."

"I'm afraid not." Kelley walked around him then picked up a pen and notepad from the desktop. "This requires something a bit more old-fashioned like labels and folders."

"There is nothing the least bit appealing about this." Yet, there was so much appealing about her. Asher pulled a box off the top of the filing cabinet and set it in the center of the floor.

"What are you looking for anyway?" Kelley asked.

"A reason," he said simply.

Kelley crossed her arms over her chest and studied him. Her eyes widened and her tone lowered. "You mean a reason for Sovereign Pride's doping."

She was smart and quick to catch on. He always admired that in a cowgirl. He nodded and took another box from the closet.

"You don't believe your dad did it, do you?" she asked.

They were waiting for the two independent labs to confirm the results of the drug test taken on the day of the race. From his research during his flight from New York to Kentucky, Asher learned the race day drug test had an extremely low percentage of false positive. He suspected the independent labs would confirm the positive drug test result. The only new information would most likely be the exact drug used.

He ran a hand over his head and said, "I know Pride was disqualified after the last race of the Laurel Legacy Circuit because of a failed drug test. That win would have cemented his place and Blackwell's in history. I know the stables were fined, Pride's winnings rescinded and our three-year-olds sanctioned from racing." The National Racing Compliance Agency would not have done all that on a whim or an unreliable drug test.

"But your dad," she said, her words soft and insistent.

"Walter wasn't like your dad, Kelley," he confessed. Her father was the retired fire chief of Gold Finch County, and he always got along with everyone in town. No one ever had a bad word to say about him. Asher always liked Neven Munroe.

"I don't believe Walter would have done that to his horse," she argued.

Asher wasn't quite so certain. Talk about being disloyal to his family. One more way he let down Walter, he supposed. He rubbed his chest.

"Walter could be curt and cantankerous sometimes, but he loved his family, his horses and this town," Kelley insisted. "He cared a lot more than he ever let on."

"I want to believe you," Asher said, surprised to realize he meant it. There was just so much history between him and his father to wade through. It was like quicksand; if he lingered too long, it would pull him under.

"Did you know we have Friday Freebies once a month at the Galloping Fork?" she stated then continued, not waiting for his response, "It's for all the first responders and medical personnel. They get to eat free all day."

Asher scratched his cheek and said, "They deserve it. That's a nice way to give back."

"Your dad was the silent sponsor," Kelley said and watched him.

"He covered the whole tab?" Asher asked.

Kelley nodded. "Never missed a month and he's been doing it for years according to Pauline."

"I'll cover it now," Asher said. "Silently. Same as my dad."

Kelley shook her head. "I wasn't pitching you on becoming the sponsor. I was trying to show that your dad..."

"I want to do it," Asher cut in then added, "And I know what you were doing."

Showing him that she had a big heart and saw the best in those around her like her own father. Risky, that. After all, the bigger the heart, the harder it broke. She should take care not to show him too much. He knew a bit more about how to break a heart like hers than protect it.

She removed the cover on a file box and asked, "Do you want this sorted by year?"

"We still haven't sorted out the catering," he said. "Until I know the state of the financials, I'm not sure how much I can pay you for your catering services."

"We can work it out." She took a manila folder from the box.

"Kelley," he said and set his hand on the folder she held. "I can't let you cater here without paying you."

She chewed on her bottom lip and considered him then asked, "How about a trade?"

Too curious not to see this through, he countered, “What kind of trade?”

“I will cater if you let Frannie apprentice here,” she said then added, “Frannie wants to be a jockey. It’s all she’s ever wanted to do. She just needs someone to give her a chance and help her become better.”

There was something about Kelley that made Asher feel better. He didn’t want to disappoint her. Still, he asked, “Do you really want your little sister to work here, given all that’s going on?”

“I really want someone besides me and my parents to recognize her potential and believe in her like we do.” Kelley set her hand on his arm. Her words were earnest. “Frannie might not have the pedigree, but she will work harder than anyone here. I can promise you that.”

He couldn’t deny another set of hands was needed and it wasn’t like the stables had a line of applicants applying to work here. Kelley wasn’t concerned about the doping allegations. Still, he would do everything in his power to make sure Frannie’s experience was beneficial, not detrimental, to her future jockey career. “Done. Tell Frannie to meet me at the stables tomorrow morning at six. We can get a feel for what she knows and find a place for her.”

“Really? Just like that?” She searched his face. Hope swirled in her expressive eyes.

“Yes.” He wanted to grin when her smile

stretched into her cheeks. He stepped away and said, "But that is not an even exchange. I will have two talented Munroe sisters helping the stables. What do you get out of all this?"

"Let's call it a chance to try out new recipes," she hedged.

"What else?" he pressed.

"You aren't going to let this go, are you?" She set her hands on her hips and faced him.

He saw it then. Just a quick peek at her grit. One more thing he liked about her. Not that he was keeping count. He shook his head. "I told you I'm looking into my father potentially drugging his horse to win. Now tell me. What's your agenda?"

She blew out a breath and brushed a strand of her hair off her face. "The diner is going up for sale. Depending on who buys it, I want to have a viable fallback plan. That's catering."

"Why don't you buy the diner?" he asked. "That seems like the most logical plan since you aren't going back to New York."

"What?" she asked, her confusion genuine. "That's not what I want to do."

What do you want, cowgirl? Wait. That wasn't his concern. Asher picked up the dessert box, reached inside and lifted a turnover out. He took a large bite and savored the blackberries inside. He had the pastry polished off in a matter of seconds. "That is phenomenal, by the way."

"Thanks," she chuckled and asked, "So, do we have a deal? I cater and Frannie apprentices."

Asher helped himself to a second pastry, ate it just as quickly then wiped his palms on his jeans and said, "We have a deal. And I still intend to pay you."

"I won't say no to that." She motioned to the boxes of paper. "You ready to get started on all this?" She held up her hand when he opened his mouth to argue. "I'm offering to help. It'll go faster with two of us."

Us. Asher closed his mouth.

A tease crossed into her words. Her expression turned playful. She said, "Not to mention, I have a vested interest now seeing as I'm something of a business vendor of yours."

The worry was when Asher looked at her, he was starting to see something between them that was a bit more personal and a lot less professional. He pointed to the box near her cowboy boots and said, "You take that one and I'll take this one."

Several hours later, the boxes were mostly empty. However, now stacks of paperwork dotted the office floor, and the filing cabinet was still full. It was going to take a number of nights to organize and sort completely. And that suited Asher given he didn't have work to occupy his evenings. Even better, they had a menu set for the weekend and into next week. Asher was already hungry thinking about it.

Outside in the driveway, he opened Kelley's car door for her and said, "Please tell me you have more blackberries so I can put in an order for those turnovers. I can guarantee the ones back in the office won't last the night."

"About that." Kelley laughed and turned toward him. "I have a confession."

Asher had one, too. He liked the sound of her laughter. It was light and easy and genuine. It filled him with joy, too. And the Kentucky stars knew he needed more of that in his life. He tucked his hands into his back pockets to keep from reaching for her as if he wanted to hold on to the feeling a little while longer and kept his thoughts to himself. "What's that?"

"Those are Blackwell blackberries." One of her eyebrows twitched, her grin was lopsided, her words unapologetic. "I sort of pilfered them from your property."

"I didn't even know we had blackberries around here," he said. Nor did he know a cowgirl's gaze could sparkle in the moonlight.

"My sisters and I found the wild blackberry briar when we were exploring our stepmom's property on one of our weekend visits years ago," she explained. "You can imagine it has now grown into a very large patch."

He was less interested in the blackberries and much more caught up on the idea that Kelley might be fairly close by. No more than a horseback ride along the river. He asked, "Are you staying at your dad and stepmom's place?"

"Only on the weekends." She shook her head, and a small smile tripped out. "It's like I'm twelve all over again and my parents are sharing custody."

Asher eyed her. "Do you mind?"

"It is how it is," she said and shrugged. "I stopped fighting it back in middle school when I realized my parents were a lot happier apart."

Are you happier alone? I'm supposed to be. And then he looked into the cowgirl's pretty eyes. He cleared his throat and said, "You never did answer my question about your blackberry stash. Do you have enough for more turnovers?"

"I'll check when I get home and let you know." She chuckled then eyed him. "If not, I know where to find more. Although I suppose I should probably ask permission from the owner."

"You can have all the blackberries on this property if you keep me supplied in turnovers," Asher said.

"I can arrange that."

"Then we have another deal." He extended his arm toward her.

She set her hand in his.

Asher stilled when he wanted to give a gentle tug. Just enough to suggest he wanted her closer. Just a nudge that would allow her to close the distance if she chose to or walk away. Yet, he never flinched. He kept his fingers wrapped around hers, his expression relaxed and his words casual. “Thanks for lending me your organizational skills tonight.”

“Anytime.” Her fingers flexed around his hand.

Now, that was a miscalculation. He had not considered the possibility that she might pull him toward her. And now he could not seem to stop considering it. He held his breath. *I dare you, cowgirl.*

Instead, she gave his fingers a firm squeeze and his arm a quick pump then said, “I appreciate you hiring me to cater. You won’t be disappointed.”

He refused to be disappointed now. After all, if she wasn’t returning to the city, Asher understood there could be nothing more between them than a professional relationship. He released her hand and said, “Until tomorrow, chef. Sweet dreams.”

She climbed into her car, started the engine and rolled down her window to call out, “Good night, Asher.”

He watched until her taillights disappeared around a bend then headed inside. And realized it was a good night. The first he had had in a long while. Thanks to a cowgirl chef and her blackberry turnovers.

But that was behind him now. He headed back to the office. He had work to do and one week to get it done. After all, his life was in New York and one “good night” could not change that.

CHAPTER FIVE

KELLEY SERIOUSLY NEEDED to keep the diner doors locked until opening. If only to prevent any more early-morning ambushes like the one they'd had yesterday.

As it was, Pauline breezed through the back door of the Galloping Fork Diner with more energy than necessary for the predawn hour. Then the diner owner clapped her hands, startling Hayes and Kelley out of their morning prep routine. Kelley set a colander of cauliflower in one of the sinks near the cold food station and turned toward her peppy boss.

"I have important news," Pauline announced. "We will be closing early tonight."

Kelley dried her hands on her apron and asked, "What's going on, Pauline?"

Pauline tapped a polished fingernail against her chin. "Last night, I came to the conclusion that there is no time to waste. We must fast-track things and that means getting the ball rolling today."

Kelley shared a confused look with Hayes. The cook shrugged as if Pauline's declaration was nothing out of the ordinary and continued cracking eggs into a large stainless steel mixing bowl.

"I've got a professional cleaning crew coming in later this evening and a photographer will be here tomorrow," Pauline explained then gave Hayes an apologetic look. "The kitchen will need to remain pristine all day tomorrow. That means if it can't be cooked on the grill outside, it can't be served."

Hayes released the whisk in the bowl of eggs and shook his head. "That's impossible."

"But necessary. We must present this place in the best light to attract the best buyer." Pauline fanned her arms out in a wide arc as if releasing her vision. "It has to be immaculate in here."

"Perhaps we should close tomorrow," Hayes suggested.

"What about our customers?" Pauline asked. "We can't upset them."

"Bringing in a buyer from the outside will upset the folks around here even more," Hayes warned, then lifted his eyebrows. "Especially when you got a potential buyer right in your own backyard."

"Hayes? I didn't think you were interested. You didn't mention anything when we spoke yesterday." Pauline's smile stretched and she snapped her fingers. "Please put something in writing and I would be delighted to discuss it with my team."

"Not me," Hayes replied and slipped his gaze toward Kelley.

Kelley gave him a small head shake.

"Oh, that's too bad. It would have certainly streamlined things on my end," Pauline said pleasantly. "But I get it. The kitchen is where you shine. Mama T always told me it's best when we know our lanes and stay in them."

Hayes rolled his eyes at Kelley and headed for the back door. "I'm going to step outside for my break."

"Don't forget to check the grill," Pauline called after him, then she strolled the length of the kitchen and paused at the prep counter. "We don't have cauliflower on the menu."

"That's not for the diner service," Kelley said hastily. "It's for the Blackwell menu."

Pauline pursed her mouth and said, "Well, this can't be here."

"It will be put away before we open this morning," Kelley said, her words reassuring. "The cleaners will not need to deal with it, either."

"No, I mean it can't be here at all," Pauline stated flatly then she spun around and scanned the kitchen as if searching for more items that did not belong.

"I thought you were okay with the catering." Kelley crossed her arms over her chest and said, "We talked about this last night."

"I am." Pauline aimed a brief smile at Kelley and then continued her inspection. "What you do on your own time in your own kitchen is your business."

Her own kitchen. That had not been part of their conversation last night. There had been no mention of Kelley cooking at her own place between talk about Kelley's supposed win-back-her-ex-husband plot and Pauline's need to spread her wings beyond Gold Finch county lines.

"It's just that your business can't be in my business because then the rest of the staff might want to conduct their other side hustle businesses here, too." Pauline met Kelley's stare and continued, "I can't have that. You understand, right?"

Kelley ran her hand over her mouth to keep from openly gaping at her boss.

Hayes returned, glanced between the women and hightailed it over to the walk-in refrigerator where he disappeared inside.

"Besides, if word gets out about your catering side hustle and you get more local customers, well, how will that look to your people in New York?" Pauline asked, her tone sounding perplexed. She gave her arms a slight flutter as if preparing to fly and continued, "Remember we agreed that we're following Mama T's sage advice from now on."

Kelley was beginning to understand that her boss, it seemed, was holding firm to the belief that Kelley belonged somewhere else, too—in New York City to be exact. But Kelley wanted her next move to be a fresh start, not a rebound back to the place she'd left behind. After all, this time her ex was not calling the shots and Kelley was not deferring to him as if he knew best.

Pauline held Kelley's stare as if expecting a response.

Finally, Kelley nodded in acknowledgment and said, "Right. Mama T did have lots of advice."

Pauline grinned as Hayes reappeared carrying a jug of milk, then she said, "Okay. I think we are all on the same page."

"We're staying in our lanes," Hayes muttered through his grin. "But I think she's at a different track."

Kelley swallowed her chuckle.

"Here's the order of events. Cleaners today. Keep it pristine. Pictures tomorrow. Showings this weekend. And a sale soon." Pauline brushed her palms together. Her expression was full of satisfaction. "We've manifested it. It shall be." A hug for Hayes then Kelley, and Pauline swept out of the diner as swiftly as she arrived.

Hayes got to work finishing the French toast batter and asked, "What's the plan, then?"

Good question. Kelley said, "We'll close after the July Fourth committee meeting this afternoon."

"And then," Hayes pressed.

And then she would have to make it up as she went. Kelley shrugged.

Hayes set his hand on her arm and said, "You keep cooking here. I won't tell no one."

"No. It's not what Pauline wants, and she owns this place." And keeping the boss happy ensured a good working environment. Kelley and her ex-husband were not good together because they were not happy. And now all Kelley wanted to be *was* happy. "I'll figure something else out for the catering."

She just wasn't sure where she would cook. Her mother relied solely on her microwave and toaster oven these days and hadn't fixed her oven the last time it broke almost two years ago. Kelley's dad and stepmother were in the middle of renovating their first floor and building their dream entertaining space. Kelley was currently advising her stepmom on the kitchen layout and design.

Just then a shout and thump echoed from the cleaning supply closet. Kelley rushed to investigate.

The busser, Shane, stood in a growing puddle of liquid soap leaking from the broken plastic industrial bottle near his boots. His eyebrows were arched into his hairline. "Sorry. I was getting paper towels for the bathroom and lost my balance."

"There's a hose out back to rinse the soap off your boots." Kelley pointed to the back exit. "I'll get this, and you can get back to clearing those tables out front."

Shane nodded and backed himself out of the soap puddle.

Kelley added, "And Shane. Thanks for taking the initiative and helping, even though it's not part of your job."

Shane's shoulders relaxed and he smiled. "Next time, I won't make more of a mess."

By the time Kelley got the soap cleaned up, she was needed out front to change out an empty CO2 tank in the soda bar and to cajole the temperamental ice machine into working again. It was a while later when she walked into the kitchen, thinking she might sneak in a minute to research possible commercial kitchens in the area that might allow her to use their space for a small fee.

"Heads up, Kelley." Hayes stopped her and aimed his spatula toward the hallway. "You got company waiting for you in the office."

Who now? Kelley headed to the office only to discover Laura-Beth inside. Her big sister's arms were braced on the desk, and her attention was fixed on a large piece of poster paper spread across the top like she was a general planning for battle.

Laura-Beth spared Kelley a brief glance as if irritated Kelley was late to her meeting, then said, "Good. You're finally here."

"But you're not supposed to be in here." Kelley motioned to the sign on the door. "It's employees only."

"Well, that's you. And if I place an order, then I'll be a paying customer with the shift manager." Laura-Beth drummed her fingers on the metal desktop and kept her focus on the colorful sticky tabs dotting the poster paper. Finally, she added, “I’ll take the ultimate breakfast sandwich on sourdough. Hold the bacon and double the avocado.”

“There’s no food service back here, LB.” It was more storage than office space. Not that her big sister was even listening. Sighing, Kelley stepped over to the other side of the desk and asked, “Why are you here, LB?”

“It’s the seating chart.” Laura-Beth spread her fingers and made circles over the poster paper. “We’ve got to shuffle again.”

“We did all that last night.” And well into the early hours of the morning, too. Kelley had prepped food for the Blackwell Stables while on a video call with Laura-Beth and Wes, who was still on the west coast, to help the couple finalize the seating chart.

“Due to recent information I received, we must rearrange seats,” Laura-Beth stated and finally straightened. Her grin stretched wide. “And since it affects you, I thought you’d like to be involved.”

Kelley stuck her hands into the pockets of the apron tied around her waist. “What have you heard?”

“It’s all good,” Laura-Beth assured her. “Really good. You have a plus-one now, so I’m moving you back to the wedding party table with us.”

“I’m supposed to be Mom’s plus one,” Kelley said flatly. That way their mother did not have to sit alone at the parents' table with Kelley's dad, stepmother and the three sets of opinionated grandparents.

"You're off the hook," Laura-Beth said, excitement in her words. "Mom found herself a new plus-one."

"Who?" Kelley asked. Her mom mentioned nothing last night.

"I'm sure she will tell us when she's ready." Laura-Beth shrugged then pulled a pink sticky tab off the paper. "It's for the best. Now you and Asher will be at my table where I wanted you in the first place." Laura-Beth peeled a green sticky off and frowned. "Only, you and Asher will then be taking Cousin Betsy and her new husband's places, so they need to be relocated."

Asher was Kelley's date? That was a newsflash. She rubbed her forehead and took a deep breath, hoping for some patience.

"You have to help me fix this." Laura-Beth eyed Kelley. "I already told Betsy she was sitting with us. She is so excited. And now she's going to feel slighted."

"They won't feel slighted and there's nothing to fix," Kelley said, working to keep her words indifferent and mild. "Because I don't have a date."

"You have to take Asher," Laura-Beth countered.

Kelley shook her head. "Why, exactly?"

"You looked really good dancing together."

Laura-Beth's chin dipped in a sharp nod as if to punctuate her words.

Kelley chuckled. "That's not a good reason, LB."

"Well, you could have like a big reveal moment at the wedding," Laura-Beth said, delight stretching through her words as she warmed to the idea. "I always love a big reveal, don't you?"

Not really. Kelley was more low-key in her approach; her big sister, not so much. Laura-Beth always wanted to make a huge splash while Kelley tended to wade in and blend in. Besides, the day belonged to her big sister. Laura-Beth deserved to shine from sunup until sundown. Still, Kelley asked, "What exactly would I be revealing?"

"That Asher Blackwell is your mystery sunrise dance partner, of course," Laura-Beth stated. "Everyone is still speculating about who the cowboy was even today."

No surprise there. The locals always enjoyed long, nonstop rides on the gossip train. Kelley frowned. "They'll move on soon enough."

"That doesn't mean you have to," Laura-Beth suggested, a gleam in her bold green gaze.

"What are you talking about now?" Kelley asked.

Laura-Beth stuck the sticky name tags on the poster paper and came around the desk. She braced her arms on Kelley's shoulders and gave her a light playful shake. "I'm talking about you asking Asher to be your date for the wedding."

"Why would I do that?"

"Because it's a chance to have fun and dance with a cute cowboy for one night," Laura-Beth said.

Asher was more than simply cute. And Kelley was more than a little aware of him as someone whom she could want to be more than a friend. If she was considering things like that. She hedged, "We don't even know if Asher is going to be in town. He probably needs to get back to the city soon. You know where he lives." And where Kelley did not.

"Stop it. I know what you're doing in that head of yours." Laura-Beth squeezed Kelley's shoulders. "You're finding all the reasons it's a bad idea."

Kelley chewed on her bottom lip rather than reply.

"You're making this into something it is not," Laura-Beth continued. "It's not a marriage. It's one date. What is the risk in that?"

Kelley blinked. Her sister was right. The end was already written. Kelley and her city cowboy were headed in different directions. There could be no messing of the heart kind of chaos when she already knew what was coming. Kelley said, "I will think about asking Asher to be my date, if it comes out that he will be in town."

Laura-Beth nodded, released Kelley then

pointed at Kelley's head and said, "Just don't think it over too long, okay?" Laura-Beth turned and set her attention on the seating chart and continued, "Or someone else is going to get to him first and you will be left watching from the singles' table."

Aha! That was the answer. Kelley smiled. "That is where we will sit."

"What?" Confusion crossed Laura-Beth's face. "Where?"

"Don't change the seating chart." Kelley motioned to the battle plan. "Asher and I will sit at the singles' table if he comes with me." And that would prove Kelley understood exactly what a date with Asher Blackwell was and what it was not. It was one night to dance with a single cowboy. No hearts on the line.

Her sister's cell chimed a double-quick version of "Chapel of Love," which Laura-Beth promptly answered. From the bright sparkle in her sister's gaze, Kelley assumed it was Wes on the other end of the line. But before Kelley could say another word, LB shoved the seating plan into her tote, muttered something about doing it herself and was gone in a flash.

A while later, Kelley was heading back to her office but quickly pulled up short before she rammed into the cowboy in the doorway. She sputtered, "Asher?"

His smile slipped out, slow and easy and private. And her pulse picked right up. He was less city and more cowboy-relaxed today, wearing a dark brown cowboy hat, faded blue jeans and denim button-down over a white T-shirt. And that jolt of awareness made her want to step closer. Instead, she locked her knees and braced her back against the door frame. "Hey. What brings you by? I was going to deliver dinner later this afternoon."

He nodded, then scratched his cheek. "I need to go to the bank. But I thought I'd stop in about my standing blackberry turnover order."

"A cowboy can't live on pastries alone," Kelley teased.

"This cowboy intends to try." Amusement flashed in his startlingly blue eyes. He moved aside and lifted a large open basket between them. "I was out near the back pasture, checking on our retiree trio and stopped to get you these."

Kelley glanced at the fresh blackberries, noting that her box from the previous night was carefully tucked inside. "You were up early." And thinking about her. Not that she was lingering on that minor detail.

"My days always start early at home," he said, satisfaction in his words. "Besides, my mother taught me never to return a dish empty. You really don't want to taste anything I bake, so I figured this was the next best thing."

If they were sharing *best things*, it was Asher in the diner again, even if it wasn't for another morning dance. *Could you stick around for a while, cowboy?* There was something about him that made her feel happy. Scratch that. She was finding that on her own these days. Still, there was a wedding venue where they could dance. For one night. *You game, cowboy?* All she had to do was stay in the moment and ask. Kelley opened her mouth.

"I overstepped, didn't I?" he asked and continued, "You wanted to pick the blackberries yourself. Make sure you got the best ones. And I read they need to be soaked or something." He sighed. "Now I've given you more work, which was not my intention. This was a bad idea."

So was a date night between friends. Still, a thoughtful cowboy was hard to resist. Kelley rubbed her forehead. "It's not that."

"Please tell me you aren't quitting," Asher said, a hint of worry in his words. "The staff was raving about your tomato egg bagel bake and mini quiches. Best breakfast they've had in years. I'd have to agree."

"That's nice to hear." Especially from him.

"You don't sound happy." He searched her face.

Are you? Happy to your core and all that. That was why she had come home. To reset and then get on with being happy on her own. But she looked at him and she started to remember the parts of a relationship she liked. The anticipation. The fun. The romance. But then there were the not-so-great parts like broken promises and broken hearts.

"Sorry. It's not you." *Although you might have been. In another time and place.* Then Kelley added, "I'm distracted. I've got unexpected logistic issues to figure out."

"Anything I can help with?" He reached up and tucked a strand of her hair behind her ear.

His touch was gentle and gone before she caught hold of the warmth. Now she was teetering. So close to leaping where she should not. She blurted, "Yes, you can help."

Remind me I'm divorced. Remind me I don't take risks with my heart anymore. A date night would only be an entanglement she didn't want.

She rushed on, "It would really help if I could use your kitchen. The food would be on site and there wouldn't be any delivery charge going forward."

He straightened and smoothed his hand over his mouth. "I'm not sure that's such a good idea."

Now she overstepped. The food would be close by and so would she. There she was feeling something he was not. Foolish cowgirl. Not a mistake she would make again. A quick course correction and she was back to putting her work first. "I meant the kitchen down at the stables of course."

"There isn't one suitable for a professional chef like you." He scratched his cheek and continued, "The one in the staff quarters is streamlined for reheating and microwaving pretty much. The oven could hold a potato or two, but not much more."

Sounded like her mother's place. She lowered her voice. "It's just the diner kitchen isn't available to me any longer." And if the diner sold, her job would not be guaranteed, and her catering might need to become more than a side hustle.

Asher glanced over her shoulder and said, "It looks like it's in working order."

"Pauline's got some ideas about keeping it that way." Kelley smoothed her hair off her face. "She wants to keep things extra clean while the diner is up for sale."

He nodded. "I'd offer the kitchen at the ranch house, but..."

"That will work," she cut in. She would make it work. This was about standing on her own, after all. She could do that with her own catering business. It would be a first step in the right direction. "I promise I won't be in your way. You won't even know I'm there."

His gaze swung back, and his startling blue eyes settled on her, intensely warm and impossibly tender.

Kelley felt her toes curl and her skin heat.

"I'm not sure that would be possible," he drawled.

Now she felt slightly breathless. Oh, he knew she was there right now. Warning lights flashed. Time to prove her heart was on the shelf where she intended to leave it. This was business and nothing personal. Kelley said, "Then I *can* use your kitchen."

His gaze flickered to her bottom lip—the one she was chewing on—then returned to her eyes. "I just don't know if…"

She set her palm on his chest. *Oh dear.* There she was getting all impulsive again. *Snatch it back.* She couldn't move. If she did move it would be toward him. *Say something.* This was the part where she went back on her word and got in his way. *Do something.* Finally, she whispered, "Please. I'll add blackberry ice cream to the rotation of after-dinner treats."

"You're making it hard to say no," he said, yet his gaze warmed even more.

She knew the feeling.

Finally, he sighed and said, "You can use the kitchen."

"We can talk more after the meeting." By then her pulse was sure to be settled.

"See you later, then." Instead of leaving, he leaned in and said softly, "And for the record, you are welcome to get in my way anytime."

That set her pulse to racing and her knees to buckling.

One touch of his fingers against the brim of his cowboy hat and he stepped out of her way. At the exit, he turned back and said, "I should warn you. The kitchen is not what you're expecting."

Kelley swallowed against her suddenly dry throat and said, "I'll make it work. It will be great."

He nodded and walked outside.

And Kelley finally exhaled.

Her city cowboy was not what she was expecting. But she was holding her own with him. Now all she had to do was keep from holding on to him.

CHAPTER SIX

WHERE WAS HIS RESOLVE?

Bad enough Asher kept thinking about Kelly all night long, but then he stopped and picked blackberries for her, too. As if he had nothing better to do. And now he granted her access to his house and kitchen. What was next—his heart?

Not likely. He was ranch-raised and covered in city grit these days. And no matter the zip code, there just wasn't room in his life for romance. Nor was he interested.

Not that anyone would know that by the way he flirted just now. *Flirted.* And badly, to boot. Talk about being rusty and out of practice. Even though he wasn't looking to change that.

Asher knocked his cowboy hat lower on his head and headed down the sidewalk to Foxglove Bank and Trust.

Asher's twin was the charmer and fluent in the art of sweet-talking. Asher was blunt and straight to the point. Not to mention, more focused on closing business deals than speaking to a cowgirl's heart. As if he wanted to do that. Not likely. He preferred a guaranteed return these days, and love came with entirely too many loopholes.

More worrisome than his poor wooing skills was that he cared what Kelley thought of his family's time warp of a kitchen. But even more, he was starting to care what she thought of *him*. As if he wanted her to like him. Because he liked… *No.* He jumped off that train of thought before it could gain momentum.

He got back to the matter at hand. The Blackwell employees needed to eat. Kelley needed a kitchen. Asher provided the solution. He would not rescind his offer. Besides, he excelled at workarounds in his day job.

There was only one obvious one now. He would not be home when Kelley was there. Then there would be no more flirting. No more getting to know her. No chance of liking her even more than he already did.

Best all around if he kept himself occupied elsewhere. Busy was his preference anyway. If he was idle too long, those memories he wanted to avoid tended to take hold. Good thing he was something of an expert on how to stay busy. Still, in an abundance of caution, Asher decided to give up turnovers, too. Just to be certain sweet treats would not draw him to his chef again, either.

Asher opened the door to Foxglove Bank and Trust, stepped inside and got back to the business of unraveling the stable's financials. He crossed the lobby of the small but well-appointed bank branch that was fully staffed yet lacking customers.

At the bank teller counter, Asher glanced at the employee's name badge then introduced himself and said, "Ivy, I'd like to get a copy of the monthly bank statements for the last three years. Will that be possible?"

"You need Valerie, our customer relationship manager over in account services," Ivy said politely. Then her grin widened. Her eyes crinkled behind the lenses of her modern, statement-making large round eyeglass frames. She asked coyly, "Could I get your signature first?"

"Sure." Asher reached for a pen in the jar decorated with colorful paper flowers and asked, "Do you need my ID, too?"

Ivy chuckled. "We all know who you are." Then she opened a drawer and took out a glossy magazine. The cheerful teller flipped to a page marked with the same kind of sticky note Kelley had stuck all over the folders in his father's office last evening. With the magazine set in front of Asher, the bank teller said, "Feel free to sign anywhere."

Asher looked at the magazine ad for Velvet Dusk cologne. A cowboy in a tailored black suit and crisp white shirt, open at the collar, sat atop a stunning white stallion in an empty intersection of a downtown city. Twilight cast a glow against the towering high-rises, and a black, wide-brimmed cowboy hat cast shadows across the cowboy's face to enhance the mystery. The tagline read: *Velvet Dusk. Where city lights fade, stories begin. Always leave a trail they'll remember.*

Asher didn't bother to hide his confusion and asked the teller, "What is this?"

"It's you." Ivy touched his arm lightly and lowered her voice as if sharing a secret with a longtime friend. "You don't have to be modest. Your brother told us all about your super-busy modeling career in New York."

Asher coughed and said, "My brother did what?"

Yet, Ivy was already leaning over the partition toward her coworker, whispering for a platinum-haired woman to get her copy. All too quickly, there were two more bank employees crowding into Ivy's station and several more glossy magazines placed on the counter in front of Asher. Each one featured a different Velvet Dusk cologne ad with the same urban cowboy and stunning white stallion. Asher brushed his hand through his hair.

Peggy, the vault teller, according to her name tag, smiled at him and said, "Dylan told us you caught the modeling bug in college and couldn't shake it after graduation. So off you went to conquer the fashion world."

Asher should not be surprised. His twin had been charming, witty and even quicker with a prank. Dylan liked a good laugh and always enjoyed watching Asher squirm. Dylan would have claimed this as one of his more ingenious and ribbed Asher about it all the way home. His brother would have been even more impressed his tale sustained this long. Asher gave his twin a silent shoutout.

"We knew you'd come home sometime so we kept these just in case," Ivy said. Her coworkers nodded in unison and the chatty teller added, "We never wanted to ask Walter about you and upset him."

That was probably for the best. Asher kept his expression neutral.

Gail, the platinum-haired senior teller, tilted her head and said kindly, "Walter missed you, even though he tried so very hard to hide it."

And that was Asher's cue to excuse himself politely and get on with his business. He cleared his throat and said, "About those statements."

Ivy nudged the pen toward him, her expression hopeful. "This one is my favorite. Someday, I will blaze my own trail right on out of here, too. Same as you."

Ivy's coworkers hummed their encouragement for the young bank teller. Gail added, "Of course you will, and it will be grand. You'll see."

Ivy considered him. "You got out. Has it been grand?" She paused then answered the question herself. "Of course it has. How could it not be?"

He could list a few ways and pop her hope bubble with a handful of lessons learned and more of his straight talk. *Ashe, you lost your fun. Mom would hate that.* Dylan had often accused Asher of being too serious years after their mom's death. His twin had ramped up his efforts to make Asher laugh despite the brothers living in different states. Asher swiftly signed the glossy cologne ads with a bit more flourish in his signature than usual. Magazines returned, the women dispersed to their workstations.

Ivy gave the ad one more glance as if setting some silent intention for herself.

And Asher surprised himself with an entirely different sort of straight talk and said, "My mother always told us stroll or blaze, boys. It doesn't matter. Just remember to kick up your own dust. It's your trail and no one else's."

"Thanks. I like that. I can kick up my own dust for sure." Ivy hopped from her stool behind her station and beamed. "Now, let's get you what you came for. Come on. I'll walk you over to Valerie's office."

Asher took the chair across from Valerie and once again made his request for printed copies of the statements for the Blackwell account. Then he asked, "Is that going to be a problem?"

"It wouldn't have been," Valerie said then frowned. "Unfortunately, you're a month too late."

Back in the city, Asher would have expected—if not demanded—a swift solution. Then he would have pulled his cell phone out and gotten to work while he waited. Time, after all, was not meant to be wasted. Yet, he was locked out of his work emails, and he had no games on his cell phone. Sidestepping his idle mind, he fished a caramel-filled chocolate out of the crystal candy bowl on the account manager's desk, peeled the shiny wrapper off and asked, "What happened a month ago?"

"That's when we were doing things the right way." Valerie pulled her keyboard tray closer to her and started to type quickly.

"What are you doing now?" Asher stuck the chocolate into his mouth.

"We're doing things the corporate way," Valerie explained smoothly and kept on typing. "Now there's all sorts of P's involved."

"Excuse me?" Asher said.

"You know, procedures and policies that must be followed." Valerie leaned forward, swiped across her computer screen, sat back and picked up her typing rhythm again.

Asher helped himself to another chocolate candy and kept himself from checking the time on his watch. A quick errand this was not, and to be expected, he supposed. The folks in Gold Finch always took the scenic route. Preferred to promenade rather than run. And if it wasn't personal, it was just bad business. Asher settled in and waited for Valerie to work through her procedures.

"Used to be I hit this button right here." Valerie hovered her index finger over a button at the top of her keyboard and eyed Asher. "Everything printed nice and neat. You went on your way, and I added another satisfied customer to my tally."

"What happens if you hit that key now?" Asher asked mildly.

"Nothing because I need to submit a work order to corporate first." Valerie shook her head and pushed her keyboard tray under her desk. "The bank was sold. We've got ourselves a central office across the border in Indiana and a whole new computer system."

"Not a fan of the new management," Asher said.

"I'm a fan of good customer service," Valerie replied. "They tell us their computer systems are faster, but I've got a backlog of work orders and a long line of customers waiting on something." Valerie's computer chimed and she smiled at Asher. "Congratulations, you've just joined the queue."

"What happens next?" Asher asked.

"You wait until I call you. It could be later today or a matter of weeks." She handed him another chocolate candy and added, "We appreciate your business. I hope you enjoy the rest of your day."

It was technically a workday. Back in New York, Asher would have been in his office. Jumping from one meeting to another and using the minutes in between to approve a final contract or smooth over a client to finally reach an agreement. There was always another investment opportunity to find and always somewhere to be. And there was rarely a spare second to even consider whether he enjoyed his day.

Asher headed back to the diner where he'd parked earlier and where Big E was supposed to meet him after he finished at the feed supply store. Noting the crowded parking lot and lack of a familiar older cowboy lingering near Walter's truck, Asher went inside and pulled up short.

The lunch hour at Galloping Fork was apparently the place to be. There was a line of customers waiting to be seated. Frannie hollered a cheerful welcome from across the diner that had more than a few locals swiveling in their chairs to look at him.

Asher touched his hat in acknowledgment and worked his way through the crowded dining area, keeping one eye out for Big E. His progress was slowed every other table as he paused to greet former friends and shake the hands of neighbors. Finally, he made it to the back of the diner and searched for a spot out of the way. Where was Big E?

The door to the kitchen swung open slightly. Kelley grabbed his arm and tugged him into the back toward the small office. Her smile lit up her eyes and had him grinning back. Now he could say he was starting to enjoy his day.

"I made you a sandwich, but you can't eat it out

there." She picked up a to-go container off her desk and handed it to him then added, "It's off-menu."

Now he was curious. He flipped the lid and smelled bacon and roasted jalapeños. His stomach growled. "Are you afraid someone might see this and try to order it?"

"Frannie will make sure they do," Kelley explained. "It's one of her favorites and she believes it should be on the menu."

"You don't," Asher said.

"It's not my choice." Kelley shrugged and added, "Speaking of my boss, Pauline should be here any minute. She's got a new policy about outside food being kept outside the diner."

Policies seemed to be a running theme for the day. "Then I'll eat fast." Asher lifted half of the grilled cheese and considered her. "Why am I getting a special order?" Not that he minded. Not even a little bit.

"To thank you." Kelley's smile was wide and warm. She reached out and squeezed Asher's arm as if to share her delight. "This is the first day Frannie showed up for her shift here smiling and happy. Even more remarkable, she hasn't made one order error yet."

"I don't think I can take credit for that," Asher said. Although he would like to take credit sometime for making his cowgirl chef happy. He bit through the toasted sourdough bread then sighed around the explosion of flavor from the blackberry jam to smoky heat and crisp bacon. He swallowed and said, "I think this just might be my new favorite, too."

Her cheeks turned a rather fetching rosy color. It was her only acknowledgment to his compliment. *I see you, cowgirl.* Asher polished off the first half and went to work on the second part of the sandwich.

"Well, Frannie is over the moon with her new job at your stables," Kelley explained. "You get *all* the credit for her newfound joy. I'm really grateful."

What he wanted was to have his cowgirl chef *all* to himself. Asher opened his mouth.

"Kelley!" That shout came from the kitchen followed by, "Five minutes until call to order."

Kelley sprang into motion, took the to-go container from Asher and tossed it into the trash can near the desk. "Come on. We need to find you a seat before the meeting. It's probably going to be long, and you won't want to stand the whole time."

"What meeting?" Asher followed Kelley into the kitchen.

"The July Fourth Committee meeting," Kelley said. "We've got quite the turnout today."

Asher slowed near the service counter and pointed to the back door. "I think I'll just slip out there and head on back to the stables."

Hayes overheard and chuckled. "You aren't going nowhere." The cook pointed his spatula toward the window in the back door and asked, "That is Walter's blue truck that you drove here, isn't it?"

Asher nodded then frowned. He traded his compact rental car for the comfort of Walter's extended cab, fully loaded truck. The four-wheel-drive diesel was upgraded, relatively new and reminded Asher how much he missed open spaces and open roads.

"Ha. The locals got you boxed in something good out there." Hayes shook his head. "I told Trudy and now Pauline the diner needs a bigger parking lot."

"More land won't matter if someone doesn't organize the parking spots out there." Kelley moved to look out the small square window then continued, "What it needs is new lines to mark each parking space clearly."

Hayes grinned. "That can be your first update when you buy the diner, Kelley."

Kelley rolled her eyes at the good-natured cook and pointed at Asher. "Come on. Let's find you a seat."

"I think I'll hang back here with Hayes." And perhaps learn more about his cowgirl chef from the friendly cook who also believed Kelley should buy the diner.

"Employees only," Kelley said, then tipped her head and eyed Asher. "Why don't you want to go out there?"

"If you must know, I don't want to talk about my land legs again," Asher said, hearing the put-out tone in his own words.

Kelley blinked then her laughter spilled out. "That's oddly specific."

"And unfortunately true." Asher lifted his cowboy hat off his head and ran his fingers through his hair. More than a handful of locals in the dining area inquired about his legs and whether he was getting on well now that he was back on land.

"That's a natural inquiry given you've been living on a cruise ship," Hayes offered, amusement in his gaze. "At least that was what Dylan told us way back when."

His twin strikes again. Asher couldn't help himself and asked, "Why was I living on a cruise ship?"

"You followed Sloane Lowry, of course," Kelley informed him, her words helpful. Her expression contained. "You met up in the city while Sloane was there chasing her Broadway dreams. Sloane is now headlining on a cruise ship and singing on stage nightly. Sloane is one of Gold Finch's success stories. Everyone loves to talk about her."

"And I followed Sloane because...?" Asher's words were slow and careful.

Kelley's cheeks turned that pretty pink again. "You were her muse, of course."

"You even wrote songs for Sloane," Hayes offered, then snapped his fingers. "Dylan was always singing it. Catchy little tune about kickin' up the sun, laughin' in the breeze and livin' it up, you and me."

Of course, his twin was singing. Dylan always claimed there was a song for everything—every mood, every situation, good or bad. *Just listen and feel, Ashe. Let go.* Asher had usually left his brother to his music sessions and gotten back to whatever he was working on, often in silence. Only recently that silence he so often preferred seemed to be closing in around him.

Asher dropped his hat back on his head and argued, "Do I really look like someone's muse?"

Kelley skipped over Asher's dry comment and asked the cook, "You don't think they'll ask Asher to perform one of his original songs at open mic, do you?"

Asher crossed his arms over his chest. "There isn't an open mic in town."

"Sure, there is," Hayes announced, his laughter barely contained. "At Lucky Lane Tavern on Friday nights."

Kelley's gaze fairly danced.

"Well, it's good I'll be sorting paperwork in my dad's office for the foreseeable future," Asher said flatly. "And nowhere near an open mic." Although being near his cowgirl held a certain appeal.

"Too bad," Kelley murmured. "I bet you have a nice voice."

He could hold his own in the shower at his

apartment. And maybe with Kelley beside him on the karaoke stage at the tavern. That would be… Asher cut that errant thought off. Karaoke would not be his first choice for a night out with Kelley. Oh, he had other ideas for a night on the town. None that he would be sharing, of course. He blamed the spicy blackberry jam for getting him all turned around again. That and his cowgirl's gold-flecked hazel eyes he kept getting lost in.

Kelley peered out the pass-through window and finally took pity on Asher. "Come on. Big E is out there with Lynette and Beatrice Arbor. They're at the end of the counter. It looks like they saved you the last seat in the corner."

Perfect. He joined Kelley at the swinging door, then paused before pushing it open. "Any other stories floating around about me that I should know about?"

"I can't tell you," Kelley said, her words playful. Her smile mischievous. "Where would the fun be in that?"

Fun. But that used to be his twin's specialty. And yet, when he looked at Kelley…

"Come on, cowboy. Get those land legs moving." She nudged him lightly and whispered, "Otherwise, we're going to be late and then everyone will start up talking."

"What's wrong?" Asher's grin stalled, totally caught by the sparkle in her gaze. "Are you afraid they might realize I'm your favorite sunrise dance partner?"

"You are not my..." She left the rest unspoken and poked him harder. "Now is not the time to discover your funny bone, Asher Blackwell."

Perhaps not. It was an even worse time to discover that when it came to Kelley, he liked the idea of being much more than just her mystery dance partner.

CHAPTER SEVEN

ADMIRING A DEVIL-MAY-CARE *grin was not the same as getting lost in one.*

And Kelley was not confused about where they stood. She touched Asher's arm before he moved through the swinging door and around the counter, drawing his gaze back to her. She said, "A word of caution?"

"What's that?" he whispered.

I know how this ends. But I like to plan ahead. If I took your hand, how long would you hold on? Kelley drew her arm back and said, "Don't make eye contact with anyone seated in the middle up front unless you want to get involved."

Asher tilted his head and considered her. "Are you involved?" His words were mild, but curiosity flickered in his blue eyes.

"I'm on the committee." *As far as us, it's best if we call it here. Skip right to the end.* "I'm in charge of the floats and parade route."

"Impressive," Asher conceded.

"Not so very much," Kelley admitted. "I had an ulterior motive."

"What was that?" he asked, keeping his voice low to match hers and his gaze fixed on her face.

"If I'm organizing, I can't be expected to participate in the parade, too." Kelley shrugged as if it was all completely settled. After all, she was more than happy to organize the saddled horses in the parade line. It was the sitting in the saddle that she was seeking to avoid.

"Is it parades or participating in general that you don't like?" he asked mildly.

She searched his gaze then asked, "You don't remember, do you?"

He forgot. She supposed that was to be expected, if not the tiniest bit disappointing. Yet, it was one fleeting afternoon years ago during another Fourth of July parade. Back when preteen Kelley took a chance and took part. Only she ended up with a sprained wrist, a severely bruised elbow and more embarrassed than she had ever been after her horse spooked and tossed her to the pavement front and center for the entire town to see. But a cowboy—a mere teenager still discovering the depths of his maverick nature back then—came to her rescue.

Kelley caught the mayor motioning for her near the front of the dining area and shook her head slightly to clear the memory. "It's not important. Remember, no eye contact."

Asher smoothed a hand over his chin and nodded. "Got it." He studied her a beat longer, then made his way over to Big E and the only empty stool left at the counter.

By the third item on the committee's meeting agenda during the in-depth review of the firework display budget, Kelley determined she was the problem. She failed to follow her own advice. Oh, she avoided making eye contact with the committee members well enough. Try as she might, it was Asher whom her gaze tracked to over and over. Again and again.

Her city cowboy was seated on the very last stool; his legs were stretched out and his ankles stacked. Arms crossed over his chest, the brim of his cowboy hat was tipped forward to cover his gaze. He might have been asleep. Except Kelley had seen him nod ever so slightly the few times Big E leaned over to whisper something to him. Fortunately, Asher didn't appear to be keeping tabs on Kelley and didn't catch Kelley watching him. Or so she hoped.

The next agenda item was Kelley's float update. She ran through the approved parade route along Derby Hollow Road and ending on Hitch Post Avenue. Then she finished up with details about the staging area and took her seat. Soon, she noticed her focus was right back to where it had started. On her cowboy.

"Very informative, Kelley." Mayor Corbin drew Kelley's attention to him. He drummed his fingers on the tabletop next to his empty lunch plate and said, "However, I still need to know the exact participation numbers for the parade."

"Right." Kelley flipped through the papers attached to her clipboard and said, "We've got fourteen floats and eight other entries."

"That won't do." Mayor Corbin frowned.

"It's almost double the entries from last year." Not to mention Kelley had officially signed up all the townsfolk available to volunteer to be in the parade. She asked hesitantly, "If the whole town participates, who will be left to watch the parade?"

"The tourists will watch," the mayor announced, certainty in his words.

"Where do you intend to find these tourists, Mr. Mayor?" That question came from one of the window booths where Sully Connelly and his family were smashed together on the bench seats.

"It's not like we can boast about our Triple Laurel winner being in the parade." That grumble came from the tables in the center, curiously close to where Patsy Richmond and her daughter Caroline sat.

Someone from upfront added, "Worse, without our Triple Laurel winner, there is no meet and greet with the colt, and that would have definitely enticed the out-of-towners to come to Gold Finch."

A hush fell over the diner. Kelley searched for the grouser. No one looked at her. There was a sudden shifting in chairs and squeaking of vinyl in the booths. A dry cough followed another. Gazes were suddenly fixed on the tabletops. Kelly eyed her cowboy. Asher did not so much as flinch. The brim of his cowboy hat remained angled over his forehead, concealing most of his face.

"What's the use of a parade with no one to watch it?" Finally, Patrick Connelly asked, then added, "We should cancel the whole thing and wait until we have something to celebrate."

"The founding of our nation is something to celebrate," the mayor countered and smacked his gavel on the tabletop. "We are not canceling the annual parade or any of the other planned festivities."

Murmurs picked up like a ripple at low tide.

The mayor added another whack of his gavel and his words gained steam. "And this will be the best Red, White and Bluegrass Parade that Gold Finch has seen in an age. Maybe even ever. I can promise you that."

"Hear hear, Mr. Mayor," Beatrice Arbor called out and lifted her teacup in a toast.

"Now, we will have tourists coming to town." The mayor smoothed a hand over his bolo tie and adopted a calmer voice. "They will be here because we will be featured on *Morning Gallop* for having one of the largest parades in the tristate area."

Oohs and *Ahhs* flowed as if that tide swelled back to supportive.

"What's the catch?" Lynette Arbor asked before Kelley could.

"There isn't one," the mayor said, his expression and words overly pleasant.

"There's always one," Patrick Connelly challenged.

Kelley nodded, despite not wanting to agree with a Connelly. A feature on the very popular and widely watched morning show for the Bluegrass Regional News was no small feat. And Gold Finch was not one of the largest towns in the tristate coverage area.

"It's simple," the mayor stated. "We just need to have at least sixteen floats to be a featured parade on their website."

The mood dimmed.

"However, if we have twenty floats, then we will be in the top three and considered top billing for the *Morning Gallop's* TV feature on Fourth of July celebrations not to be missed," Mayor Corbin explained. His eyebrows winged up his forehead and his eyes peeled wide. "And let me be clear. We must have top billing." His eyebrows slammed back down and bunched before he continued, "Especially given the unfortunate events at the Laurel Legacy. Not that we are blaming anyone, mind you."

Kelley winced. Asher looked statue-stiff. She wanted to jump up and head straight to her cowboy and stand behind him or beside him. Whatever he needed in order to know he wasn't alone and at least one person in the diner did not blame him for losing a history-making race and failing to put Gold Finch on the national map.

The grumbles began again. The naysayers gained momentum and more objections spilled out. *Impossible. That's an ask too far. Call a vote to cancel. It'll be easier and faster.*

A booming call for silence followed. The mayor stood and swung his gavel. "We can do this." He motioned toward Kelley. Resolve filled his words. "Kelley, let me see your float list. There has to be someone we've missed."

Kelley passed her clipboard over to Rosalind Sterling, the assistant Fourth of July committee chair. Heads together, the mayor and Rosalind reviewed the list.

"We can split up the high school dance and cheer teams." Amy Peterson, the head coach, raised her hand and offered, "We could put the dance team on a float to add to our float count."

"That's one down." Rosalind grinned and wrote on the paper.

The mayor rubbed his hands together. "We just need five more now."

Davis Groves adjusted his baseball cap and said, "I can ask my grandpa about driving his nineteen-fifties Studebaker in the parade."

"If Myles is driving his classic car, my grandma will be wanting to drive her nineteen forty-eight

Ford pickup, too," Sheryl Demian called out from somewhere near the back.

Lenny Culver lifted his arm and said, "My brother's got a nineteen sixty-five Ford Mustang in his garage that needs to come out. Count him in."

Mayor Corbin glanced at Kelley and said, "You'll need to ensure classic cars meet the requirements for a proper parade float."

"Of course," Kelley assured him and typed a note into her phone. "I will get right on that this afternoon."

The mayor eyed Kelley, then dropped his gaze to the clipboard.

Kelley stilled, already aware of what was coming. She scanned the audience for another classic car aficionado to add to the parade float tally. Or anyone else willing to offer up a vintage tractor or another hay wagon.

"I don't see the Munroe sisters on this list," the mayor mused.

Kelley swallowed.

Rosalind drew her finger down the list and then watched Kelley over the tops of her eyeglass frames and said, "The Munroe sisters are definitely not on this list. And if I recall they are a talented trio."

More like a duo being Frannie and Laura-Beth. Kelley squirmed under the former principal's regard and shifted. Her gaze landed on Asher and stuck. *If I fall again, will you catch me?* No. That was an ask too far. As was the idea that her cowboy could possibly witness her making a fool of herself in front of him again. Kelley started to shake her head and make her excuses.

But her little sister spoke up and said, "Not to worry, Mr. Mayor and Ms. Sterling. I'm sure it was just an oversight on my sister's side." Frannie cast a wide smile at Kelley, her words bright, "Kelley has been busy helping Laura-Beth with her wedding that's coming up real quick. What with all the dance practicing, her mind is surely twirling. Can't have a properly memorable wedding without the dancing, after all."

There were nods and murmurs rumbling around the tables. Kelley heard a reference to Kelley's mystery cowboy partner among the whispers.

"Can't blame you for being distracted by your cowboy," Rosalind said quietly. "No one can deny you two went together like a mint julep on derby day. Sweet, smooth and unforgettable."

Kelley blanched.

Rosalind nudged her elbow into Kelley's rib and whispered, "Still, perhaps you should skip another sunrise dance and the mint juleps until after the parade."

There was a lot more she needed to skip with her cowboy than dancing.

Frannie wound her way around the tables to refill water glasses and added all too cheerfully,

"Mr. Mayor, I can promise you that the Munroe sisters will have a float in the parade."

Approval spread across the mayor's thin face. "I knew your family would not let us down."

Kelley only hoped she would not let her sisters down.

"It makes my chest swell to see this town coming together," the mayor stated proudly and studied the parade list once more. "Now, by my count we need one more float to guarantee Gold Finch a spot in the top three. We can't miss out on being included in *Morning Gallop's Not To Be Missed Round-Up* and also highlighted on their website and in their weekend happenings newsletter."

Excitement filled the diner.

Kelley hesitated. The Munroe sisters had not been the only family not on the parade float list. She could think of one other.

The mayor's words were pensive and deliberate. "Used to be we could count on all our local families in times like these."

Silence spread over the dining area like the expectant hush before the bell at the starting gate on derby day.

The mayor tapped his finger against the clipboard. "However, I also don't see the Blackwells on this list."

Someone cleared their throat. Another person coughed.

Kelley peered at Asher.

Big E set his hand on Asher's shoulder.

Asher tapped the brim of his hat higher on his head. His expression was contained. Confidence spread through his words. "Mr. Mayor, you can still count on the Blackwell family. Same as always."

"I mean no disrespect," Mayor Corbin said and shifted to face Asher. "But you're gonna have to prove that."

Kelley winced.

Asher never flinched. He said mildly, "How much do you need?"

"Son, you can keep your checkbook," the mayor said, then clutched the clipboard tighter and added, "What we need is a Blackwell float."

Asher wiped his hand over his mouth and said carefully, "A float."

The mayor nodded. "There was a time not too long ago when a Blackwell float was in every parade."

"That was my mom's doing." Asher's gaze tracked straight to Kelley and stuck as if he was only talking to her. "July Fourth was one of my mother's favorite holidays."

"What a nice way to honor your mother, then," Rosalind Sterling murmured.

"Can we count on the Blackwells, then?" the mayor pressed.

Asher held Kelley's gaze and nodded. "You can."

That sounded like a private promise to her. Kelley exhaled and remembered she stopped being fanciful and foolish the day she signed her divorce papers. Asher Blackwell was getting involved, but not with Kelley.

Two more rounds of coffee refills and the meeting finally concluded. Mayor Corbin and Rosalind Sterling moved to intercept Asher to shake his hand and thank him for his parade participation. The duo called Kelley over to join them.

"Now then, Asher, you will need an approved parade float. We started the safety inspections a few years back after an unfortunate trailer hitch debacle," Rosalind explained and tapped her eyeglasses up her nose. "I don't suppose you have a trailer, do you, Asher?"

Asher glanced at Big E. The older cowboy shrugged, and Asher replied, "It's doubtful."

"Herman Whittaker has a backup trailer inspected and ready for duty," Mayor Corbin offered. "You'll be wanting to see him this afternoon."

Asher suddenly looked worried. His nod was more automatic than confident.

"I seem to recall there was some history between Herman and the Blackwell boys," Lynette Arbor piped up, then quickly waved her hands. "But I'm sure it's long since forgotten."

Doubt spread across Asher's face.

Now Kelley was more curious than concerned.

"Best if you take Kelley and a dozen of her

blackberry turnovers with you," Rosalind suggested. "Those can soften up even the sourest of moods."

"I've got some leftover in the back," Kelley offered. Although they were meant for her cowboy's private stash.

Beside Asher, Beatrice clasped her hands together and exclaimed, "Oooh, if we're going to be on TV, we've got to have flower garlands for the horses like Asher's mother used to make."

Finally, Asher flinched and held up his hands. He shook his head and said, "I'm afraid those just might be way out of my wheelhouse."

"But your sweet momma taught us." Beatrice's words were soothing.

"Everyone wanted to be on her flower committee, but she was rather selective." Lynette bumped her shoulder against Asher's and sighed, a wistful note to her words. "We had such fun weaving those flowers for the horses in the parade."

"You will, too." Beatrice patted Asher's shoulder. "When we teach you all that your dear mother taught us."

Asher's eyebrows pulled together. He was starting to look slightly ill at ease.

Up until now, he had taken everything in stride. Wanting to offer her support, Kelley said, "Count me in for the flower weaving, too."

Asher gave her a small, grateful nod.

"Well now, that will be fine." Beatrice looked

from Kelley to Asher and back. Her gaze gleamed and she murmured, “Yes. That will be just fine indeed.”

It would be fine for Kelley. Even though she only just realized if Asher was entering a float he would most likely still be in town for the parade and her sister’s wedding. That meant Laura-Beth would be expecting Kelley to ask Asher to be her plus-one for the big day.

However, asking Asher on a date would invite Kelley’s inner hopeless romantic back into the game. But that mischief maker tended to set caution aside and leap swiftly forward. And a wedding reception was the worst sort of venue. Love would literally be in the air all around her. There would be no avoiding the other dewy-eyed, lovestruck guests, even at the singles’ table.

Good thing Kelley was all about mind over heart these days. Otherwise, she might have considered it all the perfect recipe for romance.

CHAPTER EIGHT

IT WAS NOT the eye contact that did him in. It was the cowgirl in the passenger seat of Walter's truck. The one Asher did not want to let down. *Troublesome territory, that.*

Now here he was driving to Herman Whittaker's farm to find out about a trailer for a parade float that Asher would rather not design or build for a July Fourth parade he had not even planned to be in Gold Finch for. All because Asher wanted to show a certain hazel-eyed chef that he could be counted on. *Definite trouble there.*

Apparently, Asher had tossed his intention to steer clear of his cowgirl right out the window. There was nothing for it but to buckle down. He would get the trailer, get home and get back to unraveling the accounting books in his father's office alone. After all, he was good on his own. Asher knew how to succeed at being alone. He preferred it that way. At least, until recently.

Kelley laughed. The bright sound filled the car until even Asher's frown softened. He slanted his gaze toward his pretty yet bothersome-for-his-peace-of-mind passenger. Kelley was on the phone with her older sister working through what she'd dubbed just another wedding crisis before she answered the call. Kelley glanced his way and gave him a thumbs-up, signaling all was well on the wedding front.

Minutes later, the call ended yet her amusement lingered. Kelley said, "Sorry about that. Laura-Beth wants her dream day, and any little hiccup throws her into a frenzy."

"And you are making sure she gets that dream day by handling all the details," Asher said.

"I'm doing everything I can." Kelley gave a quick but firm nod. "Laura-Beth deserves it. It's her wedding. Everything should be perfect, right?"

"Was yours?" he asked, then clamped his teeth together and said quickly, "You don't have to answer that. I shouldn't have pried."

"No, it's fine." Kelley set her phone in the console and ran her palms over her jean-covered legs. "Obviously, my marriage was not perfect, seeing as we are now divorced. As for our wedding day…"

At the sudden silence, Asher glanced over and watched Kelley slowly deflate as if backing away from the memory that was suddenly staring her down. If only he stopped there. Instead, he reached over and curved his fingers around hers and said, "I didn't mean to bring up any painful memories. Again, I'm sorry. Just ignore me."

Her chin lowered and her head tilted as if she suddenly noticed his hand over hers. Asher started to pull away. Kelley was faster. One flip of her wrist and she linked their fingers until their palms pressed together. Then she anchored her other hand on top of their joined ones as if to ensure he wouldn't let go. Finally, she turned her gaze on him and said, "In case you aren't aware, you are sort of hard to ignore."

Right back at you, cowgirl. He squeezed her fingers and said, "I could say the same about you."

Asher caught a glimpse of her pink cheeks before she ducked her head again and said, "I got married at the courthouse. No fanfare. No fuss. Just a judge and a standard courtroom script."

Not what he would have pictured. It didn't sound special or dare he say magical enough for someone like her. "Is that what you wanted?"

"It was for the best," Kelley said, her words indifferent and practical. "We were opening the restaurant and putting all our efforts into ensuring it was a successful launch."

That made their wedding sound like an afterthought as if *she* was an afterthought. How could anyone consider Kelley that? He noted she did not quite answer his question, yet decided not to press and asked instead, "How do you feel about marriage now?"

"It's not on the consideration list for the future," she said, then added, "Neither is dating or a relationship." Yet, her fingers flexed around his and her hold tightened. "What about you?"

"It's not on my list, either," he confessed and turned onto the drive for Whittaker Farm.

She shifted in her seat to face him and said, "Bad experience, then."

"Not really." Asher shrugged and explained, "It's more the opposite, actually. After my last relationship ended a few years back, I dated here and there. But there wasn't a spark or a connection worth pursuing. So now I put my time and energy into things where I actually see a return."

"I like that," Kelley said, a lightness in her tone. "You've put a value proposition on dating and found none. I have to agree with your assessment."

They were aligned. That should suit Asher extraordinarily well. Why, then, did he want to change her mind? It wasn't as if he was changing *his* mind. Asher was not known to be indecisive or wishy-washy. He would not start now. He frowned. Fortunately, the Whittaker farmhouse came into view before Asher could find out how firm her new stance really was.

A reed-thin farmer in a flannel shirt, oversize moss-green waders and matching rubber boots waved and stepped off the wraparound porch to greet them.

Kelley slipped her hand from Asher's, opened her car door and hopped out, denying Asher the chance to lean in to his chivalrous side. Probably for the best. Had Asher opened her door and offered his hand to help Kelley out, he would have most likely tucked her right into his side and been tempted to keep her there. But this was not that kind of relationship in the making. He just needed to remember as much. Asher grabbed the box of blackberry turnovers from the backseat, climbed out and walked around the hood of the truck.

Kelley gave Herman Whittaker a quick, friendly embrace. She asked after his wife and grandkids.

"You just missed her and the grans. They're headed to the waterpark to swim off some of their energy." Herman's smile brightened his sunburnished weathered cheeks. "And I'm fixing to get in a spot of fishing before they get back."

Kelley grinned at Asher. "Herman has eight grandkids all under the age of ten."

"And for reasons unknown, they all want to be together kicking up a ruckus for the summer under our roof." Herman frowned, yet affection filled his words.

Growing up, Asher and his brothers had traveled as a pack, too. It was rare to find one Blackwell brother without another one close by. Now they were adults, and it was even more rare to find them together. Asher ignored that twinge of nostalgia in his chest, yet acknowledged that he missed his brothers. A lot.

Asher offered the box to Herman. "I'm not sure if you'll want to keep these for yourself as a pick-me-up. But there's plenty in there to share with the grandkids, too."

"They're blackberry turnovers," Kelley said, almost shyly.

Herman peeked into the box and whistled. "Now, don't those look delicious." He reached inside, removed a turnover and took a big bite. One long sigh later, Herman said, "Now this tastes just like my great-gran's. You can't measure the love, but you can sure taste it."

Kelley fluttered her hand as if she wanted to brush aside the compliment with little fanfare and said, "That's kind."

And all too true. Asher had tasted Kelley's food. But watching her now, he wondered if Kelley knew how truly talented she was. Either way, his chef wasn't one to easily accept a compliment. And that made Asher all the more determined to show Kelley that she deserved all the praise and more.

While Herman finished his turnover, Kelley asked, "We came to see about your parade float trailer, Herman. Do you still have it?"

"Sure do. Got it certified last month." Pride was there in Herman's thin face and words. "It's ready to make its big parade debut."

Kelley smiled at Asher. "As it turns out, we can help make that happen."

"Don't tell me Lawrence needs it. I told him the stage for his Bluegrass band would never fit on his trailer." Herman frowned. "Lawrence should've set up the band on the courthouse steps like we've always done. No reason to change a good thing."

Asher knew something about that. He had the same good thing going in New York. A successful career and an apartment he renovated himself and friends he saw on his terms. He had built a *good* life there. There was no *good* reason to change anything. Except when he looked at Kelley, he considered something different. Something more than what he had.

"No, it's not that. Lawrence is on schedule for the band's float to go into the parade as planned," Kelley assured the wiry farmer, then added, "We'd like your trailer for a new parade float."

"I see." Herman's salt-and-pepper eyebrows pulled together as if helping him to focus better. Although the perceptive farmer seemed to read things clear enough. He hooked his thumbs in the front pockets of his waders and drawled, "Hmm, that's going to cost you, then."

"Of course." Kelley patted her pockets as if searching for her wallet. "We can pay you a daily rental fee. That won't be a problem."

The farmer chuckled. "I don't want your money."

Kelley stilled and cast Asher a perplexed look.

Asher cleared his throat and said, "I'm happy to pay. Whatever you need."

"Keep your money, son," Herman said swiftly. "As it happens, I've got a different sort of deal in mind."

That was not a surprise. Herman Whittaker might look more like an unstuffed scarecrow in his waders, plaid shirt and rubber boots. But he was sharp and astute and proof that, as Asher's mom always claimed, *a dusty hat did not mean a dull mind.* Asher asked, "What kind of deal?"

"The kind where you build me a chicken coop and I give you full use of my trailer." Herman grinned at Asher. There was merriment in his gaze and delight in his words. He rolled up onto the balls of his feet and lifted his eyebrows. "Didn't think I remembered you, did you, son?"

Asher had been hopeful Herman might have forgotten the twins and their antics from their high school daredevil days. No such luck. Asher said, "I've been away for a while."

"Yes. Too busy taking a bite out of the Big Apple to see fit to come home," Herman stated, a thread of disapproval in his words.

"I've got a pretty demanding job in New York," Asher said by way of an excuse. One that suited him quite well. Until he came back and danced with a pretty chef.

"Well, Walter always claimed you wouldn't forget your roots." Herman harrumphed and plucked his straw hat off his head as if to better see Asher. "Have you, then? Forgotten your roots."

Things were certainly coming back to Asher. Yet, those he feared had more to do with the cowgirl beside him than his roots. It had been a while since he felt any sort of spark. The last time he had been captivated by a cowgirl was even longer.

There was no denying he was drawn to Kelley. Although, it was like sweet tea on a hot summer day—eventually, it ran out. Sparks faded. Distance would dim that awareness. As for his roots, there were too many city miles under the soles of his boots to feel that tug anymore.

"Perhaps we should get back to this chicken coop," Kelley cut in. "This seems like a rather big request, Herman."

But would Kelley consider dinner with Asher and a few turns on the Lucky Lane dance floor too big of an ask? Asher was only inquiring out of curiosity, of course. He crossed his arms over his chest.

Kelley continued, "Perhaps there is something else Asher might assist you with. Something perhaps less technical and labor intensive."

Asher arched an eyebrow at Kelley, amused to realize that his cowgirl doubted he could build a chicken coop.

"Don't fret, Kelley." Herman waved his hand in the air and grinned. "The Blackwell boys have experience with chicken coops. They are particularly good at knocking them down."

Kelley swung toward Asher.

"That is true." At Kelley's dismayed expression, Asher quickly added, "We also put it back together."

That was after his brother Dylan knocked the chicken coop over and released more than a dozen of Herman's excitable chickens into the field. Asher had the entire coop back to rights long before Dylan corralled the last of the agitated hens. Unfortunately, Asher had been laughing too hard watching the hens cluck and peck at Dylan's ankles to help his twin or they might have gotten away before Herman caught them. Asher looked at Kelley and said solemnly, "No chickens were harmed."

"Even so, you didn't have to come back only to knock the chicken coop down again the following day and the day after that for more than a week straight." Herman smashed his cowboy hat in his tight grip and shook it at Asher. "Don't think I wasn't watching you."

Asher straightened and adjusted his cowboy hat. He had not returned to jump the chicken coop. Not one time. Asher had been the only one to scale the coop cleanly and without incident the first time. There was no need to do it again. However, his brother Dylan could not claim the same bragging rights. Apparently, Dylan had not been so keen on giving up, either. What his twin could do, Dylan always wanted to do better. For the most part, Dylan succeeded, except when he didn't. And that was usually when Asher covered for Dylan.

Kelley shook her head at Asher and said, "What were you thinking?"

"We were teenagers. We pretty much only thought about racing fast on our horses and scaling whatever we could find," Asher argued, still defending his twin even now. As if he was still looking out for Dylan like he always had when they were growing up. Asher continued, "It was all about the dare for my brother and me. Jumping things like fences and streams and whatever seemed to be the preferred obstacle in the moment."

"Like my chicken coop," Herman muttered and propped his straw cowboy hat back on his head. Then the crafty farmer turned around and started walking across his property. "Come on, then. I've got something to show you."

Asher and Kelley followed Herman toward a vintage red barn with a second-story hayloft. Asher motioned Kelley inside, then let the door shut behind him.

Herman went over to a warped workbench where what looked to be building plans were spread across the stained wood top. Kelley moved beside Asher and leaned over to study the drawings.

The farmer's gaze flashed and he said, "I can assure you that you won't be knocking this chicken coop over anytime soon."

"I think my days of jumping and racing across the back prairies are over," Asher said easily and watched a small smile curve across Kelley's face.

Herman shook his finger at Asher, yet his words were good-natured. “Get yourself in the saddle, son. It’ll all come back to you right quick.”

“I’m in the saddle, but it’s work related.” Getting the twos ready to race was requiring all the staff’s help. Asher added, “Seeing as I’m not scheduled to be in town for long, I doubt there’s time for pleasure riding.” Or fun with a chef.

Kelley’s smile faded.

Asher shifted toward her as if he wanted to defend himself for returning to the life—the good one—he had going in the city.

“It’s not about you making the time.” Herman nudged his elbow into Asher’s side, drawing Asher’s attention away from Kelley. The farmer’s eyebrows hitched upward. “It’s about you being worried you might realize you still like it around here. Hey, you might even miss it, if you give yourself the chance to think on it too long.”

There was a certain chef Asher was starting to worry about missing. Asher grinned. “Okay, if I do ride for pleasure, I promise to stay on Blackwell land.” But staying away from his cowgirl, well, Asher knew he should do that, too.

“To be fair, I’ve expanded my corn crop so there’s not much prairie out there for you to chase now anyway.” Herman’s gaze was clear and wise. “But if you’re lucky, when you’re out riding and remembering, you might find some of those roots.”

“I’ll keep an eye out,” Asher said and earned

a quick nod of approval from Herman. He would also keep his eyes off his cowgirl.

Kelley straightened. Her arm brushed against Asher's. Her words were apprehensive. "Herman, this looks more like a small house than a chicken coop."

Asher finally looked at the plans.

"It's my chicken palace." Satisfaction and pride filled Herman's face. "My daughter has a degree in architecture. She whipped these up for me."

"It is quite something," Kelley whispered.

That was an understatement. Asher rubbed his chin, already calculating the amount of wood he would need. Well, he wanted to be busy. And from the look of things, constructing the chicken palace was certainly going to fill up his days.

Kelley's eyes widened, revealing her skepticism. "I'm not sure Asher has the time or the..."

"Or the skill," Asher finished for her.

Kelley flushed but did not correct him.

Even his chef doubted him. He should be more upset than he was. Instead, anticipation filled him.

"You still remember how to handle all those power tools, don't you?" Herman eyed Asher and rocked back in his boots. "If I recall correctly, Asher worked enough jobs around town, putting them to good use, just about every summer."

Kelley watched Asher. Interest replaced the uncertainty in her expression.

"As it happens, I remember a lot about those summer days," Asher said casually.

How things had changed. Now he simply called the building maintenance manager whenever he had a problem, big or small, in his apartment. Still, if Asher could not be behind his laptop screen, buried in work, he supposed the next best thing was having a power tool in his hand, building something.

"Well, son, you're gonna have to prove it," Herman said, his smile relaxed and his words resolved. "You build me this coop, and you got yourself a proper parade trailer."

Prove it. There it was again. First Mayor Corbin and now Herman Whittaker. Asher should be insulted at being underestimated again. Ironically, he welcomed the challenge as if he had something to prove to himself and it seemed to Kelley now, too.

After all, he promised the mayor the Blackwells could be counted on. He wanted Kelley to believe it.

Challenge accepted, cowgirl.

CHAPTER NINE

"STOP RIGHT THERE, COWBOY." Kelley aimed the vintage stainless-steel sifter at Asher and watched him pause in the archway from the mudroom to the kitchen inside the Blackwell ranch house. She arched an eyebrow at him. "I won't have you spreading sawdust all over my desserts." Or wreaking havoc on her pulse.

Too late for that. Kelley hadn't seen Asher since he had dropped her at the diner yesterday afternoon when they left Herman's farm. It was a mere twenty-four hours later, and her pulse was doing double-time as if he had been away for much longer. And she missed him every minute. Kelley gathered her grit and shut the door on her sappy sentimental side.

Asher raised his hands, palms out. "My hands are clean."

"But not the rest of you," Kelley countered.

Asher lifted his arms away from his sides and glanced down as if only just noticing he was covered in sawdust from head to boots. His words were light and playful. "Can we just backtrack to the good stuff for a second?"

The good stuff was his one-sided grin tipping into his cheek. Yet, Kelley refused to get sidetracked by a neatly trimmed, close-shaved beard speckled with sawdust and a pair of mischievous blue eyes. Tonight was about her catering work, not her cowboy.

Asher drawled, "What is on the dessert menu for this evening?"

"Black Forest brownies." Kelley turned the hand-crank on the sifter and sprinkled the last of the powdered sugar over her tray of brownie bites. "It's my grandpa's recipe. Although I have not made them in quite some time."

"Why not?" He slipped off his boots and left them in the mudroom.

"My ex-husband wanted more sophisticated desserts on our menu at the restaurant," Kelley explained and moved the brownie tray to the back counter.

"So, you don't think everyone around here has a sophisticated palate, then?" Asher asked.

"It's not that." Kelley twisted around and watched the amusement flash across his handsome face.

He padded in socked feet softly forward.

She rounded the island to block him. "I was serious about the no-sawdust-in-my-kitchen rule." And about not getting sidetracked.

"I know." His grin expanded. "It's just you've got powdered sugar. Here." He reached up and touched his finger lightly against her cheek. "It's making it hard to concentrate."

She knew the feeling. She worked on keeping her breath and words even. "How is the chicken coop coming along?"

"It's going well, considering we got the plans yesterday. Big E and I might only need to make one more trip to the hardware store for more supplies." He shifted, then brushed his finger over her other cheek. "Having any issues with the old kitchen appliances in here? I know they aren't what you are used to cooking on."

She was having issues keeping her pulse in check and her thoughts from straying. It would be simple enough to slip her arms up and around his neck. Then if she leaned forward ever so slightly, they would be less than a whisper apart. Perfect for a… Suddenly, anticipation charged the silence.

Kelley raised her focus from Asher's mouth to his warm yet all too alert gaze and said through her sigh, "Sorry. What was the question?"

"The appliances." He trailed his fingers back toward her ear. "No problems, right?"

"Nothing I can't manage." But kissing her cowboy could be more than she could manage.

Still, she was tempted.

Still, she didn't back away.

Still, she willed him to close the distance.

She would be quick. Just a touch of her lips to

his. A brief brush. Too swift to leave an impression. Nothing she could not forget.

But his kiss might make her forget. Forget this was not a first kiss, but a last one. The only one they could share. He had found his place in the city. He belonged there. The city and Kelley were not a fit. Yet, being in her cowboy's arms, well, that suited her. Quite well.

So it was one kiss. One private moment to steal. She wanted it more, not less now. *What about you, cowboy?*

The old-fashioned timer buzzed on the oven somewhere behind her.

Kelley startled and stepped back. "That would be the roast for the hot beef sandwiches tonight."

He lowered his arm and watched her.

Rattled, Kelley blurted, "It's finished." So was the moment to discover if they were of like minds when it came to a possible mutual attraction. Disappointing, that. Kelley spun around and beelined for the oven, not for her cowboy's arms.

After grabbing two dish towels, she pulled the oval roasting pan out, set it on the counter, then said, "This is another family recipe from my grandpa. I was missing..." She turned. The kitchen was empty. Her cowboy was gone. Exhaling, she finished saying quietly, "Him. I was missing him." *And now it seems you, too, cowboy.*

Kelley smoothed her palms over her apron, brushing powdered sugar on the floor to be cleaned up later. Then she retied her apron and got herself sorted. She had a dinner service to complete, not a cowboy to make memories with.

Kelley managed to get through the dinner service without being distracted by Asher. Now she was back in the outdated kitchen prepping the overnight oats for breakfast the next morning while Frannie, Owen—the stable's hot-walker turned all-around helper—and Asher finished washing and drying the last of the dirty dishes.

Frannie and Owen had been inseparable through dinner. It seemed her little sister had found a willing someone she could pass on her equestrian knowledge to. While Owen, for his part, was proving to be a skilled sous-chef for Kelley and she very much appreciated the second set of hands as she could not be on site for every meal.

Currently, Frannie and Asher were immersed in a discussion about different types of tack and the best stirrups, bridles and saddles for every different equestrian discipline. Kelley poured almond milk into the last Mason jar filled with rolled oats, vanilla and Greek yogurt. Satisfied at the consistency, she handed the glass jar to Owen.

Owen twisted the cap onto the Mason jar, set it in the refrigerator with the other dozen they'd already prepared and said, "I think they've officially discussed more than twenty different types of saddles alone. Not to mention the dozens of saddle pads and shapes."

"I'm afraid I cannot offer any clarity on tack." Kelley chuckled and dumped a bag of unshelled pistachios into a bowl. "I haven't ridden in years." Not since she tumbled off her horse in the parade.

Asher paused mid-sentence and watched Kelley too closely.

But that was old news and not worth discussing now. Besides, food was her focus these days. Kelley quickly opened the cabinet and pulled out a cookie sheet then grinned. "However, I can tell you that once these nuts are toasted and crushed, they will bring the most satisfying crunch to the overnight oats in the morning."

"Well, big sister, your horse-riding hiatus is finally coming to an end," Frannie announced and swiped a pistachio from the bowl. She opened the shell and popped the nut into her mouth, then grinned. "Laura-Beth and I want to re-create our Heart of a Horse float for the parade this year."

Not that one. Did no one but Kelley remember what happened that year? Kelley cracked shells off pistachios in swift succession, dropping nuts onto the stainless-steel cookie sheet one after another. All the while, she worked to keep her expression relaxed, not strained.

"Our heart float represented us the most," Frannie said, seemingly unbothered by Kelley's silence. "Our tagline was Three Sisters. One Bond. We each represented the three traits of a champion horse. Spirit, speed and strength."

Yet, Kelley did not have the strength to keep herself in the saddle when her horse spooked and tossed her to the ground. She lost her nerve to try again. And then her parents divorced not soon after and Kelley had retreated to the kitchen. It was there with her grandpa that Kelley discovered her passion for cooking, which only gave her another solid reason not to get back in the saddle. She hedged, "I think we should discuss this when I get home later."

"You can't back out, Kels." Frannie tossed another pistachio into her mouth and crunched down. "You promised to participate in front of the whole town. I was there. So was Asher."

Kelley glanced at Asher.

Asher stirred the large round ice cube in his bourbon and considered her. His gaze was thoughtful, his expression contained. Yet, his shoulders looked sturdy enough to back her up. His arms steady enough to hold her until she got over her unease at riding again.

Surely, in Asher's embrace, she could not be weak. Still, she was stronger now on her own. How could she not be? A cowboy rescue was not what she needed. But Asher, well, she could fall… No. There were too many reasons not to fall for him.

The fact remained she had given her word to be in the parade and would not go back on it now. Strength would not sway Frannie or Laura-Beth. That meant Kelley just needed to outsmart her sisters. Same as she would her heart. *You're off the hook, cowboy.* Kelley said, "Let's just talk later at home."

"Fine." Frannie kissed Kelley's cheek then said, "Now, I'm taking Owen to Whistle Bend Bluff. Can you believe he hasn't seen the view from the bluff yet?"

"Some people like to stargaze, Frannie, rather than go to an overlook with a view of the racetrack," Kelley teased.

"You can't fool me, big sister. I know your secret," Frannie said playfully.

That her heart was fickle and she feared already falling for a city cowboy? Kelley held her breath.

"I know full well that Whistle Bend Bluff is one of your favorite spots in town." Frannie laughed and pulled Owen toward the back door then called out, "Don't think you can fool me."

The back door slammed shut.

Kelley only really needed to fool her heart. The one that was beating faster given that she was alone with her cowboy. *At last.*

Asher sipped his bourbon and eyed Kelley over the rim of the cocktail glass. "Is she right about the bluff?"

Kelley got busy shelling more pistachios and admitted, "The overlook has quite a stunning view at sunset. And if you linger awhile, there will be too many stars to count. It is like the sky is lit up with unlimited dreams. All I ever wanted to do was catch one."

Asher's gaze softened and he leaned back against the counter. "So, you're a stargazer, then."

"More like a firefly chaser," she said, her words wistful. "My grandpa told me lightning bugs were dream catchers and wish granters." She tapped the lid on an empty Mason jar and continued, "I would make a fairy garden in one of these and then catch fireflies to put inside."

"And did your wishes get granted?" he asked, his tone casual, his gaze tender.

"Well, Drew Carson asked me out for my first ever date in the ninth grade," she said and waggled her eyebrows. "I'd been wishing for that for months. I talked him into going to the bluff." It had seemed fitting to have her first date and possible first kiss at the overlook where she spent so much time imagining it.

Asher smiled and asked, "Was the date everything you dreamed it would be?"

"It was supposed to have been," she confessed and wrinkled her nose. "But Drew discovered he was highly allergic to Kentucky bluegrass, and we never made it to the bluff. We ended up turning back halfway on the trail and heading to the store for allergy medicine. It was a tie who apologized more. Him or me for forcing him to go out there."

"That's..." Asher's laughter spilled out. "I'm sorry."

"It's funny now." Kelley's laugh joined his and she added, "But not so much at the time."

"Tell me Drew conquered his bluegrass and took you back out there," Asher said. "For a first date redo."

Kelley shook her head. "We agreed we were better as friends."

"So, you went back to the bluff on your own and caught more of your dream catchers," Asher mused, his expression pensive as if he could picture it.

"I didn't go back," she admitted. "Mostly because Trudy hired me at the diner and I was more interested in learning to cook and bake with my grandpa and Trudy than dating and dreaming."

"You learned well." Asher helped himself to one of the leftover brownie bites in the container on the island. "These might be homespun, but there is nothing unrefined about the taste. Flavorful and satisfying. Everything you could want in a brownie."

He could be someone she wanted. He hadn't pressed her on the parade and yet he found a way to get her to open up to him. No one other than her sisters knew about her fairy garden Mason jars. Kelley smiled and said, "I'm glad you like the brownies. My grandpa would be glad, too."

Asher popped the rest of the chocolate bite into his mouth and considered her. Finally, he asked, "Was the entire menu family recipes tonight?"

She nodded and explained, "Everything I have made for the stables has been a recipe my grandpa taught me when I first learned to cook. They are uncomplicated and I know each one by heart."

"Thank you for sharing a part of your family." Asher touched her arm and said, "You should consider sharing your food with more of the town."

"I tried that in the city," Kelley confessed. "It didn't go quite so well."

"But it wasn't these recipes," Asher countered. "What was it Herman said yesterday afternoon?" Asher snapped his fingers and continued, "You can't measure the love, but you can taste it. Maybe that's the difference."

But it had been about passion and love in New York. Only there had been pressure and disagreements, as well. Marriage and futures at stake. And somewhere that love got misplaced and that passion burned out. Kelley had feared it was gone completely. Yet lately, she was not so certain. She set the pistachio tray in the oven and said, "Maybe the difference is the kitchen I'm cooking in."

"Not likely." Asher picked up the pair of pliers Kelley used to turn the knob on the oven to the correct temperature and frowned. "It's not exactly easy cooking in this place."

But Kelley felt at ease with him. She liked being around him. And the more time she spent with her cowboy, the more she wanted to stay longer and share more secrets. She eased the pliers from his hand and stashed them in the drawer beside the oven to keep them in easy reach for tomorrow. "Once I figured out the quirks around here, there was nothing to it."

Asher eyed her like he didn't believe her and said, "You aren't like most people I know."

You aren't like I expected, either. And she was not certain if she was happy about that or not. She asked, "Are you giving me a compliment, then? Is it good or bad that I'm not like most people?" Too bad her cowboy was not like her ex-husband. Single-minded and inflexible was nothing she wanted in another partner.

"It was a compliment." Asher finished his drink. "I imagine most chefs would have walked in here and then walked out. Probably even most home cooks."

"I like a challenge," Kelley said.

"That's not it." Asher shook his head. "You see the best in things, not the worst."

"Not always," Kelley confessed. "Especially not after my divorce."

"What changed?" he asked.

I met a cowboy. Kelley opened her mouth.

The back door slammed and bootsteps thumped on the hardwood floor.

Welcoming the interruption, Kelley turned away from Asher and tucked her truths away where they belonged.

"Good. You're here." Big E hurried into the kitchen. There was an urgency to his words and movements. "Asher, we could really use you at the stables. It's Pride."

Asher set his glass in the sink and grabbed his cowboy hat from the stool.

Kelley turned off the oven with the pistachios inside then opened the refrigerator. She grabbed a bundle of fresh spearmint she'd bought at the farmer's market on a whim, rather than take Asher's hand. Facing the two cowboys, she realized they were watching her. She said weakly, "It's just spearmint. I read horses like it."

"It certainly can't hurt," Big E said, then spun around on his boot heels. "Heaven knows we've tried everything else with that colt. Something has gotta work."

Asher smashed his hat on his head and said, "Well, we aren't giving up on him. That's for certain."

Kelley knew one thing for certain. Sharing silly childhood stories with Asher was nothing compared to opening her heart to him.

I can't trust you with my heart, cowboy. It was nothing personal. Kelley didn't trust herself with it really.

And that meant no matter how much Kelley enjoyed Asher's company, there could be nothing more between them. Even if her heart wished otherwise.

CHAPTER TEN

ASHER STOOD INSIDE the Blackwell Stables, opposite Pride's stall, and watched the colt pace in a tight circle. Pride's muscular frame was too tense and too taut, as if he was preparing not to jump out of the stall but instead bust right through the wall. His ears twitched side to side, refusing to still. His eyes were narrowed. And his tail swish was more like the snap of a whip.

Most of the Blackwell staff were crowded in the stables, including Joe and Joe's second-in-command, Elliot James. One of the trainers approached the stall, his movements careful, his steps ginger.

Pride bared his teeth and slammed his back hoof against the stall door. The powerful thud vibrated around the stall dividers. The trainer retreated. Pride started up pacing again. Edwina, their longtime stable hand from the filly horse barn, hummed softly and stepped up. Another vicious kick followed. The sound thudded inside Asher. He winced. Every time Pride reacted, Kelley edged closer to Asher.

Elliot took a turn, adding calming words to his

approach. Pride pinned his ears back and shook his head as if to stop the grating sound. Once more the colt kicked the stall door. Then again.

Kelley's hand found Asher's instantly; her grip was tense, her posture stiff.

Elliot dropped back beside Joe and spoke quietly to him. The worried staff spoke to each other. Their murmurs only seemed to stir up the tension already thickening the air. Pride's gaze widened until the whites of his eyes were revealed.

Pride wanted out. Yet, the colt was trapped. Nowhere to go to escape. Asher knew something about that. He knew how to run far and fast. And when he eventually did, he ran all the way to New York City.

Pride's nostrils flared as if he scented the strain in the air. His tail whipped back and forth. The colt snorted, the sound distressed.

Kelley's fingers tightened around Asher's as if she was in pain, too. Worry pinched across her face.

Before the next trainer stepped forward, Asher said, his voice low and commanding, "Everyone out." All eyes landed on Asher. He kept the warning in his words and added, "Now. Leave. Now."

Joe said, "Asher, I don't think…"

Asher cut him off. "Look at him. He can't breathe with everyone hovering. He needs space." The horse was hurting. The cowgirl beside Asher was hurting for the colt. Asher intended to make it stop. Immediately. He added, "I mean no disrespect. You all tried. Now let me try my way."

"Pride responded to Asher when Asher first arrived." Big E set his hand on Asher's shoulder and said, "I'll be outside. Holler if you need me."

Asher gave him a small nod.

The staff all looked toward Joe. Finally, Joe motioned to the door and said, "Let's give them some space."

And then it was Asher, Kelley and Pride. The stable was quiet. The horses in the other stalls were still and silent as if waiting and watching.

Pride circled once more, then paused. One forceful shake of his head and the horse exhaled hard and finally stood in place. Asher held the colt's gaze.

"I think he would feel better if he could run," Kelley whispered. "That's what he's trained to do. It's what he knows. All he really knows."

Asher nodded. "Now we have to figure out how to get him out of here safely and to someplace he can run as he wants for as long as he wants." His words were pitched low. "I can't move him until he settles. It could be a while."

"Then we wait," Kelley said and kept her hand in his.

Asher slanted his gaze toward Kelley. "It could take him all night, given his spirit and stamina."

"I don't mind." Kelley looked at Asher. Her grin was small and wry. "Besides, helping you and Pride gives me a very good excuse for not answering any wedding SOS texts or calls tonight."

"Aren't you obligated to answer as the maid of honor *and* sister of the bride?" Asher said, enjoying the spark flaring in her hazel eyes.

She chuckled. "I think I've more than earned a night off."

Pride nickered.

Asher was not sure what made him happier. Knowing Kelley would be with him longer or the sound the colt made.

Kelley's eyes widened and she leaned into Asher. "Tell me that was a good noise."

"I think Pride wants you here, too." *So do I.* Yet, Asher knew he should let her go. And he would. Just not yet. He kept their fingers linked and kept his attention on Pride. "I think Pride likes the sound of your voice or perhaps it's your laugh."

"No one has told me that before." Kelley chuckled again; her amusement spilled out into a soft tinkling laugh. "In fact, I put Frannie and Laura-Beth to sleep whenever I read out loud, even now."

Pride's ears twitched and then held in place, alert and open. Asher relaxed and said, "Well, I believe you have one admirer in that stall over there." *And one right beside you. But I can't confuse things.* After all, when Asher's emotions got involved, everything tended to go awry and everyone ended up hurt.

"I don't think it's me," Kelley protested albeit half-heartedly as if she hoped it was true.

"Only one way to test it," Asher said, gesturing to her. "You have to keep talking."

"About what?" Kelley asked.

Anything. Everything. Asher wanted to know all about her. He said, "I know you haven't ridden in a while. You don't need to explain." He included the last words when he felt her stiffen beside him. He asked quickly, "But are you okay now? Because we're going to have to get much closer to Pride to calm him and move him."

"I think talking is easing my own nerves." She squeezed Asher's hand and asked, "Still, you won't leave my side, right?"

"I'm not leaving either of you," Asher said, the promise in his words. "Until Pride is someplace where he feels safe and calm." *And until you tell me to go. And mark my words, cowgirl, you will.* His heart was off-limits. It had been for a while. There was no use denying he intended to keep it that way. And she deserved a cowboy who would love her without limits.

Kelley moved slowly forward with Asher and said softly, "Frannie should be here. My little sister has got the natural sense for horses."

"I was thinking the same," Asher said. "Dylan was built for this, not me."

"You don't really believe that, do you?" Kelley eyed him. Surprise crossed her face. "You grew up riding alongside your brothers. You are as talented as them."

"That was a lifetime ago." He had long since traded dust and denim for deadlines and dress shoes. It was not a move he regretted or even reconsidered. Until recently. Lately, he'd felt a pull for the trails he thought he left behind him.

"I know how that feels. When I look back it feels like some things were in a different lifetime," Kelley said, still in that soft tone. "Sometimes I wish I could go back, if only for a day."

"Any particular day you would choose?" He guided her closer to Pride's stall.

The colt was quiet yet alert and diligently tracking their progress.

"Not a particular day, but rather a place." The wistful tone in Kelley's words caught his attention. Her face was upturned. A subtle contentment smoothed her expression. "It will come as no surprise to you that I had a garden of my own growing up."

The joy in her expressive hazel eyes drew him in completely. He wanted to wrap his arms around her and pull her into him. *Wrong time. Wrong place.* And he was certainly the wrong cowboy for her. He asked, "Did you release your fireflies in your garden?"

"Of course." Her laughter swirled through her words. "It was also the place where the garden gnomes played, and the fairies danced all night. I know this because the gnomes were never in the same place the next morning when I checked on them."

He wanted to dance with her in that garden. Except he could only picture himself walking along city streets solo. He said, "I suspect you checked the garden every morning."

"Like clockwork," she admitted. "There were also stones moved. Doors open on the mini-houses. A new plant. Sometimes even butterflies and hummingbirds were fluttering around."

"Sounds like quite the place," Asher mused.

"It was enchanting," Kelley said and sighed. "Do you know even when I found out that it was my grandparents rearranging the garden every night, it still didn't lose its appeal. It meant even more, knowing they went out of their way for me."

His cowgirl was enchanting. No way around that. Kelley deserved a cowboy who would give more to her than to his career, and make her the priority. But Asher's relationship track record was mostly losses and not exactly the sort of stellar achievement worth betting a cowgirl's heart on. Asher released Kelley's hand, albeit more reluctantly than he wanted to admit, then propped his arms gently on the stall door, working not to crowd Pride or Kelley.

"What about you?" Kelley asked, curiosity in her words. "What day would you go back to?"

"Any day spent with my brothers in our treehouse." Asher welcomed the childhood flashback. "We built it with my dad and Joe out by the hay barn pasture. My brothers and I spent hours there and even camped out on more than one night."

"A home away from home," Kelley mused.

"It was everything." Asher smiled. There were too many carefree summer days to recount. But the treehouse and his brothers were featured in all his favorite childhood adventures. "It was our hideout. The place where we shared our secrets and lived out our dreams."

"Is the treehouse still there?" Kelley asked.

"I don't know," Asher admitted and slanted his gaze toward Kelley. "I haven't looked for it." Ah, but the feelings—the delight and thrill and pure fun of being with his brothers—was there inside him still. And surprisingly simple to recall even after so much time spent apart.

"Why not?" Her eyebrows pulled together.

The same reason he had yet to go down to the brothers' wing at the ranch house where their bedrooms were and instead chose to sleep on the couch in the family room. The treehouse was abandoned. Same as the brothers abandoned each other to follow their own paths. It was not right or wrong. It just was. There was no sense looking back now. He asked, "Have you returned to your special garden?"

She shook her head. "It became a vegetable

garden and stayed that way until my grandfather died."

"And now?" he pressed.

"It's overgrown with weeds. I can't see the path anymore," she said then added, "And the truth is I haven't taken the time to try."

"Same here." Asher extended his arms over the stall door and held his palms out, inviting the colt to come to him. "I don't have the time to go chasing days gone by." And so he kept looking ahead. Always.

"All the same, it was nice to revisit just now." She bumped her shoulder against Asher's. "It reminded me how much I could use a proper vegetable garden right about now."

He grinned. "You should talk to Edwina. She used to tend to the garden my mom started near the staff quarters. I'm sure Edie would share if she has anything growing there."

"I will track down Edie tomorrow." Kelley reached into her pocket and pulled out the spearmint leaves. "Speaking of garden fresh, maybe we should see if Pride might like some organic mint."

Asher shifted his attention back to the colt and away from Kelley and things not meant for him. He said, "Let's try and see."

Kelley rubbed a leaf over her palms, then set another one in her hand and reached over the stall door. Her words were soothing and calm. "You want to move, don't you, Pride? But you're not sure who to trust. I know that feeling."

Pride's ears perked up. His nostrils flared.

"Who don't you trust?" Asher asked Kelley and watched Pride extend his head toward her.

"Myself," Kelley said, then worked to soothe Pride before Asher could ask her more.

That, he supposed, was as it should be.

Kelley continued, "You can trust me, Pride. I won't hurt you."

Asher did not want to hurt his cowgirl. The only way to do that was to get her out of his head. He trusted himself to do that. Because he could not be trusted with a cowgirl's heart as big and tender as hers.

Pride breathed heavily and took a tentative step toward Kelley, who held herself in place. Her focus remained fixed on the colt. "He's coming to me." There was a smile in her words. "You can do it, Pride."

One minute there was no connection. And the next, the colt was nuzzling Kelley's palm while Kelley cheered him on. She chuckled. "He likes it."

The next thing Asher knew, Kelley was pressed up against him, crushing a spearmint leaf against his hands and explaining to Pride that Asher was one of the good ones, too.

Asher very much wanted to be, if only for his cowgirl. And a good one would know when to let go and walk away. Pride searched Asher's palms for more spearmint and Asher said, "Let's open the door and see if Pride will let me in."

Another spearmint branch and Asher was inside Pride's stall. Kelley stayed on the other side and rubbed her fingers over Pride's muzzle. Asher ran his hand over Pride's back, noted the still tense muscles and set out to give the colt a massage that he'd seen his father treat his horses to after a hard-won race.

A short while later, Kelley said, "I think the spearmint and massage are working. Pride is looking much more at ease."

Asher was feeling the same. There was something soothing yet energizing about winning over the racehorse. He heard Pride breathe heavily on Kelley and smiled. "He likes you."

Kelley said, "That is because Pride knows I understand him. We get each other."

"What do you mean?" Asher smoothed his hands in a circular motion over Pride's hind leg.

"His world went from traveling to one racetrack after another to this tiny stall," Kelley explained. "Now Pride is scared and unsure. That was how I felt after I got divorced and lost my restaurant."

It was not lost on Asher that the more Pride relaxed, the more Kelley did, too. Both the colt and his cowgirl were starting to trust him. Heady stuff for sure. Asher would need to tread carefully. He picked up a grooming brush from the bucket and asked, "Do you mind if I ask what happened between you and your ex-husband?"

"We should have worked," she said. "We did work on paper. We were aligned in our culinary passion and goals. We cared for each other."

"But," he pressed.

"I realized I lost myself in pursuit of some vision I could no longer see," she explained. "My ex-husband enhanced the menu so much, he edited me out. Still, I was convinced he loved me, and he was making the right decisions for us as a team and for our future, not just his own success. Turned out I was wrong."

"So, you came home, rather than reset in the city," he said, his words casual.

She nodded. "The city is his place, not mine."

Asher wanted to argue. The city was a place of opportunity. There was room for Kelley. With him. It could be their place, too. Now Asher sounded like he wanted a relationship. With her. Coming home certainly turned him around in more ways than one. Nothing he couldn't straighten out once his boots hit the hard pavement alone like he preferred. Frowning, Asher worked the brush over Pride's back.

"My ex-husband is thriving in New York," she stated, her words flat and indifferent. "He is with an investment company that is more interested in profit margins than culinary experiences for their group of restaurants. From what I've heard, he is making quite the name for himself and surpassing their expectations."

Asher was not all that interested in her ex-husband's achievements. It was his cowgirl who fascinated him. He asked, "What do you want to do now?"

"I want to do something that matters. That has an impact." She paused and shifted to look around Pride's head. She met Asher's gaze. "You're going to tell me that's what everyone wants."

He finished brushing Pride's tail and gave her his own truth. "That was not what I wanted when I moved to New York permanently."

"What did you want?" She searched his face.

He considered her, considered even more keeping the next truth to himself. But it was best if she understood exactly the kind of cowboy he was. Driven. Singularly focused. Selfish and emotionally unavailable. Those were only a few of the things his ex-girlfriends accused him of. He said, "I only wanted to prove my father wrong."

"And have you?" she asked tentatively, then more boldly. "Have you proven your dad wrong?"

"He's not here to ask so you'll have to tell me." Asher dropped the comb into the grooming bucket and reached for the halter and lead rope hanging from a hook on the wall. "My father warned me I would never become anything without the Blackwell name and his stables to lean on."

"So, you went to New York where the Blackwell name carries no weight and became successful on your own terms," she said, approval clear in her tone. Her grin was playful, her mood light. "It is safe for me to assume you are successful, aren't you?"

His chuckle was short and abrupt. "According to the partners at the investment firm, I'm the best they've got." That was not by accident. It came from hard work and an uncompromising resolve. "According to the articles written about me, I'm at the top of my financial game." Where he had fought to be.

Her eyebrows winged up.

He held her gaze and said, "If financial security for myself, my family and future generations is a criterion, I have that, too."

Because it was not enough to prove Walter wrong. It was about standing as his father's equal and providing for himself and his own, rendering his father's so-called goodwill unnecessary.

"Impressive," Kelley murmured. "I would have to say you achieved your goal."

"I'm not even sure it matters now." The words slipped out before he could stop them and yet he continued to spill his truths, "Dylan isn't here. Walter is gone, too." As was the reason Asher pushed himself. He never wanted to give his dad a reason to tell him that he should have—or could have—accomplished more. Now Asher was more alone and more restless than ever.

"What is next for you?" Kelley asked.

Asher slipped the halter on Pride's head and paused to give the colt a moment to adjust. He said, "When I finish up here, it's back to the city and my job." Where he would certainly find his new reason to keep moving forward like always. He took hold of the lead rope. "Right now, it's time to get Pride someplace he can run like he's meant to."

"You look like you have a place in mind." Kelley opened the stall door.

"There's a trio of retirees out in the farthest pasture," Asher said, then guided Pride from the stable and straight outside into the evening. "They'll teach Pride how to be a horse again."

Kelley walked beside them and smiled. "I like that idea. Pride has earned the freedom to enjoy himself."

Asher could not deny he was enjoying himself. It was a far cry from his fast-paced days of back-to-back meetings, conference calls and heated negotiations where he chased improved bottom lines, and business came before all else.

The night air was cool, and the hum of nature surrounded them. And for the first time in a long while, Asher was content in the silence.

It was just a cowboy, a cowgirl and a horse.

Suddenly, Asher wondered what more he could ever want.

CHAPTER ELEVEN

It was confirmed. Asher was headed back to the city. Back to the job and life he had there. As it should be.

The only missing piece was when. When exactly would Kelley have to tell her cowboy goodbye for good? That was as it should be as well. After all, Kelley had known there would be an end from the beginning.

Honestly, the more time Kelley spent with Asher, the more she was starting to dread that last goodbye. And that was not quite as it should be. Still, that was her worry for later.

Right now, it was about Pride and helping the horse finally settle.

Up ahead, a familiar older cowboy waited at the last pasture fence. A horse with a coat the color of the fallen leaves in autumn and a white star between its ears stopped grazing and lifted its head to peer over the fence at them.

"That stunning boy is Maple Moonlight," Asher explained. "He's calm, mild-mannered and patient."

"That's good. That's what Pride needs," Kelley said, as if the colt was suddenly hers to look after. Her worry dimmed slightly from her words. She scanned the pasture. "What about the others? You mentioned there were three."

"That would be Wintermint and River Run Rebel," Asher said. "Both thoroughbreds were retired early last year. According to Joe, Walter and he decided the pair had lost their desire for winning."

Kelley eyed Asher. "You don't agree."

"Not particularly." He lifted one shoulder and led Pride toward the pasture. "But then again, what do I know?"

Kelley frowned. Her cowboy knew more than he let on. Of that she was certain. He claimed his brothers were better suited to care for the horses. However, there was nothing she had seen that made her think Asher was not suited to be there, too, right alongside his talented brothers. And he certainly had a way around horses and cowgirls. Asher kept Kelley calm right along with Pride and that allowed Kelley to realize how much she missed being around horses.

Big E greeted them and swung open the pasture gate. "Figured you might be headed this way, if you sprung Pride from his stall." Big E paused and tipped his head toward a trail outside the fence. "Frannie and Owen took Wintermint and River Run for an evening stroll to give Pride some space."

"That makes Maple Moonlight your welcoming committee, Pride." Asher reached up, rubbed Pride's neck and removed the halter. "Ready to see an old friend from the stables?"

Pride shook his head, then trotted toward Maple. They met halfway. There was a nose-to-nose greeting. A shared breath moment. Then Maple returned to his grazing and Pride explored the pasture. Kelley glanced at Asher and Big E then asked, "Is that all?"

"That was exactly what we wanted." Big E's shoulders shook from his soft laugh. "No fuss. No drama. A quick hello and a get on with your business type of introduction."

Why then was she still anxious for Pride? She didn't want to just leave the colt or her cowboy. Kelley asked, "What now?"

"We wait and watch." Asher climbed onto the wooden fence, propped himself on the top railing and then reached out to offer assistance to Kelley.

Kelley scrambled up beside Asher and notched her boot heels on the lower post to help balance herself.

"Pride is okay for now, but far from recovered." Asher smiled at Kelley. "And you are not the only one worried about him."

"Was it that obvious?" Kelley wrinkled her nose.

"It's not a bad thing to care about everyone

around you, including the animals," Asher said, understanding in his gaze.

Who do you care about? She said, "My ex often told me I cared too much. That I needed a little more grit when dealing with the staff and such." If she wanted to be successful.

"Grit has got its place to be sure. But kindness, well, everyone could use a little more of that in their day," Big E mused and braced his arms on the fence post. His gaze was fixed on the pasture. "And I always tell my family don't go changing to suit someone else if it doesn't suit you first."

"Big E, I could've used you before I got married," Kelley said lightly. Then she and her ex-husband might have realized sooner that they were not suited for each other.

Asher shifted until his knee touched Kelley's and he asked, "Do you know what suits you now?"

You. Or rather he could, if staying single wasn't already perfectly suitable for her. Still, Kelley kept her knee against Asher's as if the contact somehow anchored her even more, and said, "I'm figuring it out."

"As it happens, we are currently figuring things out for our trio as well," Big E said, smiling.

"Big E and I have come to the conclusion that the retirees in this pasture have more to offer than lounging about out here." Asher chuckled and added, "It seems there is more to their story and racing is not the end of their story."

"This sounds like a second act," Kelley said.

"Everyone deserves one." Big E grinned. "Not that there is anything wrong with pasture patrol. But if you've got more to give, you should get the chance to do it."

Kelley agreed. Although, to be clear, she was not confusing a second act for a second chance at love. After all, Kelley already gave up her heart once and it was returned broken. Now it was packed away, too fragile and worn for handling.

"Looks like the rest of the pasture patrol is returning." Asher hopped gracefully off the fence.

Kelley glanced over her shoulder, waved to her sister, then shifted to jump down. Only her cowboy got to her first. He gripped her waist. Her hands barely settled on his shoulders, and he swung her gently off the fence. Her boots landed softly in the grass. Her breath swooshed out. Talk about careful handling.

Fortunately, she caught her heart before she went a step too far. She retreated to catch her sister and meet Wintermint and River Run Rebel. It didn't take long before she learned Wintermint had the stamina for an endurance trail rider, Maple the temperament for pleasure trails, while River Run's next gig was still being sorted. Introductions were made between Pride and the thoroughbred duo over the fence. Once again, there was little fuss between the horses.

Owen and Frannie headed back for their evening chores at the stables. Big E joined the pair after announcing that he could not be late for his evening check-in with his great-grandkids.

Once again, Kelley was seated on the fence with her cowboy right beside her. Asher hadn't seemed in any rush to leave. That suited Kelley as she was in no particular hurry to call an end to their time together. The sun was only now setting, and night was still a while away.

Kelley said, "Sounds like you've got the pasture patrol's second act pretty well figured out."

"Apparently, Walter was working with them when he wasn't focused solely on Pride," Asher admitted.

"So, you're going to pick up where your father left off," she said.

"I didn't say that," he hedged.

"But you aren't denying it," she pressed.

"I'm considering it," he said. "It means extending my time here. If I start, I want to see it through."

"Is that a bad thing? Sticking around longer." Because it sounded like a very good thing to her.

"It's not a problem," he said. "I've got the vacation time."

"But..." she said and shifted toward him. This time it was her knee that connected with his.

"But if I stick around longer, I'll want to see you more." He scooted closer and motioned between them. "Like this."

"And that's bad?" Only it felt right to have him so close and all to herself. Except that was her hopeless romantic putting foolish thoughts into her head.

Asher nodded slowly and less than convincingly as if trying to convince himself. "I'm not the best long-term choice for anything romantic. I want to be clear."

Now it was time for Kelley to be clear for her hopeless inner romantic and her cowboy. She did not want there to be any misunderstanding. "Asher Blackwell, what if I told you that you are not my second act?"

He tapped his cowboy hat higher on his forehead, revealing his sharp blue eyes, and blinked at her.

Clear enough for you, cowboy? Because she had just put her inner romantic on notice, too. Kelley continued with more of her clarity bombs. "You have nothing to worry about. You see, it's very simple. I won't be choosing you because you can't choose me."

"Fair enough," he said and scratched his cheek. "What is your second act, then, if I may ask?"

"I'm sort of a work in progress, like River Run," she said decidedly. "But it's not a rebound relationship or any relationship for that matter."

"Understood," he said softly.

Yet, he kept his gaze fixed on her as if he searched for her secrets. Or maybe she was looking for his. Or something to make her change her mind or his. Their knees still touched. It was too much and not enough contact. She wanted to lean in, and she also wanted to hightail it right out of there.

Kelley curled her fingers around the fence post rather than reach for her cowboy. But if he reached for her…all bets were off. She tightened her hold. Splinters were far better than a bruised heart. And her cowboy could hurt her heart badly if she let him.

She sighed and tried to sound casual when she said, "I wonder if Big E made it on time for his family conference call."

Asher held her gaze for a beat, then gave the tiniest nod as if he approved the conversation detour. He shifted and straightened away from Kelley. There was a hint of laughter in his words. "I don't think I've ever looked forward to an evening call with quite as much enthusiasm as Big E."

"Well, clearly, you've not participated in one of Big E's video chats with his great-grandkids." Kelley chuckled. "I was only on one for a minute or so the other night, but it was entertaining and mostly full of giggles."

"Not a bad way to end an evening." Asher braced his arms on his knees.

Neither was sitting on a fence at a pasture with a cowboy. Kelley asked, "How do you spend your evenings?"

"Mostly working at my downtown office or my home office," he explained. "And if I'm on a phone call at night, there is usually very little to be amused about."

Sounded lonely. Not that she was there to fix that. Still, Kelley pointed toward the pasture and said, "You're technically working now. You can think of this as more of an open-air office if it makes you feel better."

"For the first time in a long while work doesn't feel like work." He rubbed a hand over his mouth as if perplexed by his own confession.

Kelley shifted her gaze back to the pasture and asked tentatively, "How does it feel?"

"Like a really good way to spend an evening," he said, his words quiet and pensive.

He read her mind. She smiled and said, "Maybe you, Asher Blackwell, are finding your second act, too."

His laugh came and went like the breeze. He shifted toward her again. His gaze was thoughtful. "You know you bring up a good point. If you are helping me find my second act, it seems only fair I return the favor."

But they'd already established they could not be each other's second acts. She had been clear about that much.

"This isn't about us. This is about your second act." His eyebrows lifted as if he really could read her mind. He reached over and took her hand in his then said gently, "I remember what happened at that Fourth of July parade when you fell that time."

Kelley inhaled and curved her fingers around his. "You were supposed to have forgotten it. That's what I assumed." Same as she would forget this time with him. She had to. Otherwise, she just might feel like she had lost something precious.

"But you haven't forgotten that day," he said.

"It's hard to do that when I was the one who got tossed," she said, grumbling.

Asher adjusted their hands, then rubbed his thumb in a slow circle across her palm. "You know what I remember the most about that day?"

"Me sprawled out on the pavement," she said, her voice crackling like dry leaves. But his small caress against her skin was soothing in the most impossible way.

"You were barely on the ground long enough to get gravel stuck to your jeans." He shook his head and continued, "One second you landed on your backside and the next you were up and standing as if nothing happened."

But something had happened. And if she wasn't careful, she could find herself falling again. "You helped me up, which was why I was standing," she said, yet her tone lacked conviction.

"That's not how I recall it." Asher shifted and considered her. "I handed you your cowboy hat, then went after your horse. You got yourself back up all on your own."

It was embarrassing all the same. She asked, "Why are we talking about this?"

"Because you have to get back in the saddle." Asher held her gaze, his expression understanding. "It's past time."

"That's an old wives' tale. You don't have to get back in the saddle and try again when you've fallen." She tugged her hand free. "In fact, sometimes it's safer for both the rider and the horse if everyone takes a break." One small hop and she was off the fence. Her awkward landing aside, she was standing on her own once again.

"Except you do need to ride." Asher joined her, his boots thudding softly in the grass. "You sort of agreed to be in the parade this year. Frannie is really looking forward to this. She's been talking about it every time I see her."

"That's a bit of an exaggeration." Kelley blew a raspberry at him, then asked, "Why is this so important to you?"

"Because it's about your second act." Asher eyed Kelley. "You know the one I told you I would help you find."

"Horse racing is not my second act," she said dryly.

"No, we'll leave that for Frannie's first act," Asher said rather cheerfully. "I'm going to help you remember the cowgirl who was practically glowing that day in the parade. Because that is what I remember. A fearless cowgirl, front and center, thrilled to be there on her horse, surrounded by friends and family."

Growing up, Kelley had always kept to the background, content to give her sisters their center stage. But that day in the parade, Kelley had risked and stepped forward and for a moment felt like she really belonged. "I was having fun. I was with my sisters, and we were riding together. I couldn't imagine anything better. Of course I was enjoying myself, until my horse spooked."

"Because of a rabbit skittering out of a bush," Asher added. "You lost your balance and fell. Even an experienced rider would not have been able to keep their seat."

"You would have," she said quickly. "You would have at least been on guard and prepared, just in case." Kelley had let herself get lost in the thrill of the parade excitement. She had relaxed and quit watching out for potential hazards. And she'd been unseated for her mistake.

"I've had my share of falls that I did not anticipate," he said. "That they happened in the back pastures and woods doesn't mean they don't count."

A more vigilant cowgirl would have anticipated a cowboy like him. Not that she was spooked. She was simply on guard now. Kelley crossed her arms over her chest. "I don't even have a horse."

"But I do," Asher said and whistled. Minutes later, Maple Moonlight trotted over and bumped his nose against the back of Asher's hand. "Frannie and I think Maple here would be a perfect parade partner for you."

What if I wanted a different sort of partner? Kelley shook her head. "I can't ride him."

"Fine," Asher said, much too agreeably.

Kelley narrowed her gaze at Asher and asked, "Why don't I believe you are going to call it a night and let me go home?"

"Because I'm not." He laughed and caught her arm before she made it to the gate. He tugged her toward Maple. "We will start slow. Tonight, you just sit in the saddle."

"Not to point out the obvious." And there was a lot to point out. Like how gently protective his hold was on Kelley's arm. And how kind Maple's large brown eyes looked. And how much the idea of riding did not scare her as much as she thought it would. She blamed that on her cowboy's good nature. Kelley's mouth quirked up, and she continued, "But there is no saddle."

"It's metaphorical," he said, a tease in his words. "Besides, you don't need one to sit on Maple's back."

Kelley held out her arm, keeping her fingers curled in like an open fist just like Asher had shown her in the stables and waited for Maple's greeting. The horse didn't hesitate and bumped his nose against Kelley's hand. Kelley grinned and introduced herself to Maple. "I've never ridden bareback. I'm quite certain Maple does not want me to start now."

"And you won't be," Asher said, gesturing toward the corner. "Although, Wintermint could carry us both if you might be interested in riding double sometime."

A ride with her cowboy. That appealed more than she wanted to admit. But that would not happen if she did not get back on this horse. No pun intended. She rubbed her forehead. "How long do I need to sit on Maple?"

"However long you want to. It's just to give you a feel for Maple and give him a feel for you. We can call it a refresher," he said. His eyebrow hitched up. "I won't move him unless you ask me to."

"I won't," she said.

"Care to bet on that?" he asked, a challenge in his half grin.

Her cowboy had enough confidence for them both. She said, "If I agree to do this, then we can call it a night, right?"

"Whenever you want," he said, his gaze gleaming. "Now, are you done thinking about this and ready to get back in the saddle?"

She was stalling and apparently, Asher knew it. Her divorce had taught her not only the folly of following her heart, but also the folly of not thinking things through thoroughly enough. Finally, she sighed and said, "No offense, Maple, but I'm nervous."

"Nothing wrong with that." Asher took her hand in his and pulled her toward him.

Kelley leaned against him and corralled those nerves.

"I'll be right here," Asher said. "If it's too much, we'll stop."

Right then, in that pasture with her cowboy and a horse, Kelley realized this was a fear she did not have to face alone. Something settled inside her. She didn't want to disappoint her sisters or Asher or even herself. But more than that, she was ready to finally ride.

With the assistance of Asher and the fence and Maple's endless patience, Kelley found herself seated on the horse's back. And just as her cowboy predicted, standing still was not enough for Kelley. It was not too long before Asher led Kelley and Maple on a slow stroll around the perimeter of the pasture. They paused only when Kelley spotted a blackberry patch on the other side of the fence and asked Asher to pick some for the endearing thoroughbred as a thank-you. And with each pass around the pasture, her passion for riding started coming back.

The first stars twinkled in the dusk-filled sky when Kelley finally called a halt. Her feet were planted back on the ground, yet her joy still swept through her. She spun around and all but threw herself into Asher's arms.

Her cowboy caught her easily and gathered her closer to him.

"Thank you for that." Kelley beamed up at him and held on tighter. "Just thank you."

He smiled and said, "Welcome back, cowgirl."

She never thought of herself as a cowgirl. Always believed she needed more grit and poise, and most especially, strength. But the way Asher looked at her, it was as if she was all that already and more. A sigh built from her boots.

A cowgirl for a cowboy. But only in that one moment. But it would be enough. It had to be.

Things were more clear than ever. Kelley liked Asher beyond what was wise. She had to ride a trail for herself, not get caught up with a cowboy distraction.

Nothing for it, but to put her heart back on that highest shelf. Out of reach and out of sight where it belonged. No more sharing with Asher. No more *almost* falling for a cowboy.

CHAPTER TWELVE

THE CREAK OF the mudroom door opening woke Asher. The heavy fall of the boots on the hardwood floor alerted him that it was not his chef. Kelley's steps were lighter and more brisk as if she was always in a rush, hurrying to catch a rainbow. Definitely not her. Asher's mood dipped.

"If you don't have coffee, turn right back around," Asher muttered and smashed the pillow into place under his head. "And come back when you've got some."

The boots stopped. A throat cleared. "Asher."

"Morning, Owen," Asher said and gave up going back to sleep.

"Sorry. I didn't mean to wake you." Owen moved into the family room. "Well, actually I did."

Asher rubbed his hands over his face, then peered out the tall windows across the room overlooking the back porch. It was still dark. "What time is it?"

"An hour or so before dawn," Owen said, his words hesitant as if the sunrise was slightly further off than sixty minutes.

His chef would be heading to the diner soon for her morning shift. The day would be in full swing by the time Asher saw Kelley. If he got to see her. His mood failed to improve. Asher tipped his head until he eyed Owen from an upside-down perspective. The quick-to-help stable hand hovered near the end of the couch, looking unsure and out of place.

Asher stretched his arms above his head and yawned. "You don't have any grocery bags, so I take it Kelley didn't ask you to prep something for breakfast."

"The French toast casseroles are all set," Owen said. "I just need to put the casserole dishes in the oven later to heat up."

"Then what brings you by?" Asher asked and shifted before he got a crick in his neck. He swung his bare feet off the couch and onto the floor. "I take it whatever it is couldn't wait until breakfast."

Uncertainty cast a deeper shadow across Owen's face. He tugged at his hair, until the red strands stuck out in every direction. "It's Derby Dreamer."

"Derby Dreamer." Asher stood, quickly folded the blanket he was using and tossed it on the back of the couch. "What happened?"

"Nothing specific." Owen gave one last yank on his hair and lowered his arm. "But he seems off. I mentioned it to Elliot yesterday. He was supposed to talk to Joe about it."

In flannel shorts, Asher headed to the office

where his suitcase was, and not wanting to disturb Big E in the guest room down the way, he motioned for Owen to follow him. "Did you hear anything from them?"

"Just that Joe said Derby Dreamer had a decent workout," Owen replied.

Asher pulled a plain light blue T-shirt from his suitcase and yanked it over his head. "And yet you are here. So, what's really bothering you?"

Owen set his hands on his hips and said, "My gut."

"I keep telling Asher there are several perfectly fine bedrooms in this house to set up camp in," Big E said from the doorway. The older cowboy was already dressed in his usual jeans, button-down plaid shirt and well-worn boots. He looked well rested and not the least bit fazed that the sun wasn't even up and there was no coffee brewing.

Asher knew he could stand to learn more than a thing or two from the old cowboy. As for those bedrooms, well, they belonged to Asher's brothers. Asher was fine where he was. Besides, he wasn't there to make himself at home. In the common space the trips down memory lane were more manageable. But if Asher went down the brothers' wing, he feared he might get lost in the past. "I fell asleep watching TV and didn't feel like moving."

Big E frowned yet kept his thoughts to himself. He shifted to eye Owen as if taking the young man's full measure. Finally, Big E asked, "What's wrong with your gut?"

Owen touched his stomach.

"He's got a feeling in it about Derby Dreamer," Asher said when Owen remained silent.

Big E nodded and asked, "Are you sure it's not indigestion? Got a spell of it myself. My wife told me I need to cut back on the homemade ice cream and pie."

Asher knew a little something about cutting back. He needed to cut back on the time he spent with his chef. If only to make his goodbye easier. Selfish, certainly. But true, nonetheless.

"I told my wife she needs to taste Kelley's food." Big E chuckled and shook his head. "Then she would understand that her request is impossible to do."

It also seemed impossible that Kelley was always on Asher's mind. First thing on his mind when he woke up and last thing on his mind when he fell asleep. And on his mind every other minute of the day.

Owen frowned. "It's not indigestion, sir."

And it wasn't anything serious for Asher, either. Nothing for him to be concerned about, really. It was admittedly more than a mild interest in a cowgirl. A passing interest to be sure. As in, it would pass when he left and returned to the city. At least, he hoped.

Asher ran his fingers through his hair and

walked toward the bathroom. "Give me five minutes and then we'll head to the stables."

"Maybe it's nothing," Owen hedged. "Elliot didn't seem all that concerned."

"What did he say?" Asher asked.

"He told me Derby Dreamer was just adjusting to his new training schedule," Owen explained. "And I would understand when I'd been here longer and had more experience with performance animals at this level."

Perhaps. Yet, the concern on Owen's face was genuine. Not only that, Owen proved he was capable and attuned to the animals over the past few days when Asher had been working closely with him.

"Clearly, your feeling is bad enough to have you out here waking us up when you should be sleeping," Big E mused.

"No, sir, can't ignore that," Asher said and stepped into the bathroom.

Minutes later, they piled into Owen's truck and drove to the stables. Inside the twos' stable barn, it was not Derby Dreamer that caught their attention. It was Starcaster. The colt's lip was curled, and he swung his head toward his abdomen as if to bite it. Beside Starcaster, Kentucky Ember eyed his flank. Asher was instantly alert. Unlike the others, Derby Dreamer kept his head down and stood still. Too still.

Asher had seen this before years ago in his

mother's favorite horse. When Asher had been too young to understand. His mom had been taking Asher for a ride, but they'd found her favorite mare rolling in the pasture. And the afternoon took a bad, unforgettable turn. Asher had not been able to help his mom or her horse back then. But he could do something now.

His gaze collided with Big E's and Asher blurted, "Colic."

Big E nodded and peered into the stalls across from Derby Dreamer. "We need Doc Julia."

Asher pointed at Owen. "Get Doctor Eisler on the phone. Keep calling until she picks up." Asher stepped into Starcaster's stall and grabbed a lead rope. "Then get Edie. We need more calm hands."

Owen greeted Dr. Eisler, set the call on speaker and handed his phone to Asher, before he rushed outside.

Big E and Asher worked in tandem, following Doc Julia's instructions, moving from one stall to the next. They recited vitals, pulse and breathing rates and checked coats for sweating. Owen, Frannie and Edie arrived, and each got assigned the care of a horse. Asher was leading Starcaster back into his stall after a slow walk when Doc Julia arrived and began checking on the horses.

Joe and his second named Elliot came into the stable barn not long after. Neither one looked overly pleased. Asher did not have the time or patience to deal with their pique at not being called in sooner. Doc Julia determined Starcaster needed to be taken to her veterinarian clinic in town as soon as possible. Big E and Asher were occupied loading the colt into the trailer they attached to Walter's truck as quickly and safely as possible. Then leaving Doc Julia to tend to the other sick colts, Big E and Asher drove Starcaster into town.

A while later, with Starcaster in the hands of Doc Julia's capable staff, Asher and Big E headed back to Walter's truck. Asher was barely out of the clinic's parking lot in town when his phone rang. He checked the name on the screen and answered, "Joe, tell us what you've found out."

"It looks like it was a feed mix-up," Joe said, his voice calm over the truck's speakers. "As best Elliot and I can tell it was a delivery error. Elliot is already looking into it with Cedar Post Farm Supply."

"That's not our usual vendor," Asher said. That much he knew from the invoices he had filed in Walter's office from Hoof and Harvest Supply dated for the past five years.

"The special blend was on backorder at Hoof and Harvest," Joe explained. "Elliot researched other supply houses nearby and found one with the feed blend in stock that we prefer."

"That was lucky," Asher allowed.

"I'm fortunate to have Elliot," Joe said instantly. "Elliot has stepped in as if he's always been here and hasn't missed a beat. And I know it hasn't been easy what with everything going on, but thankfully Elliot hasn't hightailed it out of here yet."

"What about the rest of the twos? Any news from Doc Julia?"

"Fortunately, Derby Dreamer, Foxhall Wind and Kentucky Ember seem to have milder cases of colic," answered Joe. "Lucky, that. Their training can get back on schedule within a few days."

"As long as Doc Julia clears them," Asher cautioned. "Not before."

The other end of the phone line was quiet. Finally, Joe said, his words serious and solemn, "Asher, you do realize what is at stake here, don't you?" There was a rustling, then Joe spoke again. "You do know what we do. You haven't been gone so long you forgot what made these stables."

Racing built the stables. Racing was the reason. Asher ground his teeth together. "I know what's on the line." The stables needed wins. Quickly. Anything to help temper the looming doping investigation.

Joe continued, "Then you know full well why these horses must race in the Rising Star Classic this coming weekend."

"I won't risk any horse's health or safety for a possible first place finish," Asher said, his resolve firm and true.

"I don't believe it's your call to make," Joe said evenly. "I have been here for the long haul. I know what is best for these horses and this stable."

And Asher did not. That was implied. It might have been Walter talking now to Asher, so similar did Joe sound. The truth was Joe was not wrong. Joe had been there while Asher had been away. But Asher was here now. And like it or not, Asher had a stake in all of this, too. "Let's not make any decisions right now while we're still in the thick of things. We've got time to let the horses recover."

"Looks like we understand each other," Joe said and hung up.

Asher understood Joe was not on his side.

"Don't forget Joe is grieving," Big E said into the silence inside the truck cab. "Walter was his best friend. He's hanging on to what he has left."

"I know," Asher conceded and let go any lingering irritation. "And Joe is the only one other than my dad who knows the stables and the business inside and out."

"True," Big E agreed and shifted in the seat to look at Asher. "You might as well get out whatever is on your mind. Otherwise, it'll pick at you worse than a mule with an opinion."

"It's not really my place," Asher said. "I have not been here day in and day out. Not like Joe. Walter trusted him." Asher was just as green and just as inexperienced as Owen by some measures.

"But you got a feeling," Big E said.

Same as Owen had earlier. Asher nodded.

"Got one myself," Big E murmured.

Asher exhaled. That weight on his shoulder

lifted and his words came more freely. "It's just the doping allegations aren't alleged anymore. We know Pride was drugged and with what. Now we have a feed mix-up that by coincidence happens to affect the only horses we intend to race this coming weekend."

Big E hummed. "Could be simple bad luck."

"Could be," Asher allowed.

"But your gut says different."

Asher nodded. And if he had learned anything from Owen that morning it was to pay attention.

Big E asked, "By the way, where are you at with the financials?"

"Still waiting on those bank statements."

In truth, Asher had not been in much of a rush to follow up with Valerie at Foxglove Bank and Trust. The more time Asher spent at home, the more he dreaded finding some inconsistency in the financials that might point at Walter and his possible guilt and downfall. But there was another urgent reason now to clear Walter or call him out.

"In the meantime, it might be worth doing a little asking around about the feed supply," Big E said. "Nothing too overt or obvious, mind you. We don't want to stir things up over what might be an accident with the delivery."

Accident being the keyword there. Asher and Big E talked for the rest of the ride back home about where to start and who to start casually questioning. Both feed supply stores were their obvious places to begin. By the time Asher drove through the stable gates, he was feeling slightly more optimistic.

He had been keeping his own counsel for so long, he had forgotten how gratifying it was to talk things through with someone he trusted. Even more, Big E listened and offered wise insight without any judgment. And the more Asher was around the older cowboy, the more he started to believe he was a part of something rather than just alone.

Asher was feeling a lot more assured than he had expected about being home. Curious, he did not mind it as much as he thought he should. Still, it was smart to keep his so-called *feels* in check. Otherwise, Asher might follow one of those *feels* that made him consider a cowgirl and something like forever.

But what did a rusty heart like his know about a love like that?

CHAPTER THIRTEEN

"WHAT'S GOT INTO you today?" Hayes frowned and aimed his spatula at Kelley.

Laughing, Kelley turned up the volume on the upbeat country song playing on the radio in the diner kitchen. She sashayed from the prep counter to the walk-in refrigerator and back.

"She's been like this since I got here at opening." Hayes flipped the hamburgers on the griddle and asked, "Did we get an espresso machine, and I missed a double shot?"

Chuckling, Frannie removed a batch of French fries and clipped the wire basket above the deep fryer for draining. "Not what, Hayes, but who."

"Why can't it simply be a good day?" Kelley tugged Frannie into a twirl before her little sister could blame Asher for Kelley's sunny attitude. "There's no rain in the forecast. It is not blistering hot for once. It's a perfect summer day."

Frannie took herself out of the second spin and shook French fries onto two plates. "You don't like to be out in the summer humidity. It makes your curls frizz."

"That's what a cowboy hat is for," Kelley countered and got back to sprinkling fresh bacon bits like fairy dust over a Cobb salad.

"I told you, Hayes." Frannie waited for Hayes to slide the finished cheeseburgers onto the two plates with fries, then added them and the finished Cobb salad to her serving tray and started for the dining area. She called out cheerfully, "It's all about a cowboy."

Except Kelley had not seen her cowboy in two days, not that she was counting. But she had been keeping tabs on him. Thanks to Frannie's daily insider updates about the Blackwell happenings, Kelley knew Asher was sleeping at the stables to watch over the sick horses. If he wasn't in the twos' barn, he was putting the finishing touches on the chicken coop or spearheading the parade float design or working with the pasture patrol trio.

Asher was busy. As was Kelley. Sure, he was on her mind, but that hardly meant anything. Kelley frowned at her little sister. "It's not about a—"

"Careful, big sis." Frannie's joyful burst of laughter cut Kelley off. "I do believe you just might be protesting a bit too much."

Kelley snapped her mouth closed and watched the door swing shut behind her sister. She peered at Hayes and said, "I can be in a good mood. Wear a cowboy hat. And want to enjoy my summer days without it being about a cowboy."

Hayes hummed and nodded, then a grin appeared. “But there is a new spark to your cooking that’s been missing. And that does make it about a cowboy.”

Kelley dipped her head and concentrated on mixing up more salad dressing. True, she was feeling more inspired in the kitchen than she had in a long while. Ever since Asher encouraged her to ride Maple Moonlight earlier in the week. It seemed she’d rediscovered more than her childhood passion for horseback riding that evening.

It was as if facing one fear centered her and lifted her spirits. She was ready to do rather than just consider what was next. To finally hit Submit on those résumés. To reach out to colleagues on the west coast and find that culinary hot spot where she could make her mark.

It seemed she had a cowboy to thank.

The back door opened. Sunlight streamed in. Anticipation wove through Kelley. But the newcomer was not Asher. Instead, Pauline breezed in; her long white sundress floated around her tall, dark brown cowboy boots. And hot on her boss’s trail was none other than Eric Grahame, the owner of Lucky Lane Tavern. Kelley refused to be disappointed. With her good cheer in place she greeted the new arrivals.

A quick hug and air kiss for Hayes, then Pauline followed Kelley into the small office and said, “Kelley, please tell Eric why we can’t stay here.

Why we need to stretch our wings and leave town for good."

If Kelley wanted to prove she was as good as her ex-husband, she needed a bigger culinary stage. Moving out of Gold Finch made practical career sense. Still, Kelley felt the sudden urge to argue and countered with, "Why can't we stay here again?"

Eric leaned against the doorway to the office. A small smile filtered across the bar owner's weathered yet distinguished face.

"Because..." Pauline said and wrapped her fingers around the amethyst heart pendant on her silver necklace as if grounding herself. "We must leave because we are following Mama T's advice like she would have wanted us to."

Kelley would have agreed not a month ago. It was always about leaving. Yet, now there was something about staying that was not quite as easy to dismiss.

Eric pushed his cowboy hat higher on his forehead, eyed Pauline and said, "Your mother wanted you both to be happy."

Kelley opened the closet and took out several stacks of napkins to refill the holders before the lunch rush and considered how to maneuver around the pair. They were in a face-off and blocking Kelley's exit.

"Mama T wanted Kelley and me to be deliriously happy." Pauline repeated, "Deliriously." Although she sounded anything but at the moment.

Kelley did not know about the delirious part. That might be pushing it. But recently, she was happy. More so than she had been in a long while. Kelley found herself looking forward to being in the kitchen and yet she was just as eager to step out again, especially if it meant time with her cowboy. Not that she was making this about Asher. Kelley tried to sound helpful and upbeat. "Hey, I want everyone to be happy, too."

"Never mind." Pauline's lips were pursed and her words were low. "We're getting off point."

"What is the point?" Eric asked, patiently.

"I'm selling the diner," Pauline said, her words clipped. "Once that happens, Kelley and I won't have any reason to stay."

Eric turned toward Kelley and said smoothly, "Kelley, I'm offering you a job at Lucky Lane. I could use someone with your culinary talent at the tavern."

Kelley blanched. He wasn't serious, was he? She was flattered of course. Not that she was seriously entertaining the idea, was she?

Pauline set her hands on her hips and stood her ground. "Eric, what are you doing?"

"I'm giving Kelley a reason to stay in town." Eric's smile remained in place yet there was something of a challenge in his gaze as if he had all day and was more than prepared to counter every one of Pauline's arguments.

"You can't just hire my best employee." Pauline's foot tapped a noisy beat on the tile floor.

"I just did. Now you both have a reason not to go. Kelley has another job. Thanks to me," Eric said, a soft smile on his face. His amusement and affection were clear. "And you, Pauline, have—"

"Don't say it." Pauline's mouth quirked up on one side. Her focus never strayed from the bar owner.

Kelley would have sworn she'd seen sparks fairly flash between the pair.

"My sister doesn't need to work at the tavern." That no-nonsense comment came from Laura-Beth. Kelley's big sister squeezed her way around the tall bar owner and popped into the cramped office like Kelley's protector. Laura-Beth smoothed her hand over her slicked-back ponytail, then down over her fitted sundress as if to ensure all was in order. "What with all the locals asking about Kelley's catering services, I could have her calendar filled in no time."

"I've had similar inquiries," Pauline said and frowned.

Kelley sputtered. "What have you told them?"

"Oh, me?" Laura-Beth pointed at herself and smiled at Kelley. "I invited them to the rehearsal dinner on Friday night, of course. I figured it's a really good showcase of your food since you are cooking."

Catering inquiries were news to Kelley. Surprising and welcome and intriguing all at the same time. But catering was supposed to be a temporary side hustle. It was not the statement-making exclamation mark Kelley warned her ex-husband to watch out for. Kelley hugged the napkins against her chest.

"We will need to update the menu now," Laura-Beth stated, entirely unfazed. She waved her hand about the tiny room. "But not until we discuss the issue with the flowers. That's why I'm here."

"Well, we are not growing the diner business by offering catering services," Pauline announced. "Given that we are selling the place."

"On account of your whole cut-and-run-to-the-city exit plan," Eric drawled. "I believe we've got that part."

Pauline silently fumed. Kelley could spot the tell.

"What city, Pauline?" Laura-Beth perked up and added, "I've heard Charleston is lovely. I've always wanted to visit. But perhaps you were thinking someplace even larger."

Eric shook his head. "Don't get her started."

Kelley did not know where to begin. Until another familiar face stepped into her view. *Hello, cowboy.* Kelley exhaled. Her good cheer began to expand again.

Asher shook Eric's hand. He scanned the crowded room and asked mildly, "Am I interrupting something?"

"Asher. Perfect timing," Pauline piped up and grinned. "Can you please tell Eric why people like us belong in the city and not here?"

Asher cast a perplexed look at Kelley.

"Pauline, you already roped Kelley into this," Eric said, caution in his words. "Don't go roping Kelley's cowboy into it, too."

Kelley's cowboy. She should set the bar owner straight. And yet, Kelley liked the sound of that. Her gaze collided with Asher's and stuck.

Asher raised his arms and held his palms out. "I'm just here about a possible special sandwich request. A blackberry bacon grilled cheese for Big E."

He was not there for her. Because Asher was not Kelley's answer. Besides, this time around, Kelley intended to find her own reasons to leave and expand her career the way she wanted, or even to stick around, possibly. Either way, she was not following someone else's dreams, believing they were her own. She already knew that was a recipe for failure. Kelley cleared her throat and said loudly, "Out! Everyone needs to get out. Now!"

Pauline's foot continued its chaotic beat. Her words were cool. "You can't order me to get out. I own this place."

Not for much longer if Pauline had her way. "I just did," Kelley countered. "And I am."

"But we are not finished," Pauline argued.

"I have work to do. Customers to see to and food to cook." Kelley guided Pauline closer to Eric and nudged her boss none too gently. Yet, that put Kelley within hugging distance of Asher. Kelly pretended not to notice and concentrated on her boss instead. "Pauline, you and Eric clearly have things to figure out. But out there. Not in here."

"About that grilled cheese," Eric said in the hallway.

"I could use something to eat, too," Laura-Beth chimed in.

Kelley rolled her eyes. "Fine, fine, fine. Grilled cheese all around, if you all just sit down at the lunch counter." And give Kelley a moment to gather herself. She was much too close to gathering her cowboy to her and holding on.

"That grilled cheese is off-menu," Pauline muttered, although her pique seemed to have leveled off.

"Well, it should be *on* the menu. When you taste it, Pauline, you will know why," Kelley retorted. She propped the swinging door open and motioned everyone through. "I've been told my grilled cheese is a mood buster and problem solver."

Kelley waited until the quartet was seated at the lunch counter with Big E and the Arbor sisters before she returned to the kitchen to a round of applause from Frannie and Hayes.

Hayes drummed out a celebratory beat on the stainless-steel counter and grinned from cheek to cheek. "About time you found your voice around here."

Now Kelley just had to keep using it.

"And Kelley actually thinks this is not about a cowboy." Frannie huffed good-naturedly and scooted back out to check on her customers.

To prove her little sister wrong, Kelley kept her attention on the griddle. It wasn't long until she delivered six excellent grilled cheese sandwiches with two sides.

Kelley secretly loved every ooh and aah she heard as the crowd tucked in to all that cheesy, fruity goodness. She tried to focus on diner guests besides Asher and when that failed, she joined Hayes in the kitchen. The lunch hour winding down, Kelley set several dessert plates in the pass-through and noticed the soft blush on Pauline's face. Kelley's boss whispered to Eric, then the pair stood and quietly slipped outside. Laura-Beth had her giant wedding planner open on the counter to the delight of the town's favorite retiree sisters, Lynette and Beatrice. Even Big E seemed to be involved in Laura-Beth's rather animated conversation.

Kelley shifted and her gaze connected with Asher's. His eyebrow twitched. His smile followed.

And Kelley's cheeks warmed. Feeling good and caught, Kelley grabbed two pie plates and made her way out to the counter. Grinning, she said, "Looks like everyone is ready for dessert."

Big E rubbed his hands together and eyed the slice of cherry pie Kelley placed in front of him. "I sure appreciate the double scoop of ice cream, Kelley. I need the pick-me-up after all that plowing this morning and we're not done yet."

"Don't let him fool you," Asher said. "I've been plowing the second field at the Skyline Drive-In. Big E has been critiquing my work from a chair in the shade with Warren Malloy."

Plowing. Kelley did not bother to hide her surprise.

"I heard we're getting another picture screen at the Skyline. Seems the double features are quite popular." Lynette leaned in and cooed, "I can tell you, Warren's snack shop is not to be missed. Their caramel popcorn won first place at the fair the past three years in a row."

"I prefer their s'mores bark," Beatrice offered. "I always buy extra on account that it tends to sell out during the first showing."

"I'll have to see about getting some of that when we head back after lunch," Big E said around a bite of pie.

"We should have that on the dessert table at the rehearsal dinner." Laura-Beth wrote a note in her wedding planner. "Can you make s'mores bark, Kelley?"

Kelley could not make herself look away from Asher. "Since when do you know how to drive a tractor?" Kelley wondered, only to realize too late she'd spoken out loud.

"Since my grandpa taught me," Asher replied, amusement flashing across his face. "Someone needed to haul hay around our property, and I was chosen. My grandad told me it was a skill that would serve me well."

"Sure has come in handy today," Big E said.

Her city cowboy could drive a tractor. It made sense, given where he grew up. What did not make sense was that Kelley wanted to know about Asher's other hidden talents. She wanted to know his secrets. She wanted to know *him*. Not the cowboy. Or the city businessman. But rather *him*. Bad idea, that.

She already liked Asher. There was no need to level up her like into something stronger that hinted at a connection. Still, Kelley asked, "Why are you plowing the drive-in and not some local landscaper? What happened?"

Asher polished off the last of his cherry pie and said, "Herman Whittaker's chicken coop is what happened."

"I am beginning to think we could live quite comfortably in that coop," Big E marveled. He glanced down the counter at the others who were now paying attention and added, "I swear this chicken coop is more state-of-the-art than my RV."

"Warren is a professional welder by trade." Asher wiped his mouth and set the napkin on his plate. "We had to go see him about the motorized doors that open and close according to the sunrise and sunset. And the sunroofs for the chicken coop, which are all now installed thanks to Warren."

"Sunroofs," Kelley repeated. Those she had not noticed on Herman's professionally drawn coop plans. But she did notice Asher had a new look about him, even if she could not quite place what was different. His dark blond beard was still trimmed short, more stubbly shadow than substance. He wore another coordinating button-down plaid shirt and fitted T-shirt as usual. Even his cowboy hat was the same chestnut brown.

"We had to bargain quite a bit to convince Warren to help us out," Big E said and arched accusing eyebrows at Asher.

There. She spotted the difference. Her cowboy was relaxed. His blue gaze was remarkably mellow. The laugh lines around his eyes soft. Even his posture hinted that he was in absolutely no rush to get on with his afternoon. And Kelley was suddenly keen to extend the conversation and keep Asher right there. She held back her grin. "Wait. Don't tell me that Dylan has history with Warren Malloy as well. What did Dylan jump and knock over at the drive-in?"

"We never rode our horses across the Skyline property. It's a bit too far from the stables," Asher replied, sounding unconcerned. "But it wasn't Dylan who Warren has an issue with. This one is all on me."

Big E shifted toward Asher and propped his boots on the footrest as if settling in to hear the story, too. Beside the older cowboy, Lynette and Beatrice swiveled their stools to listen in.

"What did you do?" Kelley propped her hip against the counter.

"I might have gotten distracted trying to get a cowgirl's attention," Asher said, a hint of regret inside his easygoing tone.

Kelley knew a little something about getting distracted. She picked up the hot water carafe and refilled Lynette's and Beatrice's tea mugs.

"One summer I worked for Mower Goats." Asher glanced at the others and explained, "I delivered goat herds to customers who wanted targeted grazing for their land. Warren Malloy was a customer. He liked the goats to clear his empty fields near his house."

"I can't picture you as a goat herder," Kelley said. Although, she could picture Asher and her somewhere else. Like a porch swing. Or the bluff. Somewhere less crowded. On a date night. Kelley swapped the hot water for the coffeepot.

"Come on, Asher, don't leave us hanging," Lynette said and leaned around Big E. Her eyes peeled wide. "Did you get the cowgirl's attention or not?"

He certainly had Kelley's full attention.

"The cowgirl is Nora Malloy, as in Warren Malloy's youngest daughter." Asher chuckled and shook his head. "As it turned out, Nora had her eye on Dylan, not me. It would not have mattered anyway. Warren would not have let me take Nora out."

"Some folks can't appreciate an overabundance of devil-may-care as much as others," Lynette said, her words consoling.

But Kelley could. And apparently did.

"My devil-may-care, as it were, was not the problem," Asher said, blandly.

"Warren didn't approve of that dam you built up in the stream to make your own swimming hole, did he?" Beatrice asked as if she already knew the answer.

Asher swiped his hand over his mouth and said, "Only my brothers and I know about that swimming hole."

Lynette harrumphed and eyed Big E. "These young folks don't understand that we always know things."

Big E laughed. "Many things, in fact."

"Then you must already know what happened between Warren and me," Asher countered.

"But the rest of us don't know." Big E motioned toward Kelley and Laura-Beth.

Kelley nodded.

"Bea and I only know Warren's side," Lynette said, helpfully. "Last I checked there are two sides to every saddle blanket."

Asher sighed. "If Warren told you that I'm the reason he missed showing his hybrid tulips at the fair and missed out on the blue ribbon and the biggest cash prize that year, well, he would be right."

The retired sisters looked unmoved by that information. Kelley decided it was old news, indeed.

"What Warren doesn't know is why I forgot to latch the gate." He stared at his boots but only for a beat. "I was rushing to talk to Nora before she left for the lake." Asher tilted his head toward Big E and said, "I figured I had one shot with the girl, so I better take it."

"Here's to putting it all out there." Big E lifted his iced tea glass in a toast. "Nothing wrong with that."

Kelley put everything on the line once, too. Only to end up with nothing more than a list of lessons learned. And a big reminder not to do that again.

"The goats all went out in record time," Asher recounted. "I swear they were out of that pasture before I said hello to Nora. And they'd devoured every flower in Warren's private garden before Nora even turned me down for that date."

Kelley would not have turned Asher down. Not then. Not now.

"Well, you've got yourself a second chance with the cowgirl," Lynette said, excitement in her expression. "Nora happens to own and run the local floral shop. Magnolia and Mint is just down the street. And she is still very much single."

"It's Nora you need to see, Asher, for the bulk flower order," Beatrice explained. "We're gonna need bunches for those parade horse garlands."

"That's convenient," Asher said, with little enthusiasm.

"As convenient as a kettle already set to boiling." Lynette drizzled honey into her tea and added, "If you're pouring one cup, you might as well top off another."

"No sense boiling water twice." Beatrice snatched the honey bottle from her sister. "Unless, of course, you're like me and enjoy a whistlin' kettle."

Asher kept his gaze fixed on Kelley and said, "I like coffee. Straight. No sugar."

That was Kelley's preference. But similar tastes in caffeine hardly meant they were a good match.

Beatrice stirred her tea and considered Asher. "As long as there is more sweet in your talk than sour, you should be fine."

Asher stirred the ice in his glass. "I will make sure to stop in at the florist."

"Just so you know, Asher." Lynette's gaze gleamed, her tone encouraging. "Nora is still looking for a date to Laura-Beth's wedding."

Asher nodded. The indifference in his expression gave nothing away.

"*Nora* isn't the only one in need of a plus-one," Laura-Beth offered all too sweetly.

Kelley wrinkled her nose and gave her big sister a knock-it-off glare.

Laura-Beth tapped her wrist and mouthed *tick-tock*. Then her big sister made eyes at Asher.

Worried the eagle-eyed retirees would catch on, Kelley blurted, "Speaking of the parade horse garlands, Asher and I still need to have our first flower weaving lesson."

"That we do," Asher said casually, although something sparked in his blue eyes.

"I've got a brilliant idea." Beatrice clasped her hands together and grinned. "Skyline would be the perfect place. There's more than enough room to spread out and work. If we need more flowers, we just pick them."

"Unless Asher mowed the wildflower field on the knoll." Lynette frowned.

"I believe the wildflowers are still standing and all good," Asher said.

"Oh, and there's a double feature playing tomorrow night," Lynette said, looking rather delighted herself. "I do so adore romantic comedy movies, and we get two for the price of one. It's double the dose of feel-good."

Beatrice laughed. "We're practically guaranteed to feel our best when we leave."

"Can't ask for more than that," Big E offered.

"A double feature date night." Lynette grinned wide. "What could be better than that?"

Kelley was struggling to come up with something better than spending an evening with her cowboy. A worry if she allowed it to become one.

All she had to do was double down on her heart lockdown and remember Asher was not her second-chance romance.

CHAPTER FOURTEEN

AT SKYLINE DRIVE-IN, Asher spotted a familiar cowgirl standing in the middle of a wildflower patch. Her curly hair fell past her shoulders and her laughter floated across the knoll. *Finally.* He caught his breath, even though he was standing still.

Kelley saw him and waved. "Hurry up, cowboy!" She shook a large blanket out and let it float down to cover the grass. "You don't want to miss all the fun!"

He had been missing his cowgirl all day by mere minutes. He missed her at breakfast. When he was with Derby Dreamer that morning, she was prepping in his kitchen. When he headed back to his house, she was already with the staff in the break room barn. And so it went for the entire day, from the Blackwell Stables to the Galloping Fork and everywhere in between. Their paths did not cross. Until now. And now he realized how much he missed her.

Asher turned to look for his carpool crew and said, "I see the others. They're heading this way."

Then he wasted no more time and made a beeline straight for Kelley.

Up on the knoll nearby, the Arbor sisters set a basket of wildflowers on another blanket and smiled brightly.

"I recruited extra hands to help weave," Asher announced by way of a greeting.

"We are more than happy to have them." Beatrice scooted around Asher to hug Frannie, Owen and then Big E. She linked her arm around Owen's. "The more, the merrier, in my mind."

He was feeling slightly merry himself suddenly. Asher dropped down onto the blanket, barely giving Kelley time to make room. As it was, he sat close enough that their knees and shoulders touched. Just where he wanted to be. Right beside his cowgirl.

"Sorry, we are late." Big E eyed Asher under the brim of his cowboy hat and added, "We got a bit delayed riding out on the trail."

Kelley glanced at Asher.

He kept his expression contained and shrugged, even though he knew full well he was the reason for that.

"We took the pasture patrol trio out for some exercise." Frannie joined them on the blanket. "Pride is enjoying his new friends, by the way."

"I know," Kelley said, meeting Asher's gaze. "I checked on him first thing this morning."

Asher was not surprised, only disappointed he had not thought to catch up with Kelley then.

"We would have been here to help collect flowers," Owen said, good-naturedly yet not regrettably, it was clear. Excitement beamed from his face. "But Asher and River Run were jumping. Asher thinks River Run might be suited for hunter-jumper competitions."

Kelley's eyes widened. She did not bother to hide her surprise. "Is that so?"

Outed, Asher nodded. "I was only following River Run's lead and going where he wanted to go."

"Straight over the stream," Owen added, his enthusiasm buffering his words. "Three different times."

Big E frowned, yet there was affection in his words. "And that doesn't include everything else that pair jumped along the way."

After that first leap, Asher could not seem to stop. Sort of the same way he could not seem to stop wanting to be around his cowgirl. "River Run needed the exercise."

Kelley's eyebrows arched higher. She tipped her head and said, "You enjoyed every minute of it. I can see it on your face. Don't try to deny it."

"Old habits and all." Although he sort of had a new habit. A cowgirl kind of one. Asher chuckled. "What can I say? You inspired me after you rode last Sunday."

"That was nothing," she said, brushing dried grass off the blanket. "It was a short, slow walk around the pasture. Hardly worth mentioning."

Everything about her was worth mentioning. "It was more than that. We both know it." Just as he suspected there might be more between them. Although, he supposed, if they did not acknowledge it, then there was no cause for concern.

"Well, I know we need to get ourselves down to the snack bar before the line gets any longer," Lynette announced, her gaze fixed on the increasing crowd.

"It'll be the first task for our extra helping hands," Beatrice declared and turned Owen toward the long lineup. "You can help us carry our snack bar loot."

Frannie jumped up and said, "I've been looking forward to s'mores bark all day."

"Come on, Elias," Lynette said. "I see Sully Connelly heading that way, too, with his son and nephew. Never hurts to find out what the competition is up to."

"You're not wrong about that." Big E held his arm out for Lynette and said mildly, "However, I suspect they are loading up on snacks. Same as us."

"Well, then, we best head 'em off before they get all the good stuff." Lynette laughed.

"Wait for us," Kelley said and started to stand.

"You two stay right there." Beatrice waved her

back into place, then pointed at the basket of wildflowers. "You're both already comfortable and those flowers need to get sorted by color and size."

Kelley shifted on the blanket.

"Don't worry," Frannie said. "We'll get you something sweet."

Asher wasn't certain he needed any more sugar. He was already sweet on his cowgirl. Asher slid the basket closer and said, "We better get to work."

Kelley scooped a handful of flowers carefully out of the basket. "You can go with them, if you want. I got this."

"I'm fine right here." He followed her lead and took out a bunch of flowers, then slanted his gaze toward her. He left the tease in his words. "Do I not look fine?"

She shook her head and chuckled. "You look really relaxed."

"I guess that's the thing about a good day. You just feel better all over," he mused. "And it's been a really good day."

"You sound surprised," Kelley said.

"I am," he admitted and set a yellow flower to the side. "I checked my email today."

Kelley laughed. "That can't be unusual."

"It wasn't for work," he said and watched Kelley reel in her amusement. "I checked my email for a coupon code after I signed up for the rewards program at Hearthstone Market."

"Well, you have to be a rewards member at

the grocery store." Kelley's laughter slipped free again. "They have exclusive BOGO days just for members. They're not to be missed."

Asher's laughter mixed with hers as he said, "That is exactly what the cashier told me."

Kelley sorted her flowers and asked, "Do you miss your day job?"

"I like what I do. But I have not minded this change of pace nearly as much as I thought I would." Especially the part about getting to know Kelley. But it would all be coming to a close soon enough. Best to let the sharing stop here and now. "I guess that's the most surprising thing. What about you? Any surprises in your day?"

"My mom and stepmom helped me prep for the rehearsal dinner this afternoon and they got along." She smiled. "Thank you for letting me use your kitchen for that."

"Anytime," he said. "They weren't bothered by the less than modern appliances?"

"My mom and stepmom both claimed they felt right at home and welcomed the blast from the past." Kelley continued, "Mom even showed me a trick to get the light in the second oven to turn on."

"That will come in handy," he said.

"It was a good day for both of us," she said softly.

And looking to be an even better evening. "We rode the pasture patrol trio to one of my mom's favorite places this afternoon. She called it her own personal thinking spot." It was on the opposite side of the property, far away from the stables and the constant buzz of activity. "I swear I heard my mom's laugh mixed in with the rush of the water in the stream."

"Was this before or after you jumped the stream?" she asked, her gaze bright.

"You should know it was my mom who taught me to jump," he said wryly and reached for another handful of flowers. "She was the daredevil in the family and always up for an adventure."

"So, she would have encouraged you today," Kelley said, understanding in her words.

"She would have jumped first." Asher smiled, welcoming the childhood memories. "Then she would have told me to lean in to my fear, go for it and trust it will work out."

She nodded and bit into her bottom lip. "How did you know River Run, and you, for that matter, were ready to make that jump today?"

Some risks were easier to take. Leaps of the heart… Those were not so simple. And Asher did not make those lightly, if ever. He twisted a flower stem in his fingers. "River Run and I had an immediate bond. We've been learning about each other. Getting used to each other. The trust has been building."

"Still, why today? Why not wait until tomorrow or next week even?" She brushed her hands together and searched his face. "Didn't it feel too soon? Too rushed?"

"It felt right," he said, simply.

Kelley pulled back and gaped at him. "Asher Blackwell, are you telling me that you jumped the river today because of a *feeling*?"

She did not have to make it sound so out of character. He had emotions; he just chose not to let them get the best of him. "Haven't you ever followed a feeling?"

"Yes. I got married and opened a restaurant because of a feeling. Then lost both," she stated flatly. "I think we can both agree feelings are not exactly reliable."

Point taken. That was why he would not pursue whatever was building between them. Whenever he jumped into love, the landing was never clean. And he did not trust this time would be any different. Asher said, "You weren't afraid to follow your heart. There's nothing wrong with that."

"I fell in love, and I followed my ex-husband," she explained. "I went along with him not to simply get along, but because it was all supposed to be leading somewhere."

"Where?" Asher lifted his leg and rested his arm on his knee.

"To a fulfilling life." Kelley touched her finger lightly against the white petal of a flower. "The kind where work is challenging and frustrating and rewarding. Yet, it all fits because you are part of a team. You have a partner and life balance and a full heart." She tossed the flower onto the growing pile and frowned. "My ex-husband sold me on that vision."

"What's the vision now?" Asher asked.

"Create it for myself." She notched her chin higher.

"That's probably for the best. It will save you disappointment."

"What part don't you like?" She shifted toward him and tipped her head to consider him. "The full heart or the work-life balance?"

He met her gaze and said softly, "I don't like that your ex-husband let you down and hurt you."

She pressed her lips together, then whispered a soft thank-you for that.

The others returned, carrying their snack bar loot and showing off their good cheer, before Asher could explain to her there had not been much reason for him to pursue a work-life balance. At least, until recently. Yet, that was only a consequence of an idle mind. Once he got back to New York, his job would occupy his days and nights, just as he liked. He resumed sorting flowers to avoid losing his good mood entirely.

Snacks and drinks distributed to all, Lynette and Beatrice wasted no time getting down to the business of how to weave the flowers into proper parade horse collars. Everyone received a long, flexible branch of trailing greenery to serve as the base. Wildflowers were woven in with string and wire. More of Asher's flowers fell off than stayed attached; however, Asher kept at it like his mother would have told him to. It was slow and meticulous, but the company was fun and lively. And soon enough the first movie started.

A while later, Beatrice called for a break to rest her fingers during the intermission between movies. Big E and Owen headed out for drink refills. The rest of them stood to stretch their backs and gather more wildflowers. An upbeat country song played over the loudspeakers. Kelley hummed along beside Asher.

Lynette walked over and dropped a bundle of freshly picked flowers into the basket Asher held. There was a glint in her perceptive gaze. "Kelley, this sounds like one of those songs you were dancing to at sunrise in the diner that morning with your cowboy."

Kelley's hum disappeared. She did not look at Asher and said lightly, "There are so many great country songs to dance to these days."

"Indeed. You'll certainly get a chance to kick up your heels at Laura-Beth's wedding this weekend," Beatrice called out and shimmied her hips. "I've always fancied a turn or two around the dance floor with a handsome cowboy myself, same as you, Kelley."

"I do like a dance floor," Kelley replied, her words sounding slightly strained.

Asher abruptly set the basket down and got busy gathering flowers, rather than taking Kelley's hand and twirling her around a field as if to prove no dance floor was required.

"You've asked him, haven't you?" Beatrice asked and wiped the back of her hand across her forehead. "Trust us. The singles' table is not a place you want to spend your sister's wedding."

Kelley yanked at the flowers and dropped them into the basket.

Asher noted there were more weeds and grass than flowers. He eyed Kelley and spotted the rather fetching flush in her cheeks.

"I sat at the singles' table at my cousin Patsy's second marriage." Lynette grimaced. Her nose wrinkled. "It was much more dull than I expected it would be."

"And not full of eligible bachelors like we thought." Beatrice frowned yet swayed back and forth to the beat of the music. She sighed. "Not a dancer among them that night. But you won't need to worry about that with your mystery cowboy, Kelley."

Asher was worried. His cowgirl's cheeks could not get any brighter. He barely swallowed his laugh.

Frannie carried over her armful of flowers, glanced from Asher to Kelley and then grinned at the Arbor sisters. She said slyly, "Beatrice and

Lynette, you should both know that Kelley's plus-one does not know he is a plus-one yet."

Lynette's mouth formed into the shape of an O.

Beatrice's eyebrows winged up under her silver bangs and hid there. "Kelley? You haven't asked him yet?"

Kelley shook her head.

Lynette bustled toward her sister and motioned for Frannie to join her. "Come on, ladies. We need to give Kelley a moment to work this one through on her own."

"There's no time to waste, dear." Beatrice tapped her wrist and pointed at Kelley. "We can't tell you how many eligible cowgirls we saw at the snack bar line."

Frannie grabbed the flower basket, blew her sister a kiss and escorted Beatrice and Lynette back toward their blanket.

Asher moved beside Kelley and whispered, "Do you have something to ask me?"

"I have to go to the florist to pick up the arrangements for the rehearsal dinner." Kelley turned and faced him. "If you want, I can place the bulk order with Nora, then you won't have an awkward run-in with your former crush."

Asher leaned in to the silence and decided to wait out his cowgirl. Clearly, she was working something out for herself.

"Unless you were planning to talk to Nora," Kelley continued quickly.

And Asher continued to keep quiet.

His cowgirl rattled on, "Of course, you need to talk to her. Once you do, you will likely hit it off and you will ask her out obviously." One exhale. One longer inhale. It was as if she was gathering her thoughts and steam at the same time. "Or, Nora might want to take you to Laura-Beth's wedding."

Asher waited a beat to be certain Kelley was finished.

She chewed on her bottom lip like she might be wanting to say more. Her gaze was locked on his but she was silent.

"I'm not asking Nora out," Asher said, finally, and edged closer to Kelley. "As for a crush on a cowgirl, yes, I've got one of those. It's a bit of a recent development. And quite a new feeling for me."

"You've never had a crush before?" Kelley asked.

"Not quite like this one." This one had all the potential of being one for the ages.

"I think I have one, too," Kelley confessed.

"What should we do about it?" Besides not to encourage it. That did not appeal, not even a little bit. Even if Asher knew it was the wise choice.

"Go to a wedding, sit at the singles' table and pretend it's not there," she suggested.

He grinned at her and shrugged. "Or we could go to a wedding, skip the sitting and dance the night away."

"One night, then." She held out her hand. "No pressure. No expectations."

And no promises hidden between the words. Asher shook her hand gladly. "Agree. It's one night and we walk away the same as we were before."

The noise around them seemed to die off as she lifted one pink flower up between them and asked, "Asher Blackwell, will you be my wedding date?"

"I thought you'd never ask." He took the flower from her grip and tucked it carefully behind her ear. "I would be honored to be your date, Kelley Munroe."

And he left it at that. Because if he kissed his cowgirl, he would have a complication of the heart kind. And he was already on borrowed time.

CHAPTER FIFTEEN

We walk away the same as we were before.

That was what Asher told Kelley at the drive-in only two days ago. Those were the same words Kelley was clinging to hours before her big sister was set to walk down the aisle and recite her vows to the love of her life. Laura-Beth would walk away from the evening married.

Kelley intended something different. She intended to walk away with her head held high.

And my heart still mine.

She traced her finger over a red-tipped yellow rose in a vase of a dozen that the floral shop delivered to Kelley's mother's house that morning with a note that read: *I know today is about your sister. Wanted you to know someone is thinking about you.*

"The card isn't signed." That came from Kelley's mother, who was finishing adding loose beachy curls to Frannie's hair at the kitchen table. They had decided the natural sunlight filtering through the oversize bay windows was ideal for their wedding hair and makeup session.

"It doesn't matter. We know they're from Asher." Frannie lowered her cell phone and peered at Kelley. "Who else would they be from?"

Who, indeed. Kelley picked her eyeliner pencil out of her makeup bag, leaned toward the portable mirror propped on the table and concentrated on applying her makeup.

"Now, listen to this," Frannie said, and read from her phone, slowly and carefully. "It says right here that yellow roses are for friendship."

Kelley ignored the pang of disappointment in her chest. Friendship was what she wanted. Same as Asher. She switched to her other eye.

"How…ever," Frannie continued, stretching the one word and pitching her voice low as if sharing a secret. "Red-tipped yellow roses are for new relationships and…" Frannie paused and waggled her eyebrows at Kelley. "A crush." Her little sister gave Kelley a smug, *I told you so* look.

Kelley worked to keep her hand steady and her smile from getting away from her.

"Well, I can't wait to see Asher Blackwell again," her mom said, pleasantly. She twisted part of Frannie's hair into an intricate updo and let the rest fall past her sister's shoulders. "Asher was always so helpful with the yardwork and such when we still lived over on Bridle Creek Circle."

Kelley set the eyeliner pencil down and glanced at her mom. "When was this?"

Her childhood home was on Bridle Creek. They

had lived there before and after her parents' divorce. Surely, Kelley would have noticed Asher being there.

"Asher's mom volunteered in the library every week." Kelley's mom placed a bobby pin into Frannie's hair, then stepped back to inspect her work. "Priscilla and I became good friends. She always checked on me after the divorce. She would send Asher over to mow the lawn or trim the hedges, so I had one less thing to worry about and she never let me pay him."

That was kind. Kelley said, "But I don't remember Asher ever coming by."

Frannie curled the strands framing her face and said, "Neither do I."

"That's because Priscilla and I waited until you were at your father's house for the week." Her mother chuckled and shook the hairspray bottle. "I didn't want you to think things were not under control, or worry that I couldn't handle the house, the property and everything else."

"We would have helped you," Kelley said. Their childhood house was quite large, not to mention it sat on an extensive property. The landscaping and upkeep alone would have been a lot for both her parents, never mind her mom on her own, who was working full-time and looking after three daughters.

"You had enough adjustments between a new stepmom and jumping between houses." Her mom shook her head. "I wanted something to remain consistent. It was important we stayed in that home."

"No wonder you downsized when we moved out," Frannie mused and glanced around the cottage house as if appreciating it even more.

"And now we are back together..." Kelley said and took in the wedding paraphernalia scattered all around the kitchen. "Cramping your space."

Her mom wrapped her arm around Kelley's shoulders and squeezed. "I'm thrilled to have my girls here."

"And you will be thrilled to see us move out," Kelley said playfully.

"I will only be cheering because I will know you are ready to move into your next chapter." Her mom laughed and dipped her head toward the dozen roses. "I can't wait to see what that might be."

Well, it was not a cowboy chapter. Of that, she was certain. Kelley gathered her makeup and tossed it into her small cloth bag with her initials. Then she checked her phone and said, "LB just texted. She is ready and waiting for us to pick her up so we can get to the venue and help her get ready."

"Mom, start the car and crank the air-conditioning to blasting. Otherwise, all your hard work on my hair is going to wilt away in the heat." Frannie gave her hair another shot of hairspray and grinned. "Kelley and I have something to do quick."

"Don't forget the essentials bag. Frannie and I will get the rest." Kelley picked a duffel bag off the kitchen chair beside her and handed it to her mom.

"Wow, this is quite heavy." Her mom settled the strap on her shoulder and asked, "Whatever is in it?"

"Everything." Kelley stood and started reciting her checklist. Bridesmaids' gowns were already hanging in the car. Shoes were in the trunk. That left bouquets and boutonnieres. Kelley walked toward the refrigerator. "There is something for every sort of bridal emergency in that duffel."

"When did you pack all this?" Her mom filled a to-go tumbler with ice and water.

"I've been filling it the last few months as I thought of things that might go wrong," Kelley explained.

"You can't plan for every potential crisis." Her mother frowned.

"I can certainly try." Kelley chuckled. "And I think I did with that duffel."

"Did you pack safety pins in case the straps on her dress break?" Frannie peered into the snack bag.

"Of course," Kelley said and grinned at her little sister. "There's also a sewing kit stocked with matching thread for both bridal and groomsmen attire in case a button fails or whatnot."

"Good call." Frannie went into the pantry and returned with a bag of honey mustard pretzels. "What about backup shoes in case one of Laura-Beth's heels malfunctions before the ceremony?"

"Yes, we've got those, too," Kelley said. "And two stain remover sticks, superglue and extra ribbon in case the ring pillow fails."

Frannie glanced at their mother. "I think she might have planned for everything."

"Dear, there is nothing wrong with figuring things out in the moment," her mom stated. "Sometimes the spontaneity takes you to unexpected places and you learn something about yourself."

"Yes," Kelley said dryly. "You learn you should have planned better."

Kelley's mom chuckled and pressed a kiss to Kelley's cheek, then headed for the back door. "All right, hurry up, ladies. We can't keep our bride waiting."

"This will only take a minute," Frannie called after their mom. Her sister snatched a rose from the vase, then claimed the box of bridesmaid bouquets from Kelley.

"What are you doing?" Kelley asked, confused. "Laura-Beth was very particular about the flowers. You can't tamper with the bouquets."

"I'm not tampering with it. I'm enhancing yours." Frannie plucked one of the six bridesmaid bouquets and in Frannie-seconds, had one flower removed and gently slid Asher's rose into its place. Grinning, she said, "Get me the scissors. I need to trim the stem to match the others."

Kelley opened the junk drawer and handed the scissors to her little sister.

Frannie finished and admired her handiwork. "Asher's rose blends in beautifully with the others."

It really did. Kelley asked, "Why are you doing this?"

"It's like a silent acknowledgment of his crush on you." Frannie beamed at Kelley. "And now you get to take him down the aisle with you."

"I don't think that's necessary." Or wise. She should not be thinking of Asher and aisles together. After all, it was a night of no pressure and no expectations. She needed to start setting some firm ones for herself.

"It's very necessary." Frannie tucked the bouquet back inside the box and said, "It's time for you to have more than a crush, big sister."

"It's not going anywhere between me and Asher." Kelley shook her head and took the boutonniere box from the refrigerator. "We are sitting at the singles' table. What does that tell you?"

"Everyone is single before they are a couple," Frannie argued and started for the back door.

Kelley scanned the kitchen for any forgotten items, then followed her sister outside. "It's better this way. Asher and I talked about it. We've decided."

"So, change his mind," Frannie stated matter-of-factly. "Or better yet. Change yours."

Kelley's mind was set.

The doubt didn't set in until hours later, when Kelley was standing at the front of the chapel barn at The Willows on Laurel Lake. The sun was going down beyond the hills while her sister and her soon-to-be brother-in-law recited their vows under a flower-bedecked archway.

Kelley brushed at her damp eyes and then caught sight of her cowboy.

He was standing at the back of the historic wooden-floored, tin-roofed open-air barn behind the guests seated on rustic wood benches. His crisp white dress shirt was unbuttoned at the collar. His deep blue suit jacket and dress pants were well tailored and well fit. And his barely there smile was sweet, private and aimed entirely at Kelley.

Just like that, Kelley's crush teetered toward something bigger.

Yet, letting herself fall for Asher would only end in heartbreak. Kelley held the thought for a breath, loosened her grip and let it sink with the setting sun.

She kept that thought in check after the ceremony, too, when Asher offered his arm to escort her into the reception. Seeing Asher at the back of the chapel barn, Kelley thought him impossibly handsome. But a scooch away from being tucked right up against his side, she found her cowboy impossible not to fancy. Still, to have this one evening in Asher's company, she anchored herself in the moment and willed time to slow through the sit-down dinner, the toasts, the speeches and even the cake cutting.

As the event progressed, Asher was charming, funny and so very attentive. He chatted with her family and friends as if he was always a part of their circle. And he won more than one admirer when he accepted the flower girl's shy request for the first dance.

And Asher kept his promise to skip the sitting and dance the night away with Kelley. The party was in full swing. High heels were kicked off under tables, and the band kept the guests dipping and swirling from one song to the next.

During the band's intermission, the evening took an unexpected turn. Kelley accepted a glass of wine from Asher, propped her bare feet on a chair and wiggled her toes. Laughing, she said, "I'm not complaining about the dancing, but this is a welcome rest."

Asher dropped into the chair on her other side. His jacket was draped on the chair. And if Kelley was not mistaken, one more button was unhooked on the top of his dress shirt.

He tapped his glass against hers and said, "Not ready to call it a night, then."

"Not even close." She sipped her wine and eyed him over the rim. "How about you?"

He smiled. "I'm just getting started."

Kelley tipped her head back and laughed. "And who thought the singles' table would be dull?"

"I'm rather enjoying it," Asher said then turned to lift his glass in a toast to Beatrice and Lynette sitting at a table across from them.

The widowed sisters wore matching grins and their gazes gleamed. Kelley was not given time to wonder what the crafty duo was up to. Frannie, Owen, several regulars Kelley recognized from the diner and a handful of other locals surrounded the table.

Frannie lifted her arms as if accepting she was the group's spokeswoman. Her grin was wide, and her gaze was bright. "There's a bit of a buzz going around."

Kelley curved her fingers around the stem on her wineglass.

"Seeing as there is a live band and we have a songwriter in our midst." Frannie stopped chuckling long enough to blurt, "We think Asher should sing."

Kelley caught her own amusement and slanted her gaze toward her cowboy.

He swirled his wine in his glass, sat back and said easily, "I'm not sure that's appropriate. The night is about celebrating Laura-Beth and Wes."

"It's also a gathering of friends and family,"

Frannie countered. "What's more fun than our friends and family performing?"

The group grinned and nodded.

Kelley immediately thought of kissing Asher. She dismissed the image quickly and asked, "What would he sing?"

"One of his originals of course," Owen offered, grinning sheepishly. "I've been hearing all about your cruise ship adventure."

Kelley coughed.

Asher arched an eyebrow at her and said good-naturedly, "Yes, well, I've been rediscovering my sense of adventure since I've been home."

"An adventure is fine, so long as you come home," Beatrice said and jostled her way to the front of the small crowd. "Although you don't need to leave to find what you're looking for. We got it right here."

Asher smiled. "I'll keep that in mind."

Kelley reminded herself the cowboy beside her would be leaving. And she refused to mind.

Lynette stepped beside her sister and added, "Come on, Asher, how about it?" Her gaze sparkled. "You gonna give us something to remember you by or not?"

Kelley held her breath.

"You know. Why not?" Asher said and put his wineglass down.

Kelley could think of several reasons. He was

not a singer. The story was a rumor. And there are too many other things to remember him by.

"Seeing as this is a celebration of the new couple," Asher began and pushed his chair back. He took Kelley's hand in his and continued, "I think a duet would be more appropriate."

That gained a round of *oohs* and *aahs* and cheers.

Kelley couldn't not smile. Yet, before she could backpedal, Asher tightened his grip, stood and tugged her with him toward the stage.

"Please tell me you have a song in mind," he said, his voice pitched low and on the edge of panic. "I obviously don't have an original. We need a song."

"We," Kelley squeaked.

"For our duet," Asher said. "In celebration of the happy couple."

"This was supposed to be *your* solo," Kelley countered.

He relaxed beside her. His smile grew. "This will be much more fun."

"How do you figure that?" she asked, hearing a note of dread in her own words now.

"Simple." He squeezed her fingers, drawing her gaze back to his. "I'm with you. That makes everything infinitely better. You make everything better."

That flutter of attraction she felt every time she was around Asher gained traction. Unstoppable and, she supposed, unavoidable. Her laughter swirled through her sigh, and she said, "You're right. We need to make this fun."

A quick debate with the band and they landed on an upbeat song, one certain to get the guests onto the dance floor and singing along. They were barely into the first verse when the guests joined in. The performance went from an upbeat duet to an all-inclusive karaoke. And the sing-along did not end there. The band asked any guest with a song recommendation to join them on stage. That was when the fun really began.

As for Asher and Kelley, they danced, sang, sipped wine yet did not sit until they were inside Asher's truck, heading home. Asher parked beside her mother's house and Kelley slipped on her heels. She said, "I can't recall the last time I closed down a wedding reception."

"I don't think I've been the last one to leave the dance floor ever." Asher cut the engine, opened his door and got out.

Kelley met him in the driveaway and asked, "It wasn't so bad, was it? Being the last to leave."

He shook his head, took her hand and walked with her to the front porch. "I would've stayed if the staff hadn't kicked us out."

Kelley chuckled. "That view of the moonlit lake from the reception hall was magical. We should've strolled along the shore."

"And missed all that two-stepping and line

dancing?" Asher said, his words wry. "I don't think so."

They arrived at the front door and Kelley turned toward him. "Thank you for tonight."

"It was my pleasure," he said simply.

And then Kelley bent the rules. Wanting something even stronger to remember. She leaned in and pressed her lips ever so softly against his. She felt him still. Felt his breath on her skin. Then she started to lean away. Only he framed her face in his hands gently and Kelley met him halfway for a different sort of kiss.

One that buckled knees.

One that whispered of everything they would—and could—not express in words.

One that promised to linger in every heartbeat.

But, she reminded herself, whatever was between them could not last.

Finally, the kiss slowed. Kelley pulled away and waited for her breath to even out and pulse to stop racing. And all the while, Asher kept her anchored in his arms as if he needed to ground himself.

Kelley started, "That was..." *Amazing. Addicting. Habit forming.* She exhaled and said, "That was simply us giving in to a mutual curiosity, right?"

His gaze traveled over her face like a caress. His voice was quiet and tender. "Exactly."

"Then there is no need for a repeat." Even if she very much wanted to kiss him again. Right now.

Right there. One deep sigh, her words came out thin like vapor. "Because we know all we need to know."

"Right," he said, his voice more gravelly than drawl.

"I should go in." *I should let go.*

He nodded but gathered her even closer.

Kelley settled against him. Rested her cheek over his heart. And let her cowboy hold her on the front porch under the moonlight. She closed her eyes. After all, this was not an evening for stargazing and firefly wishing.

It was not a forever kind of night.

It was a cowboy. A cowgirl. And an unforgettable memory made. That was all it was ever meant to be.

Kelley released her hold, rolled onto the balls of her feet and pressed a kiss on Asher's cheek. "You were right," she whispered. "The evening was infinitely better with you."

He chuckled and tucked a curl behind her ear. "See you at the singles' table."

"Save me a seat, cowboy." Finally, she stepped away and walked into the house alone.

CHAPTER SIXTEEN

THE NEXT MORNING, Asher reached over the stall door to greet Derby Dreamer. The colt nudged the back of his hand and nickered softly. Asher grinned, even though he knew he was going to ruffle some feathers soon enough. Although, the sooner the confrontation was over, the quicker he could get to the good part of his day, like seeing Kelley and taking her on a sunset ride out to the stream.

If he was lucky, perhaps there would be another opportunity to pull his cowgirl into his arms and give in to his new curiosity. After all, he was dying to know if a second kiss would be just as spectacularly world-altering as the first. Something told him it would be all that and more.

The slam of the stable door alerted Asher that he had company. Asher gave the colt one last stroke, tucked his curiosity away and prepared himself. After all, it was not every day he meddled in stable business.

"Elliot tells me you want to pull Derby Dreamer from the Rising Star Classic this afternoon." Irritation tightened across Joe's face and echoed in his heavy footsteps down the center aisle of the stable. "Care to tell me why?"

"He's not ready." Asher turned away from the stall door.

"Doc gave him a clean bill of health," Joe said, with resolve. "He's cleared to compete."

A clean bill of health was important, but Asher held firm. "It's not his health. It's his conditioning I'm concerned about."

"I know full well how to properly train and prepare a horse for competition." Frustration tightened through Joe's words.

"I know that." Asher tipped his hat back. "But even you admitted their training was accelerated. Walter always told us there were no shortcuts. No speeding up the process." *The horse is ready when it's ready. And it's for us to have the good sense to know when it's not.*

"Don't think to lecture me on Walter's training program." Joe braced his hands on his hips. His motions were tense and curt. "I helped him create it all these years."

"Then you have to agree there are risks if Derby Dreamer races," Asher argued.

"There are always risks," Joe stated, his voice flat and matter-of-fact. "That's the nature of this business. Your father and I understood and accepted it. You need to do the same."

"Protecting a horse is not a mistake. You taught

me that," Asher countered. "What has happened to you?"

"Me." Joe jerked back. "I've been here pouring everything I have into this place. Year after year. Day after day. I've been more loyal to the Blackwell name than Walter's own blood. You of all people cannot deny that."

Asher barely kept from flinching. As it was, he stepped into the aisle to face Joe and widened his stance as if to steady himself.

"Look, Asher, I get what Big E is trying to do here." Joe flicked his arm between them. "Sure, I appreciate good optics as much as the next person."

Asher folded his arms over his chest and asked, "What exactly is Big E trying to do?"

"A couple of turns on the dance floor with a local cowgirl and a parade float aren't going to fix things around here," Joe explained. "We need wins at the racetrack. Wins are all that matter. They certainly mean more than having a Blackwell walking around the property."

"Any Blackwell or me in particular?" Asher asked, his own level of frustration rising.

"You know what I'm saying," Joe said.

"I'm not wrong about Derby Dreamer."

"I mean no disrespect. I care about you like you're one of my own." Joe lowered his shoulders and his words mellowed. "But this is the part where you let Elliot and me do what we do best.

What I've been doing since before you were born. What the stables pay me to do."

"And what? I can go back to parade floats?" Asher said, impatiently.

"We know that's temporary, too. And everyone needs a little timeout for some fun and parade games," Joe said. His eyebrows lifted, his tone tempered even more. "But you know where you're meant to be. You made that choice a long time ago."

And that was not at Blackwell Stables. That much was clear to Joe. Asher ground his teeth together.

"From what I've heard, you've carved quite a trail for yourself on Wall Street. You should be proud of that," Joe added. "No sense taking a detour from what you know."

Asher may not have been Walter's protégé, but Asher worked the stables the same as his brothers growing up. He knew something about this place. "This isn't about me. It's about the horses and their health and safety."

"I recognize that better than anyone," Joe said, lashing out. "All you are going to do, if you pull Derby Dreamer out, is make us look weak and tarnish the Blackwell name and reputation even further."

"It is one race." Asher stood firm. "One horse."

"Perhaps that is exactly what you want." Joe's laugh was bitter and sharp. "To take control and run the stables so far into the ground that there's no coming back."

"You think I would do that?" Asher asked and heard the sudden chill in his own words. He had left so he would not ruin the stables.

"I think you are not Dylan." Joe held Asher's gaze and held his ground. "You aren't sticking around, Asher. You never intended to. It's not in you. We both know it. There's no use pretending otherwise."

Asher absorbed the stinging truth of Joe's accusations.

"The horses need to know who they can depend on. Same as the staff. Same as me," Joe said, more calmly. "At the very least, Dylan cared enough to stick around."

Translation: They did not trust that they could depend on Asher. He could argue. He could claim he cared. But Joe was not wrong. He was leaving. There was no use interfering now, only to be second-guessed later. In fact, he was second-guessing himself right now.

Joe eyed Asher for another beat before he glanced away and called out, "Let's get Derby Dreamer ready to load. We've got a schedule and a racetrack to get to."

Owen stepped into Asher's sightline, hesitation clear in his expression.

Asher inhaled and exhaled, then finally dipped

his chin and said, "Joe has made the call. You heard him. Get the colts loaded."

Owen gave Asher one last look and got to work.

Joe gave Asher a curt nod, then walked around him. At the tack room door, Joe called out, "See you in the stands this afternoon, Asher."

"Right," Asher muttered and shook his head. "Best not forget about those optics."

Outside the stable, Asher slipped on a pair of mirrored sunglasses and walked over to the UTV parked outside the filly barn. His phone vibrated in his pocket. He slipped a wireless earbud into his ear and accepted the call without checking the caller ID.

His boss's greeting boomed over the line followed by, "Now that I know you're okay, I'm going to make my pitch. I'll double whatever Fletcher and Rowe Capital offered you."

Asher propped his boot on the step bar of the UTV and rubbed his forehead. "What are you talking about?"

"Fletcher told me he had a call in to you," Pierce explained. "I figured since you weren't immediately back online first thing yesterday when your access was restored, well, it was obvious. Fletcher and his team got to you with an offer you could not say no to."

Asher tossed his cowboy hat onto the passenger seat of the UTV and scrubbed his fingers through his hair.

"I will take your silence as an affirmative." His boss sighed, the sound more irritated than resigned.

Asher considered how to play this unexpected turn of events.

"I'm changing my counter," Pierce said suddenly. "We will do whatever it takes to get you to stay. Whatever. It. Takes. Asher, just name it."

"You're serious."

"Absolutely," his boss said, determination in his voice. "We need you. And we are prepared to fight to keep you here."

We need you. Wow, wasn't that what anybody wanted? To be needed. Perhaps Joe had the right idea after all. Everyone should stay in their lanes. Stick to their own trails. Skip the work of clearing a new one. Asher sighed and said, "What if I told you that I have not spoken to Fletcher and Rowe Capital and there is no job offer?"

"Well, there will be," his boss insisted. "They recognize talent and know what you bring to the table. I will have an offer and contract ready when you get home. I'm not losing you to any rival."

"Fair enough," Asher said.

"When will you be back?" his boss asked.

Asher paused and watched Elliot back the trailer toward the twos' barn, then said, "I'm catching a flight out later today."

"Excellent," Pierce said. His boss quickly set about getting Asher up to speed on the current deals and negotiations in the pipeline. Pierce ended their call with a pleased, "Looking forward to seeing you in the office tomorrow."

There was one goodbye Asher was not looking forward to. Yet, the sooner it was done, the sooner things would seem right. Asher stuck his phone in his pocket. Big E hollered his name before he could climb into the UTV and head back to the house to pack up and prepare for that last goodbye.

Big E closed the door to the filly barn and walked over to join Asher. "I see they're loading up Derby Dreamer."

Asher nodded yet did not turn around to look. He kept his tone indifferent. "It is Joe's call." That was Joe's lane. No sense believing otherwise.

"But you don't agree," Big E said and nudged his hat higher on his forehead to eye Asher.

"Not the decision I would have made," Asher admitted.

"You've got a say around here, too." Big E set his hands on his hips.

"Let's be honest," Asher said, taking a page from his conversation with Joe. "The time to use my voice passed years ago."

Big E's nod was slow and pensive. "Or perhaps you needed all this time to find your voice?"

"You should know that was my boss on the phone just now," Asher explained. "He needs me back in New York to close a few deals before we lose them." Asher needed to go before he lost his way again.

"I understand," Big E said, easily.

Asher did not understand why this was suddenly difficult, as if he was somehow letting Big E down, too. This was always the way things were going to go. Asher cleared his throat and said, "When I get home, I'll talk with my brothers and figure out next steps."

Big E hummed his acknowledgment.

"You don't need to stay, either," Asher said.

"I think I'll hang about for a bit longer," Big E said quietly. "Feels like there's a lot of dust left to settle around here yet."

"I appreciate it." Asher stuck his arm out to shake Big E's hand.

Big E gripped Asher's hand and pulled Asher in for a tight embrace. One that Big E ended with a hearty thump on Asher's back and Asher's word that he would call when he landed in New York. Big E touched the brim of his hat, then walked over to join the others at the trailer.

Asher finally climbed into the UTV and drove back to the house.

Hours later, his flight confirmed, the office set back to rights and his bags packed, Asher heard the familiar bootsteps in the kitchen. Kelley was there. Asher sat behind the desk and rubbed his palms on his jeans and fought to find the words for one final goodbye.

Here we go. And for the record, cowgirl, I am really sorry.

HUMMING A COUNTRY love song, Kelley set the picnic basket she prepared for her sunset ride with Asher later on the kitchen island, then went in search of her cowboy. Stepping into the office doorway, she caught sight of Asher's packed suitcase and grinned. "I see you are finally moving into a bedroom. That will surely be more comfortable than the couch."

He stood, came around the desk but didn't close the distance between them.

Okay. The love song broke apart in her suddenly dry throat. Kelley swallowed and searched Asher's very composed face.

He leaned against the front edge of the desk, fluid and graceful yet reserved and guarded all the same. "Actually, I'm heading back to New York."

Oh. Okay. Kelley locked her knees and braced herself. "When?"

"My flight departs at four thirty." He held her gaze, steady and undaunted. "Today."

That was the same time they were supposed to be out on a trail ride with River Run and Maple. The same trail ride he had invited Kelley on yesterday in a late-night text, wishing her sweet dreams. She clenched her jaw until the burn of disappointment receded.

This was the goodbye she knew was coming. This one she prepared for. This one she expected. It was not supposed to change her. *No.* She would not allow that.

"Big E wants to ride with you later," he said, his words smooth and refined as if all was as it should be. "I'm sure Frannie and Owen would like to go as well."

But not you. She forced herself to stand tall. Her shoulders back. Her heart in plain sight. *Don't hold back, cowboy.* She would not flinch. He could count on that. She asked, "What about the parade?"

"I worked it all out with Owen before he left for the Rising Star Classic," Asher explained. He anchored his arms, no tension in his grip around the desk edge. No strain in his words. "It's been more of his vision and his project anyway."

Kelley matched his indifference. "What about the pasture patrol?"

"Big E is already looking for buyers," Asher said simply.

Kelley curled her fingers into her palms and let her nails bite into her skin. "What about the stables?"

"I need to talk to my brothers," he explained, easy and sure. "We need to decide how to move forward together."

She nodded. "You certainly have all the answers, don't you?" *What if I dared you to stay, cowboy?* Kelley planted her boots. *Got an answer for that? Didn't think so.*

"They want me back in New York. My boss

called this morning," he said, so very cool and unflappable. "I have to go. They need me."

I need you more. What do you think of that? Kelley smashed her lips together and waited out the tremble before she said, "It seems your mind is set."

"It always was." He did not blink. He stayed the course and said, "We both knew this was always how it was going to be."

"Of course, we did." Kelley took in a careful breath, steadied herself, even while her pulse beat wild inside her. She forced a small smile. "Don't worry. My heart is not breaking or anything like that." He could not break what she did not give him.

"That's good." His gaze trailed over her face. His words gentled, revealing the slightest hint of regret. "I never wanted to hurt you."

Oh no you don't, cowboy. He did not get to flinch now. There was no folding. No retreating. This they would face head-on. She said, "You never wanted to do a lot of things."

"What does that mean?" he asked, carefully.

It was time for a little straight talk. *Call it a parting gift.* "You're starting to care, Asher Blackwell," she said, a challenge in her words. "You're starting to care about the horses. The staff. The town." *Me.*

He reached up and wiped his hand over his mouth as if catching his response.

But Kelley was not waiting for him to gather his thoughts. There were more things ready to get off her chest and she let those truths free. “And all that caring has you running scared all the way back to the city.” She inhaled and let another truth fly on her exhale. “Not that it really matters. You were out before you were ever in.”

“This hasn’t ever been my place.” He extended his legs, crossed one ankle over the other as if to prove she had not shaken him. He added, “This is not where I belong.”

“You made that decision a long time ago and you’ve been proving it to yourself ever since,” she challenged. “Maybe it’s time to try a new narrative and realize you are enough. Just as you are. You always have been.”

“You should take your own advice.” His grin was brief. “You’re thriving in a small-town diner in a barely-on-the-map Kentucky town. Doing what you love surrounded by people who love you.” He arched an eyebrow at her. “What’s so wrong with that?”

She would be doing it all without him. She caught the catch in her throat and evened out her voice. “You didn’t come back because it was a convenient excuse to get away from work. You came home because your family needed you.”

“Is that so?” he drawled.

“Everyone knows it,” she said, ignoring caution. “But the truth is, Asher Blackwell, you need them and this place more." *I could be everything you ever needed.*

"What do you need, Kelley Munroe?" he asked, his words icy-cool. "Because as far as I can tell, you're so afraid to fail again, you're standing still. You're existing, not living."

Kelley notched her chin up. "At least I've put myself out there, my heart and all." Perhaps she was standing still, but better that than tossing him her heart and watching it land in the dust around his boots.

"Is that what you want?" he asked and tipped his head to consider her. "Do you want my heart?"

She wanted his whole heart, not the pieces he chose to give her. All or nothing. *Broken bits and all, cowboy.* She shook her head. "It was never about that, remember?" Because she was starting to.

"Then what is this?"

"Just a cowboy and a cowgirl clearing the air for the last time." Now it was time to call it. She met his gaze. "Bye, Asher."

He waited for a beat and finally said, "Kelley, I wish—"

"Please don't say anything else," she interrupted him. If she bent an inch, she just might splinter. "There's really nothing left to say."

He closed his mouth.

She straightened, kept her head high and walked out of the office.

Because Kelley was not chasing love. She was not going to try to hold on to a cowboy who was already gone.

She was letting go. Making a clean break. Moving on.

CHAPTER SEVENTEEN

THE WORK WEEK was kicking off. Yet, there was a noticeable, rather inconvenient hitch in Asher's get-up-and-go. One that Asher blamed on jet lag. One that he was convinced caffeine would immediately rectify.

So Asher found himself jostling through the business suit-clad crowd jammed around the pickup counter at the coffee shop on the busy city corner close to his office. There was no greeting from the harried barista. No *nice to see you* from a local. No funny bits of gossip being traded. Cell phones were the focus. Personal space was guarded. And everyone was in a rush.

Except Asher. His phone was tucked in his pocket. His cowgirl was not calling or texting. He did not need to look at his phone for that bitter reminder. At least his mobile order was ready and waiting. Although, his first sip of coffee revealed it was tepid and bland. No matter. There were any number of shops in the blocks surrounding his office building. Surely, he would find a decent cup of joe. It did not have to be the best. He already knew where to find that. He just needed good enough until he lost his taste for diner coffee and put Kentucky completely behind him.

Asher walked into the offices on the forty-fourth floor of the high-rise, only to find himself pulled directly into a meeting. Fortunate, that. Even better, he went from one conference room to another and was not given a chance to be alone with his thoughts. He barely had time to trade his coffee for a soda.

It was well into the afternoon when Asher finally made it to his office and unwrapped a deli sandwich his administrative assistant had delivered.

A quick rap of knuckles on his door and Asher's boss strode in. Pierce Rylan dropped a folder on Asher's desk and snatched the other half of Asher's sandwich. Pierce folded his tall, lean frame into the chair across from Asher and said, "Thanks. Didn't realize how hungry I was until I saw your sandwich."

Asher tossed him the bag of chips and said, "Help yourself."

Pierce popped open the bag, fished out a chip and aimed it at Asher. "You'll want to read that."

"What is it?" Asher brushed the crumbs from his hands and opened the folder.

"Your next step up the ladder." Pierce stuck the chip into his mouth and crunched down. He smiled around the bite. "Figured you might like a new challenge in a new location."

Asher chased his bite of sandwich with a deep sip of soda as he scanned the top page. "The London office." That was unexpected. And not entirely off-putting. With more distance between him and Kentucky, surely the memories would fade faster, and he would finally be back to himself. Asher asked, "When do you need an answer?"

"Take as long as you want," his boss said. "But don't take any calls from anyone at Fletcher and Rowe Capital."

How about a call from a cowgirl? Asher avoided checking his phone. Kelley was not calling him. He made sure of that before he left Gold Finch. Asher wrapped up his sandwich wrapper and tossed it in the trash bin. "I'm late for a meeting. I'll let you know what I decide soon."

"I'm just going to hang here and finish this sandwich." Pierce stretched out in the chair and grinned. "Don't tell anyone where I am."

"You got it." Asher tapped the offer letter, then asked, "Do you think this counts as a second act?"

"Are you looking for one?" Pierce took a bite of the sandwich and stared at Asher.

Asher shrugged. "Just recalling a conversation I had back at home." With a cowgirl he could not quite get off his mind.

"If that's what it takes to get you to accept the offer, call it whatever suits you," Pierce said. "Just sign it so I can sleep well knowing you're working for me and right where you need to be."

Asher nodded and headed to his next meeting,

but he could not shake the feeling that he needed to be somewhere else entirely.

That night, all Asher could do was pace around his empty flat. He did not notice before how sterile his place was. There were no photographs. No pictures on the walls. Just a modern metal art piece the staging company had left when he bought the flat and the furniture in it. Yet, it was the silence that sat heavy around him. He opened the sliding glass door, letting the nighttime buzz of the city sweep in. His ears strained for something different, something more like laughter and easy conversation.

Too restless to sleep, he reached for his backpack and his no-fail distraction: work. Only he pulled out a large yellow envelope with a Foxglove Bank and Trust return address. The financial statements for the Blackwell Stables were inside. Valerie had hand delivered them to Big E at the diner when she caught the older cowboy eating pie there. Asher opened the envelope, pulled out the paperwork and discovered a familiar magazine inside.

He flipped to the sticky note-marked page and chuckled. It was another Velvet Dusk cologne ad with the same cowboy and same white stallion and same tagline about leaving a trail they will remember. Except there were colorful signatures and well wishes from the bank staff covering the page. On the sticky note, someone had written, *don't forget you can leave a trail and follow it back home whenever you want.*

Asher picked up the bank statements. He might not be following that trail home, but he could take care of some unfinished business. Logging in to his laptop, Asher got to work on the stable's financials. The sun was a few hours from rising when Asher finally crawled into bed. He missed his cowgirl and did not know what to do about the ache in his chest. But he knew one thing. There was no financial crisis that drove Walter Blackwell to extreme measures.

That revelation prompted Asher's phone call to Big E on his way to work later that morning. He wanted Big E to know it was looking less likely that Walter was guilty of doping Pride. If only that did not bring about another set of unanswered questions. The first of which being, if not Walter, then who drugged Pride?

"We're gonna have to keep digging until we figure things out." Big E sighed over the phone line. "Seeing as I've got you, I have other news."

Asher's footsteps slowed. "You don't sound happy. What happened?"

"I suppose it's all in how you look at it," Big E said. "Got a buyer interested in River Run."

"That's good." Asher clenched his phone and switched ears. "That's what we wanted. That's real good." And Asher would be real good soon, too. After all, that was what he wanted.

"Since you're okay with it, I'll work out the contract for purchase," Big E said mildly. "And send it over for your review."

"That will be fine," Asher said quickly and walked into the lobby of his office building. "Just fine."

"And Asher… You should know you were right."

"About what?" Asher asked. Because nothing was feeling quite right inside him at the moment.

"Derby Dreamer," Big E replied. "He had a bit of a stumble in warmups at the Rising Star Classic. Nothing serious. No damage done, but he had to be pulled from the main event."

Asher rubbed his forehead with his free hand. Not exactly how he wanted that to go. "I'm glad he's okay."

"How about you?" Big E asked. "You okay out there?"

No. Not quite. But he would be. He cleared his throat and said, "I'm working on it."

Big E chuckled. "If you gotta work that hard to call it right, maybe you're in the wrong saddle, son."

Still, it was the one he chose. "Nothing wrong with wrestling a bit. Walter would've told me to keep at it. Nothing worth having is supposed to come easy."

"All the same, just make sure it's worth having," Big E cautioned, then ended the call with a promise to check in again with more information about the buyer for River Run.

Next thing he knew, Asher was on a crowded elevator, heading to the forty-fourth floor. Yet, he was not mentally reviewing his upcoming presentation; he was reconsidering his choice of second acts.

"I HAVE BEEN waiting to talk to you." Kelley set a box of cleaning supplies on the floor in the diner office and smiled at her boss.

Pauline paused in the doorway. Confusion curved across her face. "What are you doing?"

"I'm making sense of the storage closet." Kelley navigated her way back to the closet and removed another box. "Never mind all this." After all, some things just made no sense. Kelley knew that much firsthand.

Pauline straightened a teetering stack of cleaning rags and made room on the floor for Kelley's next box.

Kelley brushed her hands together and said, "I wanted you to know I'm ready, Pauline. I'm ready to fly with you. It's time for us to spread our wings."

Pauline's eyebrows shot up.

"I know it seemed like I was dragging my boots before," Kelley rushed on, her words tripping over each other as if the faster they came out, the more truthful they would be. "But I don't have cold feet now. Nothing of the sort. I'm more than ready for the next chapter. So, let's fly." Preferably sooner rather than later.

"Is this about Asher leaving town?" Pauline asked, her voice gentle.

"What?" Kelley shook her head and scrunched her face. "No."

If it was about Asher, Kelley would be standing still and picking up the pieces of her broken heart. *Nothing broken here*. Kelley tucked in her chin.

"Of course, it is about Asher." Frannie waltzed into the room and frowned at the contents of the closet strewn all over the floor. "How could it not be about him?"

Because Kelley would not let it be. She countered, "This is about business." The business of getting on with things like she should have done a long time ago. "I've reached out to my network for possible buyers for the diner." And a job for herself.

"Fine. If you're done talking business, it's really picking up out there," Frannie said, a hint of annoyance in her words. "I never actually thought so many folks would show up for the watch party this morning."

"It's *The Morning Gallop* on Bluegrass Regional News. It's not to be missed television, especially since Mayor Corbin is making his TV debut today." Kelley chuckled and grabbed an apron from the hook on the wall. "I'll take a section or two, then assist Hayes with the orders."

"I got it covered." Frannie glanced at Pauline, a plea in her words. "Please tell Kelley to stop meddling in everyone's jobs. It's not our fault she hasn't been able to sit down since…" Frannie paused and lowered her voice. "Since a certain cowboy left town."

Pauline nodded, her expression sympathetic.

"I'm helping. Doing my job." Kelley tightened the straps of her apron and the ones holding her together on the inside. "That's what I get paid for."

"She took the busing bin from Shane. Yanked it straight out of his hands." Frannie's expression fell and she added, "And she kicked Hayes out of the omelet station. That's his specialty. Kelley has never interfered with the omelets before."

"That's not good." Pauline grimaced.

"It's fine." Kelley headed for the hallway. "I was giving Hayes a break. Everyone needs one. Besides, Hayes and I are fine. Let's not make it into a thing." Same as she was not making more of that tender spot in her chest. After all, a dent in her heart she could deal with, but a break, well, she was not certain there was enough busywork to get her through that.

"Something needs to be done about her," Frannie muttered behind Kelley.

"I can hear you," Kelley called back. "I'm fine."

All she had to do to stay fine was stay in motion. Otherwise, that heartache she was avoiding might catch up to her. She only hoped she could skip town before it found her.

"I got this," Pauline said and brushed by Kelley

to speak to the cook. "Hayes, what did Beatrice and Lynette order?"

"The usual," Hayes called out. "Spinach and mushroom omelets. Extra cheese. Sourdough toast and extra crisp on the crispy bacon."

"Double their bacon. Add extra honey for their tea," Pauline stated firmly. "And Frannie, tell them their orders are being served with a side of heartache."

Kelley rolled her eyes and walked into the diner before anyone could stop her. Smiling big, she seated guests, took orders and even bused tables. She joined in on small talk across the diner and bolstered the gossip at the lunch counter. Anything to keep busy. Anything to keep her thoughts from circling back to her cowboy.

Fortunately, the dining area was buzzing. The parade showcase was proving a boon for Gold Finch. The inn was already booked solid for the weekend. And the fireworks show had been doubled for what Beatrice deemed an even grander grand finale. It was not difficult to get swept up in the excitement.

When Kelley overheard Pauline offering the diner to Edith Sterling for a Friday night parade costume prep and repair party, Kelley jumped right in and volunteered her cooking services. She was more than thrilled to have another evening arranged. After all, it was in the stillness that her cowboy walked right back into her mind.

That buzz around the diner gained momentum after Mayor Corbin's entertaining and all too engaging *Morning Gallop* TV appearance. The locals were convinced out-of-towners would come just for a chance to meet the exuberant and genuinely enthusiastic Mayor Corbin. The mayor's live shout-outs to Edith Sterling and Kelley Munroe, his efficient and dedicated committee members, were unexpected yet welcome. It was the mayor's wrap-up with a rather witty plug for the Galloping Fork Diner that had the folks truly enthralled.

"Mayor Corbin just called your grilled cheese the best in the state, Kelley." Beatrice beamed. "And on live TV to boot."

"We could not have paid for better advertising," Pauline said, sounding thoroughly pleased.

"The mayor outright encouraged viewers to head on down to the Galloping Fork, have a taste and decide for themselves." Lynette dunked her tea bag into her teacup. "I'm no marketing guru, but I do believe that was genius."

"It's sure to fill up around here," Len mused, a gleam in his gaze, approval in his words.

"Wait until word spreads about how good Kelley's grilled cheese really is." Frannie's smile grew wide. "You could turn into an internet craze overnight, Kelley, with like a huge following and all."

Kelley chuckled. "I would not go that far."

"Why not?" Frannie asked. "You've got the culinary chops as it were to lead, rather than follow."

Lynette hummed. "Let 'em follow you for a change, Kelley."

Lead, rather than follow. No one could accuse her of standing still, then. Kelley flexed her toes in her boots as if testing the fit.

"And we could add a sense of urgency by letting our grilled cheese ingredients run out each day," Pauline mused, her expression thoughtful. "When we are out, we are out. It's limited and you best get it while you can."

Kelley eyed her boss, surprised at the interest she heard in Pauline's words. They were flying, not sticking. Selling, not settling. This was not a diner conversation they should be encouraging.

"Bea and I went to a restaurant in North Carolina once with a secret menu," Lynette said and arched her eyebrows. "If you knew, you knew what to order."

"Oh, yes, I remember that. It was the special menu for the locals in the know." Beatrice's gaze sparked. "Our niece was a housekeeper at the local inn in town. There's something rather fun about being in on a really good secret."

"It helped that it was a delicious secret at that." Lynette laughed. "We certainly felt very special that night."

Kelley had felt special in her cowboy's arms under the twinkling lights on a wedding reception dance floor. She supposed that was her secret. Kelley topped off Len's coffee and said, "Aren't we getting ahead of ourselves a little bit?"

"Better that than being left behind," Len quipped.

Everyone at the counter nodded, including Frannie and Pauline.

"Speaking of being left behind." Beatrice picked up her tea mug and eyed Kelley over the rim. "When are we going to talk about you, dear?" Beatrice patted her heart, giving Kelley a silent cue as to what she was referring to.

"There's nothing to talk about there," Kelley replied. "As it happens, I'm really good."

Lynette's brow wrinkled. "It's worse than we thought."

Kelley tried to smile at that, and said, "Look, Asher and I went to a wedding together and sat at the singles' table. What does that tell you?"

"Laura-Beth was not very efficient or detailed with her seating chart," Beatrice answered.

"Nooo," Kelley stressed the word. "Asher and I knew there was nothing between us. Friends was all it was ever meant to be." If she wished for more, well, that was her heart wandering where it never should have been. But Kelley was finding her way now. Without her cowboy. And she was determined to be better for it. Forcing a grin, she added, "Let's just call it a limited special and leave it at that."

CHAPTER EIGHTEEN

ASHER LASTED ALL of five days in New York before the silence spurred him into booking a red-eye flight back to Kentucky. He missed diner coffee. He missed sunrise out on a pasture. He missed the horses. The staff. The land. But mostly, he missed Kelley.

Now he was home again. And breathing easier. Asher carried his suitcase into the house and heard water running in the kitchen. He veered that way and found Big E standing at the sink, a cup of coffee cradled in his hands.

"Welcome back." Big E's smile was slow and knowing. "This is unexpected. I thought we were having a phone call with the potential buyer for River Run, not an in-person meeting?"

"I changed my mind." About a few things. But he would get to those in time. Asher set his suitcase down and continued, "I don't want to sell River Run."

Big E placed his coffee on the island, took another mug from the cabinet and poured a cup for Asher. Handing it to Asher, he said, "I get the impression you have a lot on your mind."

Asher took a deep sip, then realized he was still

restless. Caffeine would not help. He gripped the mug and paced around the kitchen. "River Run and I have a sort of bond."

"And you don't just trade that away," Big E stated.

"Exactly." Asher paused. "I want to give River Run his second act." And perhaps have one for himself.

"That sounds like it's not only River Run who will be sticking around here." Big E tipped his head toward Asher's suitcase. "I guess my next question is where are you putting that this time around?"

Asher curved his fingers around the coffee mug. "I thought I might try a bedroom this time around."

Big E's grin drifted out. "Then you're thinking of staying for more than a bit."

"I was thinking more like *for good*." Asher leaned in to the promise. It felt like he was finally going in the right direction.

"That's the best news I've heard today." Big E lifted his coffee mug in a toast.

"The day has barely gotten started," Asher said, a tease in his words.

"Don't make light of it," Big E cautioned. "Your father would have been proud of you. I know I am."

That settled inside Asher, not lightly, but rightly. As if the words fit. He intended to keep on making them proud.

"This place needs a Blackwell caring for it. Looking after it," Big E continued. "You will do well by it."

"I hope the staff agrees," Asher said, a hint of uncertainty in his words.

"Prove to them you mean to stick." Big E put a hand on Asher's shoulder. "Show them how much you care, and they won't doubt you or your intentions."

"I should get changed so I can get to work on that." Asher picked up his suitcase and turned toward the bedroom wing.

Big E stopped him and said, "I cleaned out Walter's room, painted and changed the furniture."

Asher turned to look at Big E and asked, "Why?"

"To get it ready." Big E met Asher's gaze and held it. "For the next generation."

Asher looked away, then nodded and turned toward the private wing for the primary bedroom suite.

Big E said, "Of course, you can change whatever you like, it's yours now. And you'll be wanting to update the other rooms I'm sure, but you've got time for that."

He did, didn't he? Asher stepped into his parents' old bedroom and stopped short. He didn't recognize it. The light gray walls, white trim and neutral tones were gentle to the eye and welcoming. The natural wood furniture and other fixtures everything he preferred.

Asher set his suitcase in the walk-in closet and headed toward the French doors and patio. An old-school-style notebook on the dresser caught his attention. There was a handwritten note stuck to the cover. *Asher, seeing is believing. Found this in your dad's office.*

He picked up the notebook and sat on the padded bench at the end of the king-size bed. Opening the cover, Asher found another note, this one from his father. *Asher, you've always gone your own way. Cowboy to cowboy, I respect that. But this father misses his son. Here's hoping you find your way home one day. Dad.*

Asher squeezed his eyes closed, but that only acted like a dam, backing up his tears so when he blinked, they all fell at once. The scrapbook turned out to be a photo album of Asher's highlights growing up. Each picture was labeled and dated in his father's handwriting. In the back was a collection of articles written about Asher during his years in New York.

It was a bittersweet, but necessary walk down memory lane. He knew there would always be regret for not making the time for one last conversation with his father. And he would always miss his twin. But for the first time, Asher was at peace in his family home and knew he was where he belonged.

Big E tapped on the door and said, "I'm heading down to the stables. Wanted to see if you are ready?"

Asher closed the scrapbook and stood. "Why didn't you give this to me before?"

"I've found there's a right time for things," Big E explained. "You might have heard me, but I don't know if you were open to listen, in here." Big E put a hand over his chest.

Asher understood and tucked the notebook carefully into a drawer in the bedside table. "Thank you for this and not giving up on me."

"You're family." Big E smiled. "I don't know any other way."

Asher was glad to have Elias Blackwell in his corner. A quick change into his jeans, cotton shirt and favorite cowboy hat, then Asher met Big E and they headed to the stables.

The lunch hour was quickly approaching just as Big E and Asher made it out to the pasture patrol to exercise the trio and check on Pride. They worked with the horses through lunch and only just finished cooling them down when Joe showed up.

Asher and Big E joined Joe at the pasture fence.

"Welcome back," Joe said. "Heard from Owen you were here. He's expecting you at the parade float this afternoon for final touches."

"I will be there." Asher grinned. "I'm looking forward to seeing it." There was a special cowgirl he was looking forward to seeing even more.

He just had not quite figured out what he was going to say to Kelley when he finally saw her. *I'm back* seemed a little less than satisfactory. And *I'm sorry* seemed hardly enough for his spirited cowgirl.

"I owe you an apology." Joe stepped forward and reached an arm over toward Asher. "For not listening about Derby Dreamer."

Asher gave Joe a solid handshake and a nod.

"I've got no excuse except pride," Joe admitted and scratched his weathered cheek. "Seems I've been fighting to prove time wrong. To prove I haven't lost a step the past few years."

"Getting older doesn't mean a cowboy stops making mistakes." Big E braced his arms on the fence and considered Joe.

Asher knew his fair share about making mistakes. He was going to get to righting a few shortly. Just as soon as he got his cowgirl alone.

"But age does give us the insight to own up to our mistakes faster," Joe said, his words wry. He took off his cowboy hat and tapped it against his leg. "And I'm doing that now."

"Appreciate it," Asher said, and noted the shadows under the older cowboy's eyes and that his hair was more gray than brown. "Looks like you've got more on your mind, though."

"I need to step away," Joe said.

Surprised, Asher asked, "For how long?"

"I'm still figuring that out." Joe brushed the dust

off his hat brim. "I watched Walter fade away on these lands. I don't want that. If the legacy I leave is that I was fully present with my wife and kids and grandkids in my final years, then that is more than enough for me."

"Family first," Big E said, with clear approval.

"Take all the time you need," Asher said, repeating the words his own boss had told him when Asher turned down the London job offer and requested an extended leave. "But can you tell me what happened? Was there something more to it than Derby Dreamer?"

"Watching Derby Dreamer falter on that warm-up track at the Rising Star Classic all but did my heart in," Joe confessed. "But the truth is I haven't been at my best since Walter passed. That's no good for the horses or anyone."

Asher nodded and realized he was starting to find his best. Perhaps for the first time.

"Walter and me, we did real good. We were a team. We trusted each other and we were loyal to the end. That's why we made magic on the track together," Joe explained and held Asher's gaze. "Now it's time for you to take the reins, Asher. You've got it in you. Find your own team and you will make your own magic."

Joe had his back, too. Just like that, his foundation was feeling even more steady. Asher asked, "When are you leaving?"

"I'll tie up a few things here. Speak to the staff

and take off before the week is out," Joe said, a small grin on his face. "I got time to make up for with my wife and family. I'm going to get to that vacation we put off for far too long. I don't want any regrets."

Handshakes all around and Joe walked away.

"I know a thing or two about regrets," Big E said and propped his boot on the bottom fence post. "I had quite a collection myself at one time."

"What did you do?" Asher asked.

"Dusted 'em off, put on my boots and got down to the business of going toe-to-toe with each one," Big E said, amusement in his tone. Yet, there was a solemn glint in his gaze as if it was a hard-won fight.

"Got any left?" Asher asked.

"Can't say that I do." Big E hooked his thumbs into his belt loops and gave Asher a sidelong smile. "Been a bit of a good run recently. Collecting memories these days like Joe is intending to do with his kin. What about you?"

"I think I've got one giant regret in the making," Asher said. And if he didn't fix things with Kelley, it was going to turn into a tumbleweed picking up speed and size until it became a thornbush barreling into his chest.

Big E adjusted his hat and said, "You're regretting not asking me to be on the parade float, aren't you?"

"You're riding with Lenny Culver in a nineteen

sixty-five Ford Mustang. Best seat in the parade." Asher chuckled. "And it's a bit more personal than that."

"Why didn't you say so?" Big E stood and faced Asher. "This is a simple fix. Listen to your heart and there won't be anything to regret."

"I can guarantee I have not ever done that," Asher said. If he had, he wouldn't have let Kelley go.

"Maybe it's time you tried," Big E suggested. "Where has not listening gotten you?"

Alone. Although he argued, "I haven't done too bad on my own."

"Can't disagree with you on that," Big E said good-naturedly. "If you're happy, well, then there's nothing wrong with going on as you have been. On your own, as it were."

Except there was that tumbleweed of regret building inside him. Not to mention he was not content quite yet. He said, "How happy are we talking?"

"Deep down to your core." Big E grinned at him. "That's where the good stuff is."

The good stuff had been his time spent with Kelley. As for really happy, he had been with his cowgirl. But was that enough to stake a future on? And was he ready to stake his future there in Gold Finch? To go all in? "I never imagined I would find myself back here. Let alone running the place."

"Sometimes you gotta leave to feel the tug of

the roots pulling you back to where you are meant to be."

"But I did not feel any tug when I left all those years ago." Asher frowned.

"Perhaps this time it's not so much about the roots you've got but rather it's about the roots you want to put down with a certain cowgirl," Big E said.

Kelley. Asher tested out that pull inside his chest. All roads seemed to be leading back to his cowgirl. A slow grin spread across his face. "I think you might be right."

"Of course, I am." Big E laughed and set his hand on Asher's shoulder again. "Son, this isn't my first rodeo with love."

"Love," Asher repeated.

"What did you think this was all about?" Big E eyed him and continued, "Even your dad knew that much. Love is at the core of it all."

Asher gripped the fence, yet it was something else entirely that started to center him. Feelings, strong ones, important ones, he supposed. For once he didn't shut them down.

"Your dad was never the same after his Priscilla passed. A broken heart has been known to do that to a cowboy," Big E said. "But then Walter lost Dylan and instead of clinging to you boys like he should have, he pushed you all away further."

Asher stepped back from the fence and straightened as if to prove to himself he knew exactly where he stood.

"Easier to push you away than love you up close, and fear the day he loses you, too," Big E added. "Walter loved you, but on his own terms."

You're starting to care, cowboy. And then he ran. Asher knew about having terms. He scrubbed a hand over his face and realized he was more like his father than he wanted to admit.

"But Walter closed himself off so tight, he never could heal properly." Big E shook his head. "Shame, that. He missed so much time with you and your brothers."

The time away from Kelley felt like years, not days. Asher accused Kelley of existing, not living. But he was doing the same. Living with his heart mostly closed. Perhaps his cowgirl was right all along. It was past time to flip the narrative. Grinning, he glanced at Big E and declared, "I am in love."

"I already knew that, son." Big E chuckled. "What I'm wanting to know is what you're intending on doing about it?"

"I'm going to take Joe's advice," Asher said, his smile spreading wide. "I'm going to build a team. My own team." And his first pick for a partner—the sort that stuck for life—was his special cowgirl.

CHAPTER NINETEEN

It was official. Kelley could fly now.

She ended the phone call where she had just been offered the head chef position at an award-winning fine dining restaurant in a luxury resort in Las Vegas.

Kelley now had everything she needed—a job. Exactly what she wanted—a place to make her culinary mark. And no further reason to stay in Gold Finch.

She pressed her palms flat on the metal desk in the Galloping Fork Diner office and searched for that joy. Any minute it was going to sweep through her and she would be beyond thrilled. Kelley watched the second hand tick around the wall clock hanging above the door and waited.

Nothing.

She was flattered, of course.

Honored to be selected.

Pleased with such a solid offer.

But ecstatic or elated or even delighted—she was not feeling that.

Pushing out of the creaky chair, Kelley gave

up the wait and went in search of Frannie and her mom to give them the good news. She was frowning when she pushed through the swinging door into the dining area and stepped into a full-scale summer garden party.

Dozens of floral horse collars were propped on chairs around the room. More flowers in a burst of rainbow colors waited in vases and buckets. There were yards of shimmery ribbon spools. So many sequins. Hot glue guns. Needles and thread. Bright costumes. Cowboy hats. Cowboy boots. Laughter. Too many folks to count. And such beautiful chaos that Kelley's smile bloomed from cheek to cheek.

The dance team shouted her name and waved from the other side of the room. Kelley found a path over to the group of spirited teenage girls, stopping to chat with locals on the way. Finally, she reached the girls, and their excitement at volunteering washed over her as they presented her with one of their floral garlands now adorned with beautifully intricate bows in coordinating colors. Encouraging them to keep going, Kelley spun around when her name was shouted again.

Frannie and Amy Peterson, the head coach of the dance and cheer teams, motioned to her from a window booth. But Kelley was stopped by the florist, Nora, who recommended that Kelley sell her miniature strawberry cake towers and signed up on the spot for a standing weekly order.

Finally, she reached her sister's booth. Frannie

promptly climbed out and dropped a gold circlet onto Kelley's head. Amy lifted up Kelley's costume for her to see, a perfect outfit representing *Strength* for their Heart of a Champion parade float—a crimson suede split skirt with a fitted top.

The dance coach looked happy with the team's efforts. "We added antique gold trim to your skirt and your top to match what we added to Maple's red saddle blanket."

"We are going for bold, deep red and antique gold for courage and heart to represent strength," Frannie explained. "We want you to feel fierce and elegant."

Kelley drew her finger over the subtle shimmer in the metallic thread and appreciated every stitch. "I approve."

Frannie fist-bumped Amy, then Frannie wrapped her arms around Kelley and said, "Glad you like it. If this is our last parade together, I want to make sure we go out in style."

Last parade with her sisters... Kelley startled and swallowed around the sudden knot in her throat. She hugged Frannie a little bit tighter. They debated the trim for the three sashes—one for strength, stamina and speed—that each sister would wear. Picked the flowing chiffon ribbons for Frannie's speed theme. And designed a flower crown for Laura-Beth's stamina costume.

The cheer team captains came to find out if Kelley had more caramel apple bites. A quick trip to the kitchen and the captains took the platters to hand out the sweet treats. More than one local recommended adding the caramel apple bites to the secret special menu Kelley was supposedly building.

Kelley chuckled and eyed Beatrice and Lynette. "I thought a secret special menu was supposed to be, well, secret."

Beatrice chuckled loudly. "It's not a secret for friends and family, Kelley."

Lynette grinned and spread her arms wide. "And we are your community, Kelley. You're stuck with us."

Stuck with them. No, Kelley was lucky to have them. She turned around to refill water glasses and pulled up to avoid bumping into Rosalind Sterling.

Rosalind wrapped her in a warm embrace. "What wonderful fun this evening has been."

Kelley nodded and said, "I'm glad you are enjoying yourself."

"I'm even more excited for the parade tomorrow." Rosalind trailed behind the lunch counter. Rosalind continued, "Now, I was talking to a few of the teachers from the high school earlier."

Kelley scooped ice into a pitcher and filled it with water, only half-listening. A burst of laughter from the widows' corner caught her attention. Smiling, she glanced at Rosalind.

The former high school principal resumed speaking. "And there are a handful of students interested in culinary arts, so we thought it would be quite beneficial if you spoke to them."

Kelley blinked and sputtered, "Me?"

"You're talented, experienced, and I believe you can offer them sound advice," Rosalind said.

Kelley set the pitcher on the counter. "You want me to mentor potential culinary arts students."

Rosalind's eyes widened, her expression delighted. "Oh, that would be above and beyond. I can only imagine how grateful the students would be."

Kelley knew how grateful she was for her grandfather and Trudy taking her under their wings for so many years. Now she was getting the chance to pay it forward. And that felt more than right. Kelley nodded. "I would like that."

"We won't overwhelm you," Rosalind assured her. "We will work around your schedule. My, this is very exciting."

It was. Very exciting. She apparently had a community behind her and now she was getting involved even more. And that joy Kelley had searched so hard for in the office after her call finally began to surface.

The diner's front door swung open, and Pauline swept in, a brilliant smile on her face and a glow all about her. She tossed her arms over her head and announced loudly, "I accepted an offer!"

The tile floor seemed to give way under her boots. Kelley braced her hand on the lunch counter.

"It's an offer for my hand in marriage!" Pauline flashed her left hand and revealed a beautiful diamond ring.

Kelley gaped and took in the bold sparkler adorning her boss's finger.

"I am going to be Mrs. Eric Grahame." Pauline pressed her hands to her cheeks. Her eyes flared wide. She hopped in place and shouted excitedly, "I'm getting hitched, and everyone is invited to the wedding."

Cheers and congratulations resounded from every corner of the dining area. Hugs followed and good cheer swelled again and uplifted the gathering even more.

Pauline finally made her way over to the lunch counter and plopped down on a stool. She set her elbows on the counter and marveled at her engagement ring. A hint of breathless wonder brightened her words. "Kelley, I'm getting married."

"Congratulations are definitely in order." Kelley set a cup of hot water and a mint tea bag in front of her boss and asked, "When did this happen?"

"Tonight. At dinner," Pauline sighed as if she still did not quite believe it was true. "Eric cooked spaghetti and meatballs at his place. You know that's my favorite."

Kelley raised her eyebrows.

"It was quiet. Private." One more long sigh and Pauline added, "Romantic and absolutely perfect."

"It sounds like it."

"Do you know he was worried it wasn't flashy enough? Not grand enough." Pauline chuckled and fixed her tea. "I told him I'm too old for such nonsense."

"Pauline," Kelley scolded her boss. "Don't say that."

"Then you don't think I'm too old to be a blushing bride?" Pauline looked at Kelley.

"I don't think you're too old to be anything," Kelley assured her. "Especially in love and happy."

"Thank you for that." Pauline took a big breath and released it. "I don't think I'll be able to stop smiling even if I try. I might fall asleep smiling."

"As you should," Kelley said and envied her boss. How precious it was to be so full of joy that her smile could not be contained.

The parade preparations continued, but wedding chatter also swirled through the conversations. The evening finally drew to a close with Coach Amy declaring it was time for everyone to go home and get a good night's rest. Parade participation required high energy and enthusiasm, no yawning or tired waves. It was some time later when, once the kitchen and dining room were cleaned up, Frannie, Pauline and Kelley collapsed into a booth and propped their feet up on the opposite bench.

"Nice work, ladies." Pauline leaned her head back and considered Frannie and Kelley across the table from her. "You know all these flowers gives this place a botanical, outdoorsy vibe."

"Don't tell me you want to do a botanical-themed menu," Kelley said, playfully.

"No," Pauline retorted. "But what about outdoor dining?"

Kelley shifted on the bench and smiled. "Like summer patio dining."

"Yes, but make it once a week," Pauline said.

"A summer Friday night date night on the patio," Frannie chimed in.

"I like that," Pauline said. "A special summertime event with a special menu curated by Kelley."

Her own menu at the diner. That intrigued her. Kelley lowered her feet to the floor and sat up straighter. Even more, she felt her excitement begin to stir. However, the idea of her own menu was just the beginning. Kelley cleared her throat and decided to stop standing still and jump in. "Pauline, I've got an offer for you, too."

"I'm happy to be your travel companion, Kelley, but my home base is here now," Pauline said, with conviction.

"As it should be," Kelley replied. "You are engaged now and from the sounds of things soon to be married."

"There's no need for a long engagement." Pauline chuckled and a blush filled her cheeks. "Why wait when we both know what we want?"

Why wait, indeed. Kelley nodded, stepped out her own holding pattern.

"I'm sorry I didn't talk to you first." Pauline

reached across the table and touched Kelley's arm. "I seem to have ruined our plans to fly the coop."

Kelley had not been in much of a mood to take off. And she was starting to realize why. What she really wanted she already had right here in Gold Finch. "I'm thinking more of a business proposal kind of offer."

Frannie's eyes widened and she pressed her lips together as if to hold back her smile.

"I'm intrigued," Pauline said and tapped her ear. "And I'm listening. Give it to me."

"I want to be partners in the Galloping Fork." And since it was her one shot and her one chance, Kelley went all in. "With full control of the menu and the kitchen."

"No," Pauline said, swiftly and succinctly. Her head shook back and forth.

Frannie stiffened beside Kelley and opened her mouth.

Kelley took her sister's hand under the table and silently encouraged Frannie not to speak. Frannie squeezed Kelley's hand harder as if shouting at Kelley to say something. Finally, Kelley exhaled around her disappointment and asked, "Why not?"

"Because I want you to buy the Galloping Fork." Pauline grinned and spread her arms wide. "I want you to own this place. Same as Mama T owned it. If it's wholly yours, you will love it like Mama T did, and you and the diner both will surely thrive."

Frannie was nodding vigorously.

Kelley released her sister's hand and touched her forehead. She said, hesitantly and not without a dose of deep discontent, "Unfortunately, I don't have the funds." And she was not certain she could afford a loan of that size, either.

Pauline held up her hand. "Just tell me you want to buy this place. That you want to own the Galloping Fork."

"I do," Kelley said. The words settled true and sure inside her. The Galloping Fork Diner in Gold Finch was where she wanted to stake her claim and make her mark.

"Then we can work out the details like how much and when to pay with the rest of the paperwork," Pauline said, cheerfully. "We can come up with a fair deal. Something that benefits us both."

Kelley grinned. "Yes, we can. We will."

Frannie whooped beside Kelley and said, "Best night ever. My big sister is sticking around. Pauline is head over boots in love. There's so much to be excited about."

Kelley was getting everything she wanted. That joy she had been pining for simmered. Yes, she had everything, but not everyone. And she sensed she needed someone, if she wanted that joy to overflow. She reached over and took Pauline's hand to better see her stunning engagement ring. "Pauline, what happened? How did you fall in love?"

"Simple." Pauline squeezed Kelley's fingers and drew Kelley's gaze up to her. "I finally let my heart fly free. I realized that was what Mama T really wanted."

Kelley sat back and touched her chest.

"Mama T wanted us to give our hearts to something—or someone—completely and fully," Pauline explained. "That's where the happiness truly lies."

Frannie bumped her shoulder against Kelley's. "Kelley already gave her heart to Asher."

"But he didn't give me his," she countered.

"Because you gave him your heart, but held on to the key," Pauline said and arched her eyebrows at Kelley. "Your cowboy is still locked out."

Because she didn't want to fall first. She wanted a guarantee her love would be returned. That this relationship would not fail. So Kelley protected herself. But it failed because she refused to try and put herself out there. Kelley blinked and dropped her forehead against the table. "I don't think I'm cut out for this whole love thing."

Frannie rubbed Kelley's back. "At least you are talking about love now."

"It's not about being good or bad at it. It's about being true to yourself," Pauline said, softly. "It's about believing you are enough, and your love is everything your cowboy needs. And then making him realize it, too."

Kelley lifted her head. "I have to tell him how I feel." How she really felt. She had to open her heart and give him the words. Trust that he felt the same.

Pauline nodded. Frannie hummed her agreement.

"I have to show him," Kelley said louder and flung her shoulders back. She had to show her cowboy that their love was worth the investment. So worth fighting for.

"Not to point out the obvious," Frannie started, "but Asher is in New York, and you are here. How exactly are you going to show him?"

"I need to get him here." Kelley tugged her phone from her pocket. "And I need Big E's help."

"Isn't it late to be texting Big E?" Frannie frowned at her.

"Are the stars out yet?" Kelley asked and tried to peer around her sister to see outside.

Frannie swatted her away. "I can't tell. And I think you need to do more than wish upon a star."

Kelley laughed at Frannie's put-out tone, and said, "Big E told me he stays up every night to count the stars."

"How many does he count?" Frannie asked, dryly.

"Is that like counting sheep to fall asleep?" Pauline asked and looked as if she was considering it.

"No." Kelley started typing a text to Big E and glanced up. "Whenever Big E is away from his wife, they both go outside and count the first ten stars they see."

"Why?" Frannie nudged her elbow in Kelley's ribs. "Either text or talk, but don't leave us hanging here."

"Sorry." Kelley hit Send on her text message, then smiled and said, "When they count the stars it's a reminder that even though they are far apart, they are still in the other's heart ten times over."

Pauline sighed. "That's sweet."

Frannie flopped back on the bench. "I want someone to count stars with one day."

So did Kelley. Her phone vibrated and she smiled wide. "Big E is awake and ready to help me."

"Are you going to share the plan?" Pauline asked, her gaze curious.

"Simple." Kelley stashed her phone in her apron pocket. "Big E is going to tell Asher that there is a serious buyer for Maple Moonlight who wants to speak to him in person about the purchase terms."

"And you're that serious buyer?" Frannie asked, sounding giddy.

Kelley nodded. She was serious. Serious about loving a cowboy.

CHAPTER TWENTY

HE HAD HIS cowgirl in his sights. *Finally.*

Although, she was still too far away.

Asher stood under the awning of Lucky Lane Tavern. The Red, White and Bluegrass Parade was rolling slowly past him, turning from Derby Hollow Road onto Hitch Post Avenue. Mayor Corbin had kicked off the July Fourth celebration earlier, leading the procession in the Grand Marshal's horse-drawn wagon.

A string of impressive floats and performers followed. The Barn Dance Blowout where the high school dance team two-stepped and twirled. The Show Ponies. The Horse and Wagon Train. And Myles Groves in his 1950 Studebaker had already gone by to the excitement of the crowd gathered on the sidewalk all around Asher. The high school band followed, and the cheer team tossed candy to the delight of the happy kids. The Hometown Heroes earned applause from the spectators and salutes from the veterans in the crowd.

Flags waved nonstop. Cheers went up nonstop like a sparking current.

Asher skipped his gaze past the Front Porch Pickin' Float and the local Bluegrass band playing a lively tune.

There.

A flash of crimson red and gold behind the 4H Farm Animal Showcase. He pushed away from the wall of the tavern. And suddenly, Kelley was there. She was radiant. Stunning. Heart-stoppingly so. Asher lost his breath and every bit of steady he thought he had.

His cowgirl was front and center of the Munroe sisters' trinity. Sitting atop Maple Moonlight, all confidence, courage and grace. Her smile flashed brighter than the sun glinting off her gold crown. There was more gold sparkling in her thick braid falling over one shoulder trailing down to her split riding skirt and Maple's adornments. Shimmery gold ribbon had even been woven through Maple's plush red floral horse collar. It was magical. Enchanting. Asher could not look away. He was caught on a cowgirl, heart and all. And wouldn't have wanted it any other way.

He was careful to stay beneath the shadow of the awning. This was Kelley's moment, and he wanted her to absorb every minute. Soon enough, Asher hoped to have her in his arms for their own private sort of moment. After he told her a few of those heartfelt truths he had been keeping to himself for far too long.

He waited until Kelley and her sisters rode past

him, then with his cowgirl in his sights, he followed her along the last of the parade route. Asher kept his greetings to folks on the sidewalk brief and matched his pace to Kelley's. The area in back of Briarwood Reserve was the parade's disbanding area. And the closer they all got, the more he fought the urge to run to her.

As it was, he lost the trio within the happy confusion of floats, band equipment and cheerful participants celebrating among themselves. Then he spotted that flash of red and gold and beelined around a trailer and dodged a door opening of a 1948 Ford pickup. The Blackwell trailer attached to Walter's truck was parked at the end of the street. A quick jog and he got to Kelley before she dismounted.

Elliot James and Edie Kincaid were about to assist Kelley. However, Asher stepped between the pair and got to his cowgirl first.

"Asher." Kelley gasped, delight sparkling in her wide eyes.

He reached for her. And with her hands on his shoulders, Asher gripped her waist, swung her down and straight into his embrace.

Her arms curved around his neck. Her head fell back, and her laughter streamed out. She shifted and squeezed him close. "I can't believe you are here."

Asher could not believe he had his cowgirl right where he wanted her. He tightened his hold, watched as Edie led Maple away, then he said, "I couldn't miss your parade comeback."

More amusement escaped. Her hazel eyes flashed. "What did you think?"

"Incredible. So beautiful. Stunning, really." He watched color bloom in her cheeks. "Truth is, you made me forget how to breathe."

She stilled in his arms as if suddenly holding her own breath.

He caught her stare and opened the door to those truths he'd been holding on to. "And if breathless is how love is supposed to feel, then that's how I want it. Forever."

Her lips parted. Her eyes went impossibly round.

Someone shouted Kelley's name, then Asher's. The moment paused as if love now held its breath.

Footsteps sounded behind Asher.

Kelley glanced over his shoulder, set her forehead against Asher's and whispered, "Pauline has spotted us, and she looks quite determined. I don't think we can outrun her."

He chuckled and hugged Kelley, then said, his tone serious, "There is still much more that needs to be said."

"So much more," she agreed.

The promise was there in the low hush of her words. That was enough for now. Asher slowly lowered Kelley's boots to the ground yet kept his arm around her waist.

"Come on, you two." Pauline jogged over, looking set to mobilize the group. "We've got to get a move on."

"Where are we going?" Kelley asked, confusion in her words. "Asher and I were—"

"Coming with me. Back to the diner." Pauline glanced quickly around, then called out, "Frannie, we need you as well." Her gaze shifted to Kelley, and she asked, "Can Laura-Beth cook?"

Suddenly, Laura-Beth appeared beside them and said, "I can serve."

"What is going on?" Asher asked and started following Pauline down the street.

"*The Morning Gallop* is here," Pauline replied, practically sprinting and talking just as quickly now. "They want to feature the Galloping Fork Diner in their Hotspots for Foodies feature."

Kelley's hand found Asher's. Her fingers entwined swiftly with his. Surprise overtook her expression. "Seriously?"

"Yes." Amusement spread Pauline's smile wide. "Apparently, Mayor Corbin's comments were very convincing. So, they wanted to see what all the grilled cheese fuss was about for themselves."

Asher squeezed Kelley's hand and said, "There is a lot to make a fuss about when it comes to Kelley's cooking."

"We know that. Now we need to show the *Morning Gallop* staff," Pauline said, looking cheerful. "But you should also know that Mayor Corbin would also like the diner to have a booth at the festival."

Kelley shook her head. "The festival in the next hour or so?"

"That's the one," Pauline said.

Frannie sputtered. "Uh. Okay. That's nothing to worry about, right?"

Kelley looked at Asher. Concern flickered in her hazel eyes.

"I'm not going anywhere," he said and smiled. "I'm here for you. Tell me what you need. I got you."

She searched his face, then her grip relaxed, and she said, "Together." Certainty came through in her words. "Together. We totally got this."

HOURS LATER, THE festival officially closed to allow families to prepare for the fireworks show, Kelley stood in a clearing on Whistle Bend Bluff. She shook her head. "This was a bad idea." Turning on an LED candle, she placed it inside a Mason jar and muttered, "What was I thinking?"

Frannie laughed, gave Kelley a quick hug and took the Mason jar from her. "You were thinking that you are in love, and you want Asher to know it."

Kelley scanned the clearing she had chosen to make her declaration to her cowboy. A large navy-and-white gingham blanket covered part of the grassy area. A packed picnic basket, several plush pillows and more blankets sat on top. Mason jars lined the entire perimeter, sitting on rocks and tucked into the longer grass. The candles inside the jars flickered, adding a mellow glow to the area.

"I think it looks amazing." Frannie set her hands on her hips and surveyed their work. "It's private and romantic and magical."

"Like a secret garden for two." That was what Kelley had envisioned. Still, she bit her bottom lip and considered the bouquet of a dozen red, white and blue roses near the picnic basket. "Maybe the flowers were a bit much. Who gives a cowboy flowers?"

"I think they are a perfect touch," Frannie countered and adjusted several Mason jars to her liking. "And remember what I told you about what each rose color represents."

"I got it." Kelley bent and straightened the tassels on the blanket. "And if I can't get the words out or if they get stuck in my throat, I'll just thrust the roses at Asher and tell him these say it all."

"You're going to get the words out fine." Frannie chuckled. "You just need to speak from your heart."

Kelley rounded on her sister. "Francine Marie, when have you ever spoken from your heart to a cowboy?"

"I haven't," Frannie said, her words soothing. "And this is why you must get this perfect grand gesture completely right so I can one day follow in your footsteps, big sister."

"Is this supposed to be a grand gesture?" Kelley blanched and shook her head again. "I don't think it's grand enough. And more importantly, will Asher consider it grand?"

"Wrong thought. Never mind." Frannie stepped to Kelley's side and wrapped her arm around Kelley's shoulders. "This is just you telling a cowboy how you feel about him. The rest of this is a pretty backdrop."

"And if he doesn't feel the same?" Kelley arched an eyebrow at her little sister.

"As if." Frannie's gaze fairly danced. "The entire town watched Asher practically push Edie and Elliot out of the way so that he could sweep you off Maple's back today at the parade."

Her first time being swept off her boots and Kelley had rather liked it. A lot. She grinned. "Asher didn't push them."

Frannie chuckled. "Well, he certainly made his presence known. And Asher had every cowgirl in town sighing all day over how he looked after you and stuck by your side in the diner booth at the festival."

That was quite nice. Asher had not hovered, yet her cowboy had seemed to know when Kelley needed him and been right there. Admittedly, Kelley liked knowing Asher was within quick reach. "I looked after him, too."

Frannie tapped her finger lightly on Kelley's nose. "And that is why you two are a perfect match."

That and so many other reasons. Kelley clasped her hands together underneath her chin and nodded. "You're right, Frannie. This is just what I wanted. And it is going to be grand."

Frannie gave Kelley's shoulders a squeeze, then checked her cell phone. "Laura-Beth and Wes are almost here with Asher. So that is my cue to leave."

The blissful couple was set to leave for their honeymoon in the morning, but they wanted in on Kelley's reunion with Asher first. Kelley inhaled and worked to slow her pulse.

Frannie tucked her phone into her pocket, gave the clearing one last survey, then said, "I'm really excited for you, Kelley. You deserve all the happy your heart can hold."

"You do, too." Kelley wrapped her little sister in a hug, then watched Frannie collect the boxes they'd carried everything in and disappear down the trail.

Now she was alone in the clearing, waiting to give her heart to a cowboy.

Finally, Asher stepped into the clearing. His gaze found Kelley immediately. One long sweep and he seemed to take it all in. His eyes held hers, warm and unwavering and settled something deep inside her. Kelley felt completely seen and finally found.

It was grounding and empowering, humbling and uplifting. And she knew with certainty she was done hiding from her cowboy.

Kelley stopped Asher's approach. "I have some things I need to tell you."

Asher pulled up. There was a quiet readiness in his stance and how his hands slipped into the front pockets of his jeans as if he was prepared to take in whatever came next.

"Pauline told me it did not have to be extravagant. Just heartfelt." She was trapped by his incredibly kind heart and his unguarded expression. "But I wanted this to be private. I wanted to tell you earlier after the parade. Then everyone was there. And then we were in the food booth in the park." Her pulse picked up. "And you should be the first to know. But it's not really about being first." It is about giving the words freely.

Asher did not move. Just watched and listened as if he was content to let Kelley ramble the long way around to her truths. It felt like he understood Kelley better than she did herself. And that only made Kelley fall for him all over again.

Kelley kept her gaze as open and honest as his and said, "I realized I don't want to stand still anymore. Not in life. Most especially not with you."

The faintest of grins filtered across his face. Still, he did not come to her.

I see you, too, cowboy. Kelley said, "I want to be the place you call home." A catch caught her words as if it was her heart that broke through her voice. "Because you're that for me. You're my home, Asher."

"Kelley."

Her name was like a promise on his lips. The tender ache in his voice undid her. The words slipped out. Quiet as the sun setting behind her. Certain as the change of seasons. She said, "I love you."

A smile, awe- and joy-filled appeared. His blue eyes glinted as if lit from within.

Warmth like so much sunshine rushed through Kelley. Her smile built from inside her. The words came again. Sure and carefree. Simple and easy. "Asher Blackwell, I love you."

He was there in an instant, sweeping Kelley up in his arms, gathering her gently and impossibly close. His embrace anchored her and steadied her yet made Kelley feel like she could soar at the same time.

Kelley buried her cheek against his chest. If she looked at her cowboy, she would kiss him and then she would be completely lost in the moment. But there was more to be shared. "I know you're in New York. And I'm buying the diner here in town. And it's really complicated."

"Say it again," he whispered against her hair.

Kelley leaned back and met his gaze. "It's complicated."

Asher shook his head and pressed his lips lightly against hers. “I meant the good part.”

“I love you.” She held him tighter.

“Kelley Munroe, I love you, too.” Asher leaned in and captured her mouth with his.

This was a kiss that joined and claimed. That buckled knees and reached the stars. That whispered of forever and celebrated now. There was nowhere else Kelley wanted to be.

The kiss slowed and Asher pulled away slightly. “I think I need to sit. I’m winded in the best way possible.”

“Me, too.” Kelley led him over to the blanket.

Asher sat and tugged her down beside him. “I can’t believe you did all this. It’s incredible.”

“I had help,” Kelley said.

He held her close. “But it must have been your idea. There are firefly catchers here in our little garden.”

Oh, how he got her. She curled into his side. “Those flowers are for you.”

He kept one arm around her and reached for the bouquet with the other. “This is the first time I’ve gotten flowers.”

“Do you like them?” she asked.

“Very much,” he said. “And now I believe I’m going to have to go all out to make sure you feel as special as you are making me feel right now.”

“That’s all I needed to hear.”

“All the same, I’ve got some ideas,” he said and

set the bouquet in his lap. "Did you know the blue rose represents true love?"

She leaned up and grinned at him. "How do you know?"

"I know what all the colors stand for. The red is for love, and the white is for new beginnings. It was not by accident that I sent you those red-tipped yellow roses. I had a real bad crush on you."

"And now it's blossomed into something so much more," she said, teasing.

He kissed her again. Then they unpacked the picnic basket and enjoyed a bit of their feast. There were apologies given for words said that fateful Sunday and new promises made. There were secrets shared and more kisses exchanged.

The food stashed away and the stars twinkling above, Asher unfolded a second blanket and draped it over Kelley's legs. He took her hand in his and said, "The only place I want to be is beside you."

"What about New York and your career?" Kelley asked and linked their fingers together.

"I thought it might be time to flip the script. I want to put a cowgirl and love first this time around. What do you think?"

"I think I want you in my life," she said. "And if that means your job is in New York, then I'm prepared to figure that out with you. But I don't want to lose you."

"I don't deserve you." He kissed her softly. "But I'm still not letting you go."

She tightened her grip but left her heart wide-open. "Neither am I."

"I want to build something with you here in Gold Finch," Asher said. "Something my dad and Dylan would be proud of. Something lasting. Something that is ours."

Kelley searched his face. "It sounds like you are talking about..." Her heart was so full already.

"I'm talking about commitment and marriage. Children and family." He shifted to face her on the blanket and took both her hands in his. "I'm talking about arguing and making up. Laughing and crying. And holding hands through every single up and down."

"And not giving up," she whispered, her heart overflowing. "Or letting go."

"Exactly." His smile came slow and curved up until it reached his eyes. "Kelley Munroe, will you marry me?"

Kelley gasped and said his name, although it was as fragile as mist.

"I should be on one knee," he said, his gaze solemn. Yet, his voice was undeniably steady and strong. "I should have a ring. And a big proposal plan."

Kelley swallowed and blinked. Still, she felt those tears coming.

"But I'm leading with my heart. And this feels

so very right." He reached up and framed her face in his hands, carefully and tenderly. "Please marry me, Kelley. I can't promise it will always be perfect. But I can promise I will love you always."

"Yes." The tears slipped free. "It will always be yes." Kelley kissed her cowboy as fireworks lit up the night sky.

And she finally knew what deliriously happy felt like.

It was wishes granted.

It was dreams answered.

It was a cowgirl and a cowboy and a love worth building a future on.

EPILOGUE

BIG E WAS back in Kentucky.

A late-night phone call from Asher Blackwell, and Big E had the wheels of his RV rolling down the highway before the sun even considered rising. Fortunately, Big E had been in Kansas City at an annual August Harvest Rodeo and Livestock Show with his grandsons and not too far from Gold Finch.

With his RV parked on the Blackwell Stables property, Big E made his way over to the colt barn.

Asher met him at the door, skipped the handshake and opted for a quick hug instead. "Appreciate you coming so soon, Elias."

"I wish it was under better circumstances." Big E frowned.

Asher ran a hand over his jaw, his tone serious. "Elliot died in a one-car crash two nights ago. I would have left it there, offered condolences and got back to the business of trying to save this place."

"But," Big E pressed.

"But then I went to collect Elliot's personal things to return to his family." Asher opened the door and started up the stairs to Elliot's former room above the colt barn. He pulled out a key and unlocked the door. "No one has been in here other than me. I wanted you to see what I found before I contact the authorities."

Big E stiffened and followed Asher into the rather austere living quarters. Elliot might have slept there, but the former assistant stable manager was not living there and certainly not making the place his home. There was a box on the bed with folded clothes and no personal keepsakes.

"Other than books and clothes, Elliot didn't leave much behind," Asher explained. "I never knew he was much of a reader, and now I'm fairly certain the books were for cover."

Big E eyed the only book still sitting on the top of the dresser under the window.

Asher handed Big E a pen and said, "Use this to flip open the cover. No sense adding more fingerprints to anything in here."

Big E took the pen and arched an eyebrow at Asher.

Asher grinned and lifted one shoulder. "What can I say? I like a good cop TV show as much as the next cowboy."

Big E chuckled, went over to the dresser and flipped the cover of the hardback book open. The pages had been carved out to form a pocket. There was a syringe and vial carefully tucked inside. Big E read the label on the vial and swallowed hard. "That matches the drug found in Pride."

"Yes, it does," Asher said, his voice low and full of emotion. "Pride was doped by one of our own."

Big E closed the book and tucked the pen into his pocket. "Now we know who did it."

"But we don't know why." Asher looked Big E in the eye. "And my gut is feeling way out of sorts on this one."

He knew the feeling. Big E nodded and said, "You should make that call to the sheriff. It sure feels like there's more going on here."

"We need to leave Joe out of this for now," Asher said, clearly determined. "Elliot was his hire. And this might be a mistake Joe can't get past."

"No sense giving Joe another regret," Big E mused. "Joe is a solid cowboy, and he was loyal to Walter for years. He should ride a little freer in retirement. I was never much for weighing down another cowboy's saddlebags if it wasn't necessary."

Asher agreed but seemed concerned. "Still, we need a team we can trust. I can't do this alone."

Now, that sort of talk sat right with Big E. He tried to hide it but grinned, nonetheless. Big E could not deny the pride with knowing he had a hand in guiding Asher back home. There was no doubt that riding his trail solo had made Asher stronger, but Asher understood now how much farther he would go with folks he could count on. Big E thumped his hat against his knee. "That leaves us one choice really."

"Family," Asher stated, no hesitation. No doubt. "We need family."

Big E's grin came easy and quick this time. After all, Big E considered family his *reason* for everything he did. Family was the center of his world.

And if Big E was a bragging sort of cowboy he would claim fixing those broken family tree branches was a kind of specialty for him.

And if Big E's legacy was a Blackwell family tree rooted deep and standing true, well, there was no finer success a cowboy like him could claim. He asked, "Got a particular brother in mind?"

"Has to be Nathan. He's got the horse experience we need." Asher walked out into the hallway, waited for Big E, then locked the door. "And besides, Matt is working undercover with the US Marshals' office. Caleb is serving overseas. And Ridge has his specialty vet practice to look after."

Big E eyed Asher. "You don't look convinced, though."

"I want Nathan. I need my little brother," Asher said, a sure set in his jaw. "It's just Nathan may not want us."

"We should call him and find out," Big E suggested.

Asher's chuckle held little humor. "Nathan won't be answering the phone or even a text. He never does. And he did that long before he became a widower."

That was the way of it. Not unfamiliar terrain for Big E. He adjusted his cowboy hat on his head and trailed down the stairs. Outside, he pulled his keys from his pocket and said, "Looks like I'll be headed out sooner than I thought. You good to hold down things around here until we get back?"

"You're that certain you can convince Nathan to come home," Asher said, skepticism clear in his expression.

"Son." Big E set his hand on Asher's arm and held his gaze. "I was told your boots would never walk this land, let alone leave a permanent boot print."

Asher relaxed and grinned. "You have quite a talent for persuasion. I will give you that."

And Big E refused to take no for an answer, especially when family was asking. "All I need from you is an address for where to find Nathan."

"Nathan is in Paducah." Asher pulled out his phone and typed on the screen. "I'm texting you the last address I have for him."

Big E checked his phone and nodded. "Give me a few days to collect your brother and keep me posted on what the sheriff has to say."

"You aren't sticking around to meet with the sheriff?" Asher asked.

"Best for me to get on the road," Big E replied, and arched his eyebrows at Asher. "Something tells me I might need more than one sit-down with your brother to make him see sense."

"If Nathan really does not want to be here,

please don't force him," Asher said. "I will figure things out somehow."

Meanwhile, Big E would figure out how to get Nathan to keep an open mind. Big E headed for his RV and caught sight of a blonde cowgirl coming from the twos' stable barn.

Asher's stress all but evaporated like a trail of steam. Asher was already starting for Kelley as if the cowgirl was his start and finish.

Love always did Big E's heart good. He chuckled and called out, "Asher, don't forget there's work to be done around here."

Asher laughed, yet his steps did not slow. His direction was already set. "I know it, and I will see to it."

"Just remember the cowboy who had fun never truly worked a day in his life," Big E said, cheerfully.

"And the cowboy who finds his special cowgirl always knows where his home is. That's precious and worth holding on to," Asher said, his grin spreading from cheek to cheek. "I'm lucky. I've got a cowgirl I intend to hold on to right now."

Love sure did a cowboy's heart good, indeed.

Big E climbed into his RV, started the engine and got to considering how best to convince a closed-off cowboy widower that home just might have more to offer than more pain.

* * * * *

Don't miss A Cowboy to Remember,
the next installment of
The Bluegrass Blackwells,
coming next month by bestselling author
Melinda Curtis!